# Morning Is for Joy

F
Jil

R·L·H

# Ruth Livingston Hill

# Morning Is for Joy

**HARVEST HOUSE PUBLISHERS**
Eugene, Oregon 97402

665

**MORNING IS FOR JOY**

Copyright © 1949 by Ruth H. Munce
Published by Harvest House Publishers
Eugene, Oregon 97402

ISBN 0-89081-523-2

**Printed in the United States of America.**

# Morning
# Is for Joy

# Chapter 1

THE MORNING SUN shone out joyously after the dreary storm of the night before, as if to say, "I'm glad that is over at last!" Every green leaf on the elms and maples all across the wide lovely lawns of the Applegate house was bright and shining, eager to begin a new day. Even the sidewalks had the look of a small boy thoroughly scrubbed and slickly combed.

The front door of the big stone house opened and Joy came out. She poised a moment on the steps looking about her with ecstasy. She was young and slender, with short blond upcurling hair and blue, blue eyes. She was dressed in yellow, with touches of crisp white, dainty and graceful. But it was not her blue eyes or her dress, or even the dimples that couldn't seem to stay in hiding, that made her seem a part of the spring sunshine. It was the lilt of her lips and the lift of her head, a look of expectancy about her whole being that suggested that some delightful thing was about to happen. It curled up the corners of her mouth leaving you to wonder whether the thoughts that were in a continual dance behind those blue eyes were dancing with mischief or for sheer delight.

Joy's lovely roseleaf coloring she had from her mother, whom Joy only faintly remembered. "Your *sweet* little mother" her father always spoke of her, with love in his eyes. Her mother had had a firm little chin, showing a firmness of character that had quietly balanced her husband's eager spirit of high adventure. Joy had her mother's sweet firmness, but that look of high anticipation, coupled with courage and softened with deep tenderness, she got from her father whom she adored.

Edward Applegate, over forty now but still darkly handsome, was prosperous. He had succeeded partly through natural ability and partly through daring much, and usually winning. He had just dared a new move in his building business, on the outcome of which he had staked a great deal. The excitement and suspense of it showed in his black eyes as he glanced out his window and saw Joy there in the full radiance of the sunshine. "My pride and Joy" he called his boy and girl. Michael, Joy's brother, was just turned fourteen.

Mr. Applegate smiled and his eyes lingered lovingly upon her as she caught sight of him and blew him a kiss before she ran lightly down the steps and out to the sidewalk. But there was a pucker of anxiety between his straight black brows as he turned away from the window.

Joy had chosen to walk the few blocks to a little corner grocery to which Emmy the cook had sent her for more bread to stuff the extra large chickens for dinner. She walked three blocks, past fine houses and grounds, then turned the corner down one block of homes less lovely, and turned again. This last block slanted downhill. Its dreary brick row houses were a hangover from an abortive development started before the War. Each house seemed to cling with forlorn perseverance to the one above it lest it lose hold and sink away to the dismal condition of the ugly shacks down in the hollow across the highway which ran at the foot of the hill.

Joy shuddered as she wondered what sort of people would be willing to live in such desolate surroundings. Her own house was so spic and span, so exquisite in every detail, and she was so accustomed to modern gracious living that it was well nigh impossible for her to imagine what it would be to live in one of these places. Her life had been warmly and lovingly sheltered, with little or no responsibility in it for her to shoulder, and she had had no contact as yet with the ragged underseams of living.

At the end of the row was a vacant lot littered with rubbish and stubble; then alone on the corner, as if unfit to associate with even the shabby brick row, huddled the little store. She rarely went to this store. Emmy always used the spotless big chain store on Main Street, halfway to town, but this was a holiday and it wasn't open. Emmy was in a hurry, too, for they were to have dinner early, since Daddy had promised to go to the big league ball game with her and her young brother Mickey.

Joy was anticipating the outing. Her father seldom had time to go with them and it was always an extra special pleasure to have him. Even Mickey, who at fourteen had acquired a teen-age superiority to parents in general, admitted that Dad was more fun than any boy. A little glimmer of maturity came and sat upon Joy's sweet face as she thought how glad she was that her father was going to the game. "Mickey needs him," she decided. "He runs too much with the gang."

In fact, she had had a little talk about him with her father the day before. "I don't like the look of some of the boys that are always after him, Daddy," she had said. "And Mickey takes too much for granted, too. He's getting so fresh and impudent."

"Oh, I don't believe Michael will get into much that's wrong, Joy girl," her father had answered, rather absent-mindedly, she thought. But she noticed him studying her brother at dinner and then he had proposed the game.

There was a sandlot game in progress across the street, Joy noticed as she walked back up the little hill. It was im-promptu, apparently, in honor of the holiday.

Joy noticed one young man, a tall broad-shouldered boy of perhaps twenty-two or so. He walked with an easy grace as he came to bat. Something in his fine bearing attracted Joy and

she paused to watch. There was a look of strength and manli-
ness about him. As he strode toward the plate he bore himself
as might a knight of old about to start off on adventure. She
had a sudden fancy that he would look best in shining armor,
astride a white horse. Then she giggled at herself. She was
aware that her foolish imagination was always running away
with her. But it was fun. She liked to imagine. She generally
set that little chin firmly as she did it, as a sort of checkrein, to
keep her balance. It kept the fancies from becoming entangled
with fact.

All at once she saw the young man throw down his bat and
run toward the street. Joy saw that a woman had started to cross
the street, right into the midst of traffic. She had stepped out
into the path of a car, which barely swerved in time to miss
her. Yet she still went on without apparently noticing the oncoming traffic. She was attractive, or had been, just under middle age, but carelessly dressed, and her steps were uncertain.
Joy tried to scream as she saw another car speeding toward
her. But just then the tall young man appeared at her side,
guiding her gently, courteously, across.

Joy caught her breath with relief. How fine of him, she
thought, to stop his game and help her!

They were coming straight toward Joy. She realized with a
touch of pleasure that she could get a nearer glimpse of the
boy. She saw that he had deep-set large brown eyes and
smooth brown waves of hair. The lines of his face were
cleanly carved and his mouth was wide but the lips were
compressed grimly.

Again as they came nearer Joy, that fleeting image of a white
horse and armor came to her, but she tossed it out of her mind
once more, with a glad feeling that here was no fanciful story-
book knight, but a real flesh-and-blood twentieth century man,
who had proved himself to be what he looked to be, and was
willing to pass up a few moments of his own fun to help a
stranger who needed help. It was unusual. It thrilled her.

But as they reached her side she glanced again at the woman and caught the heavy odor of liquor on her. A revulsion swept over Joy. How terrible! So that was the kind of people who lived in these houses she had wondered about.

For now the two mounted the low weather-beaten steps of the little house in the middle of the block. The young man opened the door and took the poor woman in.

He stayed only a few moments, and Joy, in her horror at the condition of the woman, and in her admiration of the young man, stood still where they had passed her.

Then the young man came out, a high look of stern pity on his fine face. As he passed her again, impulsively Joy reached out a hand and stopped him. "I think that was about the finest thing I ever saw anyone do," she told him, and smiled her sincere admiration. There was no boldness in her glance but she looked straight into the boy's brown eyes that were still filled with trouble.

He stopped and looked down at her, as if a fairy or an angel had alighted in his path. It seemed to him that all the loveliness of all spring mornings was in her face. He looked deep into her sweet blue eyes upturned to his, eyes that showed not a trace of a thought of herself, and what he saw there stirred all the hungers of his soul. A girl had never looked at him in that way before. And he had never seen such a girl.

Oh, plenty of girls had glanced his way in admiration. They had done more than glance. They had brazened their way into his notice. He had been much sought after in college and in his year of service, but he had had very little use for the girls. It had always seemed to him that they were seeking something from him for themselves, some notice, some flattery perhaps. But here was purity with loveliness and he drank it in, reverently, scarcely knowing that he stood gazing at her.

Then all at once his look of adoration changed and that stern look of sorrow came to take its place in his deep brown eyes. When he spoke it was as if the words were torn out of his heart, agonizingly.

"She—is—" he took a deep tortured breath—"my—mother."

The pain in his face defied the girl to speak or to pity.

Joy was stunned. But the sweet look that held high honor for him never left her face. She put out her soft little hand and laid it gently on his arm with a tenderness of sympathy that the boy had never known.

"Oh-h-h!" she said, with a world of understanding of his suffering, yet with no less admiration for him in her tone. "Then I think it was all the finer for that!" she added, knighting him again with her glance. Then with one last smile of radiance she turned and walked swiftly up to the corner, and rounding it, she disappeared.

He took two strides after her, as if he must not lose the precious thing that he had just found, then as suddenly he stopped, remembering his shame.

The stern, hopeless look came back to his eyes and his whole figure drooped. Gradually he became aware that the boys were calling from the sandlot across the street: "Donovan! Get a hustle on!"

"Hey, Steve! What's got ya? You're up!"

"For Pete's sake get a move on! *Don*-ovan!"

Slowly he turned and went back to the game.

Meanwhile, Joy walked home with her heart in a whirl. Although she had not sought admiration, she was not unaware of the homage this young man had paid her. And she was thrilled at the remembrance of the honor and respect in his look. There had not been the slightest effort on his part to take advantage of her informality. He was a gentleman, as true a knight as she had pictured him. She tried to quiet the exultant throbbing of her heart by telling herself that this whole thing had been just an unusual little incident which would be forgotten by them both in a day or two. But something within her told her that she would not forget, that the memory of this fine man would remain with her always, and be an ideal against which she would find herself measuring every other man she met.

But there was a deep gash of pain, too, as she recalled the suffering in the boy's eyes when he told her the truth about his mother. How terrible that a woman could do that thing to her son. She had been an attractive woman once, Joy could see that in her first glance. How could such a thing come to be? Joy tried to imagine what it would be like to live in close quarters with shame as this boy had to do. She found herself longing to help in some way. Yet what could she do? She did not even know his name and probably never would.

Joy sighed. She had been aware of troubles in the families of her friends, deaths, illnesses, sorrows or difficulties of one kind or another, but this had seemed to strike home with a kind of shock that set her placid world aquaking. How could such a thing happen to a fine young man like this one?

She walked more slowly on the way home, searching for the first time for a satisfactory answer to sorrow in the world. A cloud had come over her sun and a little shudder ran through her as she reached the porch of her pretty home again. But she shook it off and held her head a little higher as she remembered the fineness of that grand young man. How bravely he was taking it! She wondered if many boys would have taken it that way. As she opened the front door she wondered how she could take trouble if it came to her. Then she started down the spacious center hall to give Emmy the bread. The library door stood open and her heart turned over in terror.

There, slumped on the rug in the library, lay her father, face down.

# ～ *Chapter 2* ～

WITH A SOBBING cry Joy flung down her loaf of bread and sprang to her father's side. Fear clutched at her heart as she knelt and bent over him to listen for his breathing. She flashed a glance around for blood stains, with a wild idea that he had been shot, but there was no sign of violence. His face was ghastly white. He did not seem to be breathing. She listened to his heart but she could not be sure whether it was beating or not.

Unconscious of the icy trembling of her limbs she rushed to the hallway again and screamed, "Emmy! Emmy! Come quick!"

The faithful colored woman dropped her rolling pin onto the big table where she was making apple pies, and wiping the flour on her apron she came as fast as her weight would allow her. She was an old-fashioned servant who loved those she served and she sensed the distress in Joy's tone. She had seen trouble herself and knew much of its subtle ways. So her voice was calm and full of sympathy as she took one look at her master and gave her simple diagnosis.

"That thar looks like a stroke, honey chile. You go call yo' doctor whiles I gets him some smellin' salts. Could be he's jes' fainted."

Joy felt herself staggering from weakness as she went obediently to the telephone at the back of the hall. Her fingers fumbled with the leaves of the telephone book, and she won-

14

dered impatiently why she couldn't find the number. Then she realized she was looking under the "D's" for "Doctor" instead of under "M" for MacKenzie! She took a deep breath and tried to steady herself. She was the head of the household in these moments until her father came to himself again. She was conscious of a great relief at Emmy's suggestion that he had fainted. She had always leaned on Emmy.

Dr. MacKenzie lived only a few blocks away and happened to be in his office when she called. But the few minutes before he arrived seemed ages to Joy.

Emmy had decided not to disturb her patient, though she had rolled him in a warm blanket. The restorative had not brought him to, and Joy and Emmy were hovering over him when the doctor came.

Anxiously Joy watched his face as he made his examination. A cold hand seemed to grip her heart again as she saw the doctor's face grow more and more serious. She had to force herself to wait quietly for his verdict.

At last he lifted his kind gray eyes to hers and said as gently as he could: "It's a cerebral hemorrhage, I'm afraid." He watched Joy's face grow whiter and saw the perplexity come into her eyes.

"What is that, doctor? I mean, of course I've heard of them, but I don't know just what—how serious—" she stammered, dreading to say what she feared.

"Come over here and sit down, child," Dr. MacKenzie said, starting to lead her to her father's big chair, and unobtrusively taking her pulse. "Oh no!" she cried. "Let me stay here by him. I'm all right." She straightened up and faced the tall gray-haired man. "I want to *know* what the chances are. Tell me the truth, please," she said bravely.

The doctor nodded, giving her a keen level look to measure her stability.

"All right, I will," he responded. "Frankly, he has a slight, a very slight chance of full recovery. It is possible that this may not be an actual hemorrhage. Sometimes under high pressure a blood vessel becomes too full and a pressure is set up that paralyzes whatever part of the body is controlled by it. If there is an actual breaking of the vessel a clot is formed and there is practically never full recovery. We must get him to the hospital immediately and he must be kept absolutely quiet. We may not know for some days or weeks what the outcome will be."

Joy's tortured eyes looked steadfastly into his. "Will he—do you think he will—" again she could not bring the word out.

"Will he live, you mean?" asked the doctor. "I'm not sure yet. It is possible that he might go at any time. We will do all we can, of course."

"Yes, doctor. Thank you." Joy's firm little chin was set and her voice was steady once more, although her sweet lips still quivered and their little uptilt was gone. "What can I do?" she asked.

"Take care of yourself, mostly," he smiled. "When your father is better he will want to see you looking like yourself, not worn out with worrying."

Joy smiled a wan little smile. "I'll try," she sighed.

She waited, sitting close to her father, stroking him gently, while the doctor made his phone calls. But when the ambulance had come and she was seated in it with the nurse, watching that still white face that was so dear to her, she felt as if she would collapse. How alone she felt! She had tried to find Mickey but he had gone out with the gang, even before she had left for the store.

How utterly changed everything was since she had started out that morning. How beautiful the day had seemed. What promise of pleasure the holiday had held, with the ball game and the prospect of her father going with them! Oh, how *could* such a thing happen! Her whole life seemed to be in tatters before her. Suppose Daddy should not get well? Suppose he should be an invalid all his life? How he would hate that! She would wait on him. Oh yes, gladly. But he would suffer so under the thought that he was not free and independent any more. Her dear, straight, strong daddy, with his wonderful flashing black eyes and his warm, delightful smile.

Sickness, sorrow! They had done no more than cast their shadow near her before, since she was a tiny girl. Distant relatives had been invalids. Her own cousin had had to leave college to take care of her mother. But now it had touched Joy herself. Her world had crashed all about her and she was left standing in the midst of the ruins. Alone. Utterly alone. She had never felt alone before, for there was always her father to go to. She began to have some little realization of how tender and gentle her father had always been. How he had taken the place of both father and mother to her. Wonderful that he could do it. Where did he get the understanding? Was it because he had suffered? She sighed again, a deep sigh and then became aware that slow tears were creeping their way down her face. The nurse looked woodenly at them and offered her a paper handkerchief as she saw Joy pawing for a pocket in her dress. Joy accepted it, wondering whether that starched figure had ever known suffering herself. Was she so accustomed to it that she could take it for granted now? Perhaps that was the way to be. To become hardened to sorrows. Would that be a way out? Could that happen when there was suffering to meet day after day, perhaps year after year?

Then suddenly, like a bright light, so bright it was like a pain itself, came the image of deep brown eyes with suffering in them. Where had she seen them? Oh! This morning. That nice boy. He had suffered. He probably had his kind of suffering to meet day after day. She wondered how long it had been going on for him. It didn't seem to have hardened him. Anyway, he met it bravely. It gave her a little feeling of encouragement and almost comfort to think that there was someone else she knew who was walking this hard way of sorrow. She was not alone. There were millions of others, too, of course, but she did not know them. If she ever saw that boy again she would like to ask him some questions. Ask him how he was able to meet his trial. Ask if it never floored him as he awoke to a new day and knew it was there. But of course she probably never would meet him again. She had been ridiculously impulsive to speak to him anyway, a perfect stranger. But he did not seem like a stranger to her. It seemed now as if they had something in common.

Somehow Joy managed to live through the next few hours. She went up to the bare silent room where he lay, and watched. Watched for some flicker of life in that too still face. She kept back her sobs. Only slow tears made their way now and then down her cheeks. She was aware that if she made the slightest disturbance the nurse would put her out. She was glad that this nurse was more human than the one in the ambulance had been. This girl was pale and sad looking herself; she patted the covers gently about her patient's still form as gently as Joy herself could have done. Joy thanked her in her heart for that. She wondered whether this girl had lost her father too. For Joy had already the feeling that her father was gone. Not to be able to speak to him and have him answer was just like death. Oh, how was she ever going to bear it?

The day wore on, a faultless spring day, but it might have been dark and stormy, for all Joy saw of its brightness. At noon she called up her home and asked Emmy if Mickey had come in yet. He should be told, of course, but Joy dreaded the telling. She did not know how Mickey would take it. He had seemed so unfeeling, of late; all he looked for in life was a good time, she thought a little resentfully. The thought came to her that she was not very different herself, perhaps. Her own aim in life had been little if any higher than her brother's. Parties, gaiety, dates with one or another nicely mannered boy, picnics, a pleasant interlude of studies sandwiched in, for Joy had always liked books and did well in school and the two years of college she had had. There had been no thought in her head so far that there would be anything but fun in her future. It humbled her to think that perhaps she had been no more mature than Mickey, no more ready to understand and sympathize with some of the difficulties her father must have had to face, than the one she condescendingly called her "kid brother."

Again she sighed as she waited for Emmy to answer the telephone. No, Mickey had not come home yet. Emmy promised to tell him as well as she could.

"And make him *understand,* Emmy, how really serious it is." For Joy had the apprehensive feeling that Mickey might take his father's illness as lightly as he took every other circumstance in his life that threatened to hinder his doings with "the gang." It would seem terrible if Mickey should insist, for instance, on going to that ball game. It would be as if some member of the family should play ball when there was a funeral in the house.

"Oh, I'll talk to him, honey chile," agreed Emmy. "Don' you worry none."

But Joy did worry. And it was a great relief to her an hour later to catch a glimpse of Mickey's burnished copper curls, sleekly combed, behind the doctor's coat sleeve as Dr. Mac-Kenzie came in again to inspect his patient.

Evidently the doctor had done his share of explaining, as well as Emmy, for Mickey wore an unaccustomed look of concern which Joy had rarely seen on him before. He marched with an air of authority over to the bed where his father lay so motionless and white, as if he had come to see what all this fuss was about and straighten it out.

But when he looked at his father's still face he took one gulping, gasping breath and turned quickly away and strode out of the room, casting only a frightened despairing glance at Joy as he went. Only she saw how near the tears were to brimming over, and in kindness to his feelings she waited a

moment before stepping out into the corridor to speak to him.
She well knew he would loathe having anyone see him cry.
It comforted her a little, though, to know that he could care
that much.

"Gee, Sis," he burst out when she touched him on the shoulder as he stood gazing out the window at the end of the hall.
"Gee! Dad looks awful!" He nearly broke down again and
only just looked away out the window in time to keep two
disgusting tears from rolling down his face right in front of his
sister.

"Yes, Mickey, he does," Joy answered gently. Her own woebegone look was softened by her sympathy for him. She was
surprised that he took it this way. She had been so afraid that
he would be impudent and fresh about it, getting off some
smart remark. There must be a real heart in him after all.
Perhaps he was even going to be a help.

"Doc says he may not get well!" Mickey went on fiercely.
"Gee! what's Dad ever done to be hit by a thing like this? It
isn't right!" Mickey clenched his fists in bitterness.

Somehow it shocked Joy to see that hard look on her
brother's face. She felt she should be able to answer the question of why this had happened, but she found that she had no
answer.

"Don't feel that way, kid," she tried to soothe him. "Things
do happen, you know, to good people. And Daddy may come
out of this all right. Dr. MacKenzie said so."

But Mickey's face remained hard and he stood still gazing
stormily out the window. Joy felt helpless before his challenge.
She wondered whether anybody did have an answer for such
things. She had never heard any.

Suddenly Mickey turned and bolted down the corridor with
only a gruff "I gotta beat it. I'll be seein' ya." And he was
gone.

Sorrowfully Joy went back to take up her vigil. The doctor
had no further word for her. The waiting seemed endless.

The nurse sent her down to the little hospital lunchroom sometime that afternoon, with a command to get herself something to eat. Joy tried to choke down a peanut butter sandwich, but she could scarcely swallow.

At eight o'clock that night the doctor came again and sent her home, promising to call her if there was the slightest change. So she dragged herself out to her little car and reluctantly wove her way out to the pleasant quiet of Sherbrooke Avenue. But the big house was so empty!

Even Mickey was not there. He had been to the hospital once more that afternoon but he had stayed no longer than the first time. Joy tried to realize that his boyish energies could not be tamed to the long endurance of watching there, but she was so lonely. She tried to think of some one of her friends whom she would want with her. There was Mildred. She had played with her since they were little girls and she was fond of Mildred in a way. But lately their paths had parted somewhat, as Mildred's maturing tastes led her into rather frivolous ways in which Joy had no interest. No, Mildred would have no comfort for her. She would only try to take her mind off this trouble, by avoiding mention of it. That had always been Mildred's way; if she didn't like something she would by-pass it. But Joy didn't want to take her mind off. It would seem like deserting her father. She could not bear to leave him, even in spirit, though she had been forced to go from the hospital for the time being.

Then there was Eleanor. She was more serious. In fact, she was something of a philosopher, always taking people's feelings and thoughts apart and analyzing them. She was interesting sometimes, but she had no heart. She would tell Joy just why it was she felt badly and advise her to take a certain attitude of mind, like medicine in a bottle that could be spooned out.

Joy thought of her grandmother, her mother's mother. Yes, she was sweet and she knew how to comfort, as Joy remembered from short visits away out West when she was a child. Grandmother would have drawn her into her arms and spoken gently to her, perhaps found her some lovely words from her Bible. But Grandmother was not here, and Joy needed somebody at hand.

Strangely enough, as she climbed wearily into her bed, there came the thought of that young man she had seen on the street this morning. She had a feeling that those broad shoulders were able to carry great burdens. She had a sudden longing to have him step up beside her and put his strong hand under her arm and help her across this hard place as she had seen him do for his mother that morning. But she tossed the thought away again as futile and foolish. He was a stranger to her. He might not turn out to be a fine sort of person at all, on closer acquaintance.

Joy thought she would not be able to sleep at all that night for sorrow. But she did not realize how utterly weary she was from her day of unaccustomed trouble, and she soon dropped off into heavy slumber.

She did not hear the sound of footsteps on the front walk, or the chime of the door gong. Only Emmy was there to answer it, for she had stayed up, after getting Joy off to bed, to wait for Mickey. She felt responsible since the master of the house was not there. Mickey had come in at a reasonable time, nine o'clock or so, asked a gruff question "How's Dad?" and gone stumping off to bed.

The caller was a young man, a little under average height, very well dressed. He stepped confidently into the hall. Emmy did not have her spectacles on but she recognized him as Pembroke Harvey, Mr. Applegate's young assistant.

He bestowed a smile on Emmy which was tempered with just the right amount of concern. The smile showed perfect teeth between red lips and above the smile was a thick little crisp black mustache. His chin was rather attractive, with a small cleft in it, but it was just a bit too short for the rest of his face. His dark hair had a wave across the forehead that any girl might envy. His smile made the outer ends of his black eyebrows point upward.

"Is Miss Joy in?" he asked deferentially.

"Yassir, she is. But she's gone to bed. She's been through a mighty lot today and she was wore out. Mr. Applegate's been took sick."

"Yes, I have just heard the bad news. Miss Joy telephoned the house this afternoon to let me know, but unfortunately I was not at home. I called to offer her my sympathy."

"Well, I c'n tell her," vouchsafed Emmy, "but not tonight. I think she's asleep already."

The visitor smiled again, a somewhat amused smile.

"Don't disturb her then, I beg you," he assured her. "I will call tomorrow. Thank you. Good night."

He bowed as courteously as if Emmy had been more than a servant in the house, as indeed she was, and politely withdrew.

Emmy closed and locked the door after him with a questioning frown on her dark brow. "A mighty smooth young man," she muttered to herself. "Almost too smooth. An' he's settin' his cap fer Miss Joy shore 'nuf." Then she shook her worried old head and sighed as she climbed the stairs to her pleasant back room on the third floor.

# ~ Chapter 3 ~

STEVE DONOVAN STAYED with the game across the street until the end of the last inning. Not that he was eager over the outcome. Any mild interest he might have had when he started was gone. But it was a way to pass the holiday morning, his first holiday from his new job, and he did not want to go home. He wanted to put that off as long as possible.

When noon came and the rest of the fellows drifted away, most of them to their homes to get a bite of lunch before freshening up to go out on some date, Steve sauntered down to the corner at the highway, watching the heavy traffic, then slowly went on up the street, idly walking a few blocks before he would have to give in and go back to the house.

The Donovans had not always lived in poverty and disgrace. The years when Steve and his sister Laurel had been growing up had been reasonably happy ones. Their father was fairly well to do; their house, while not handsome, was roomy and comfortable and their father kept the grounds looking nice. The inside of the house had reflected somewhat the intense, artistic nature of their mother. If there was some disarray, there was warmth and vivid coloring in the furnishings. It is true that the family were sometimes left to the tender mercies of the cooks who came and went, for there were days when their mother was too engrossed in some musical activity to take time out to give routine orders. But there was love in

their home and that covered a good many of Charlotte Donovan's sins of domestic omission.

The calamity came during Steve's last year in college. His
father was in an automobile accident and died within a few
hours. It was a blow to them all, but it completely crushed his
wife who had loved him desperately and passionately, as such
an intense nature as hers could love.

Steve finished college, as his father had wished, and came
home only to be called almost immediately into his period of
army service. The last six months of it he was away so far
that it was almost impossible for him to get home, and then
his mother wrote that they had moved.

Sometimes her letters showed a high attempt at great bravery
but other times she would pour out her grief to her son until
he felt he could not bear to think of her suffering so. But then
that was like her. Always either up or down. She had tried
two or three times to work but for some reason she seemed
unable to keep any job. Laurel's infrequent letters were only
brief expressions of despair and discouragement over the
comedown in their way of living. But Laurel was in her teens,
just out of high school and bitterly disappointed anyway because she had to go to work instead of going to New York to
study for the stage as she had always wanted to do. Steve felt
he could not judge very accurately the state of things from
either his mother or sister.

But sometimes there came to him the memory of his
father's words during the precious few minutes they had had
alone together before he passed away. That talk came and re-
hearsed itself before him when he was on the train on his way
home after his army discharge, as if to prepare him for what
he was to do next.

"Son," his father had said earnestly, "it is going to be up to
you to take care of your mother now. I don't mean financially.
I guess you all can make out with the insurance and the bonds.
But I mean other ways." His father took a deep tortured

breath and the sweat came out on his forehead as he struggled to make clear to his son what he wanted of him.

"I knew what your mother was like when I married her, Steve," he went on. "She was dynamic and intense, and very talented, you know. She was like a flame, Steve. And I loved her! But I was afraid of that flame. I tried to stifle it. I tried to calm her down. But I failed. I tried the wrong way."

His father was breathing fast with the effort of speaking. He had to wait a moment before going on. Steve sensed that it was not the physical effort, nor the pain of his poor maimed body, but the distress of his heart that troubled him.

"She wanted to sing," he continued, speaking with many hesitations, and gasping sometimes for breath. "She has a marvelous voice, you know. She had a chance to go into opera and she would have been a great star. I knew that then, and so did she. And I was afraid for that. I had been brought up to feel that actresses and opera stars were pretty fast moving people, not generally the sort that make good honest citizens and home lovers. It didn't seem right to me. I was jealous of a career for her, and besides, my father and mother had given me high ideals of right and wrong. Your mother considered them narrow. I still don't know whether they were right or not. But my parents knew God in a way that I never did. I could have. I know that now. And I know now that that was the most important thing I could have done."

Steve bent closer as his father stopped speaking and closed his eyes. He tried to tell whether those painful breaths were still coming. Then he saw slow tears stealing from under his father's closed lids. Steve roughly brushed away his own tears and sat up to listen again as his father went on.

"I could have," he said, as if he had not stopped talking, "but I wanted to succeed first in business. And I wanted to please your mother, to make up to her for what I had asked her to give up. I guess I put her first—before God. Now I know I was wrong. If I had learned to know Him better He might have helped me with her. She has been headstrong, Son. And your sister is like her. It won't be easy for you to carry on where I've failed. But Son, remember! *The one thing I didn't try was God!"*

The sorrow and remorse in his father's voice were almost too much for the boy. He wanted to soothe him, but he realized that it was giving his father relief to be able to talk.

"I'm telling you this, boy, so that you will have a better start than I, perhaps. For it's going to be up to you to help them. I failed. They are too intense for their own good. They need a strong hand to guide them but a hand that will do it in love. They will do anything for one they love. If your mother had not loved me, and I her, with a love that will never die, she wouldn't have been willing to give up her career. I'm sorry now that I asked it of her without giving her something better to satisfy her. A quiet family life and just me was not enough. Perhaps God would have been—I don't know. I'm going to talk to her too, Son, if I have strength. But the hard part is going to be up to you. Good-bye, Steve."

His father had slipped off soon after that and had never had the talk with his wife. Steve had wondered sometimes whether he should tell his mother something of what his father had said, but the time never seemed ripe.

He had not forgotten it, although at first the activities of his senior year had pushed to the back of his mind any responsibility about his family. It troubled him while he was away the next year, but on the train on the way home from the army it came back with a rush.

He found the new address his mother had given him in her letter. But when he arrived at the house he stood still, aghast. Surely they must have had hard times making ends meet if they had come to this. There must be some mistake. He got out his mother's letter and looked up the number once more. Yes, this was right, 512 Emerson Street.

His thoughts were in a turmoil as he took the two broken

front steps in one stride. He was still uncertain so he knocked.
There was no answer. He ventured to peer into the front
window that gave onto the porch. Yes, there was their dark
red velour living room furniture, or most of it. The door was
unlocked, so he walked in and whistled as he always used to
do. He tried to sound cheerful, so that his mother should not
guess his chagrin at the sort of house they were in. But there
was no answering call. His mother always used to sing a rich
trilling note or two in welcome. He had loved her voice.
There was a thrilling quality to it that made one long to hear
more.

Steve whistled again. Then he went out to the kitchen.
Perhaps she was in the back yard and couldn't hear. Laurel
wouldn't be back from her work yet, of course.

But there was no sign of his mother either in the dark un-
kempt kitchen or in the untidy little patch of a yard.

With foreboding he climbed the steep narrow stairs, whistling on the way up. He thought he heard a stirring. The
doors of the three tiny bedrooms were open and there lying
across her bed was his mother in a soiled housecoat, asleep,
her lovely masses of long black hair dishevelled and tumbled
across the bed.

Tenderly Steve stepped over to waken her, eager to surprise
her, to hear her old time glad cry of welcome, and see her
beautiful eyes light up as they always did at sight of him. But
something in the way she lay sent a stab of fear to his heart.
She did not look natural. Perhaps she was sick. Or had
fainted. He shook her gently and she stirred and moaned a
little.

"Mother," he called. "Mother, wake up!" He tried to laugh
a little as if he had a good surprise. She opened her eyes and
they were red. With weeping, he thought. Poor Mother.
Nearly two years since Father left them, but the grief was still
gnawing at her heart.

Gradually comprehension dawned as she gazed dully at her

son. He smiled and stooped to kiss her wide awake. Then like a sword thrust, the odor of liquor assailed him and he straightened up as if she had struck him.

"Mother!" he cried in horror.

Oh, Stephen was used to liquor. They had always had it in the house, though he had never liked it himself and he knew his father did not. But they used to serve it at parties. His mother had been brought up in New York and considered it essential to a gay party. So his father had reluctantly given in. He had seen his mother many a time toss off a glass and seem the brighter for it. But it had never occurred to him all during the last year that she would seek this way of drowning her grief.

He took her by the shoulders and roused her wide awake.

At last she seemed to come to herself and recognize him. She smiled but her smile was too silly to be natural.

"Stevie! You're home! I've been waiting up for you and I must have fallen asleep," she apologized and her hands went up to smooth her tossed hair.

But Steve looked sternly, sadly, at her. "No, Mother. It's not night. You've been drinking, Mother," he said accusingly. "You've been drinking a lot. Oh Mother! Why did you do it?"

He sank down on the bed beside her and groaned, torn between his horror and a longing to have her take him in her arms as she used to do and tell him that this wasn't so, that his fears were only shadows.

The agony in his voice seemed to reach her. She roused to laugh and reassure him. But her voice was thick.

"Oh, maybe, Stevie, just a bit too much. You were coming home, you know, and I wanted to be bright. I had one of those old headaches of mine and I thought maybe I could throw it off. I'm sorry, sonny boy! Here." She reached over and drew him to her, giving him an unsteady hug and a kiss and then she laughed delightedly.

But her breath was heavy with liquor and her laugh was too gay. The shadow on Stephen's heart was real, and it had come to stay.

They sat down on the end of the bed to talk, since she was determined to pretend that nothing was wrong. She seemed really to be herself again. But when at last Steve took his suitcase to his own room and began to unpack, he was far from light-hearted. The distasteful living conditions, the tiny cooped-up room he could accept bravely and he soon could remedy all that, he thought, for he would get a job right away. But the horror over his mother's state would not subside. Perhaps it was the more bitter as he reflected that it was partly his own fault. His responsibility in the light of what his father had charged him with loomed very large now. He had not carried out his father's wishes. But what could he have done? He had not been home six weeks in all since his father had gone. He put his head in his hands and groaned.

Laurel came in just then and started up the stairs. He called her into his room and tried to greet her in the old way as he used to do to tease her:

"Hi, kid!" with a kiss on the lips and a brotherly spank at the same time. But Laurel seemed rather unconcerned. She shrugged off the caress and answered carelessly, "Hi, yourself!" She went to the mirror and began combing out her thick glossy black curls.

Steve looked at her in dismay. Then he went over and softly closed his door.

"Say, where's Mother, kid?" he asked cautiously.

"Down in the kitchen," responded Laurel without stopping her combing. "You rate high. She's actually getting dinner. And I saw a roast in the icebox this morning. I scarcely knew what it was!" She gave a hard laugh.

Steve frowned. This was Laurel's way of letting him know how bitter she felt over the state of things. But he had to find out more.

"How long has this been going on, kid?" he asked.

"What? Living in this dump?"

"No, I mean Mother. She was out like a light when I came in. Silly drunk."

"Oh, that!" Laurel tossed her hair back and patted it into a lovely wave over her forehead. A discouraged sneer came into her deep-set black eyes under their curved brows, eyes so like her mother's. She sniffed scornfully. "The old girl's like that a lot these days. Sure is a great help, isn't it?"

Steve turned on his sister and whirled her about to face him, holding her shoulders in his strong grip with both hands.

"Laurel! When did you start calling Mother 'old girl'?" he demanded.

"What's it *to* you?" she retorted. "Let go of me!"

Steve studied his sister in amazement and chagrin. This was a girl he did not know. She was no longer the gay tomboy he had loved to have as a companion. He had played with her and taught her all the boy lore he knew. She could handle a canoe as well as anyone, and pitch in a ball game with the boys. He had taken her with him proudly, when many a boy would have left his sister at home.

But in those days she had been loving and teachable. She had adored her big brother. What had come over her? He could see that she was ready to take sides against him now. She must be handled with care.

He released her arms and she swung away from him and went on with her hair. But he spoke gently.

"Maybe it doesn't matter what it means to *me*, kid," he said, "but after all, think what Dad would have said if he had heard you talk like that."

"Oh, Dad." Her voice was hard and bitter, choking back any tenderness that might have been there. Her words seemed to well up from dark depths within her. "Where is he now? Nowhere. He can't count any more."

Steve was silent a moment, trying to grasp his sister's point of view, so altered from what it used to be.

"I'm not so sure of that," he said at last, thoughtfully. "Anyway, he was our father and he was swell. He tried to teach us the right way as far as he knew it. He gave us a darned good start, I think."

"So what?" shrugged Laurel.

" 'What'? Well, there's God, of course," suggested Steve.

"Oh yeah?" sneered Laurel. "Okay, if you still think so. What's He ever done for us? I've got my own life to live now. So have you. Do yours as you choose and so will I." She glanced at him belligerently and flaunted out of the room.

He sat down and put his head in his hands and groaned again. What had his family come to? His father had spoken truly. There was a hard way ahead. Steve felt utterly baffled.

He finished unpacking and stood looking out the dirty window at the dreary vacant lot across the street. Then he sighed and went downstairs where his mother with character-istic feverishness was putting on the best tablecloth in honor of his return, although it was rather mussed, and getting out the best china which had not been used in so long it was dusty.

He took a deep breath and resolved that the first thing he must do was to get a job, tomorrow, early! Then he set his lips and determined to be cheerful with his mother on this first night at home. He certainly would never get anywhere with her if he was cross and discouraged.

All that was three weeks ago. Steve had found his job, a good one, with a lumber company, and he had mended the front steps, cleaned up the yard and washed the windows. But there was no other house to be found within reason. And so far he had made no progress at all with his mother or sister. He had only discovered with more and more shame and horror that his mother was clear-minded and sober far less than she was beclouded. It seemed hopeless.

He reviewed the whole situation as he walked around those three blocks after the ball game. Well, there was nothing for it but to go home.

He turned back and went up the hill again toward the dismal house in the middle of the block. On the pavement in front of his home he paused and looked up the street. Suddenly there flashed before his eyes the picture of that girl he had met this morning. Up at that corner was the last place he had seen her. It had seemed to him as she vanished that the brightest thing that ever came into his life had disappeared. He had deliberately put from him the thought of her as often as it came back that morning, reasoning that he did not know her, could never know her, that she was out of his world entirely. But oh, she was sweet! It suddenly seemed to him now, as he gazed at the empty corner where he had last seen her, that he would give his whole life to have one more chance to see her. The sweetness of her radiant face drew him until almost without his knowledge he found himself starting up to that corner. He had a feeling he would find her if he only looked around the last house.

But again he stopped. There was responsibility waiting back there at home. It was time he looked after his mother. Laurel paid little or no attention to her. He must get her some lunch and see that she was all right. Still, he felt that strong longing to go up to that corner and try to recover what he felt he had lost this morning. Would it be possible that he could find that girl again by searching? Or had she been real at all? So like a lovely being from some heavenly realm she had seemed.

If he found her he would not need to speak. He would not presume on her having spoken this morning. If only he could see her again. She seemed the very embodiment of hope and joy. After lunch he would go.

He hastened into the house with a feeling of eagerness for the first time since his return. It seemed as if there might be a delightful surprise awaiting him this afternoon. He kept telling himself that he was foolish, crazy, yet he knew that he was going to search for her.

# ~ *Chapter 4* ~

EDWARD APPLEGATE'S NAME was on the big airy streamlined office at the corner of Main Street and First Avenue. He had started his building business years ago in a tiny office on a side street, but his natural business ability and his brilliant personality, coupled with his propensity for taking risks, had finally won an enviable place for him in the world of commercial building.

At the present time he was bidding on an enormous plant that would soon be erected in or near the city. He and his young assistant Pembroke Harvey had been working day and night on the plans.

Pembroke Harvey was the son of an old college friend of Applegate's. The father had died but Applegate, reckoning on inherited ability and learning that the boy had already proven his brilliance since his graduation from college, had decided to take him into his office. He had been working for Applegate for two years now and was fully as talented as Applegate had guessed he would be. Besides his ability at engineering he was a nice appearing young man, a little cocksure perhaps, but then he was generally right! He did have a rather overbearing way with the office force. But he was young; a little good-natured teasing would take that out of him. On the whole, Applegate was well pleased with his choice. This new plant would be Harvey's first big job. Applegate was letting him do a large share of the handling of it, and he was putting his best efforts into it.

Mr. Applegate had been in friendly touch for some years with Sanderson, the vice president of the Atlas Company which was putting up the plant. So it was natural on the golf course one day, for Mr. Sanderson to discuss with Applegate the matter of a site for the plant. There were two places under consideration: one at the northern end of the city, and the other out near Big River. Applegate's arguments for the Big River site, wholly unbiased at the time, were so convincing to Sanderson that he carried them back to the board meeting and subsequently told Applegate on the phone that it was as good as decided that that should be the spot.

It was not without a good deal of investigation and not until after the telephone call from Sanderson, that Applegate called Harvey into his office one day.

"Close the door, Pem," he ordered and the young man noticed an undertone of excitement in his employer's voice.

But the older man was silent for a few moments, while Pembroke waited. He seemed to be weighing for a last time the wisdom of the step he considered taking.

At last he said, "Atlas is choosing the Big River site, Pem." Harvey nodded and waited.

"What would you think of going into the real estate business for a while?" Applegate's eyes had a twinkle in them. Harvey smiled since that seemed to be expected of him.

"Do you realize," went on Applegate, "that there will have to be a whole new town out there? Houses for the workers, and stores, and what-have-you. I have been looking up the prices of land near the building site. It's ridiculously low, of course. Thousands of acres will be needed. A little enterprise and advertising would make a small city of it. Get me?"

Applegate looked keenly and delightedly at Harvey. That was a part of Applegate's charm. A new idea always made him as radiant as a boy.

Harvey raised his eyebrows and a gleam began to come into his eyes too. He said nothing at once but did some quick silent figuring.

"That would take a lot of money, sir," he ventured, but there was added respect in his voice for a man who spoke in terms of hundreds of thousands of dollars.

Applegate grinned wryly. "It would!" he agreed. "Banks have money for just such occasions." Harvey could see that his employer had already accepted the challenge of this thing. A new risk was a new toy to him.

Applegate had been leaning far back in his swivel chair dangling his legs like a schoolboy, as if he had not a care in the world. Suddenly he sat up and leaned forward looking keenly at Harvey.

"Listen!" he said. "We'll be ahead of anybody else on this if we snap it up now. I have it all figured out. Come over here."

He got out a pencil and drew a pad of paper toward him. For the next hour the two men sat together going over figures.

At last Applegate pushed back the pages and turned to the young man.

"And so, if you care to put in the twenty thousand you say you have, you and I will go into this thing together. I may as well tell you that I have been considering taking on a partner before many years anyway and it might as well be you. If this thing really goes through you will have a sizable amount to put into the business some day."

Harvey's eyes held subdued excitement. His tongue crept out and carefully wet all around the edges of his red lips under his mustache and he took a deep breath before he answered.

"Thank you, sir. I feel it's a great opportunity to be let in on a deal like this, and a greater honor even to be considered as a partner of Edward Applegate!" He bowed his head toward Applegate deferentially.

Applegate nodded, dismissing the honorary mention as inconsequential, and started immediately to make plans.

"You scout around and see if you can get the ground for any less than I have figured and I'll take you over to the bank and arrange for you to sign checks covering what we may need. I would rather not have my name appear in this just yet, or some of these property owners may smell a rat. I have to see my lawyer about power of attorney for my daughter on account of that trip I have to take soon and I will attend to this at the same time. I may be delayed so it's as well that you have full authority while I'm gone at least.

"But let's say nothing to anyone at all about this real estate deal, Pem," cautioned Applegate. "I'll have Thorne do all the desk work on it here. I can trust him to keep his mouth shut."

And so it was agreed. Everything went well for two weeks. Then, after commitments had been made and a good deal of the ground bought outright, Applegate met his friend from the Atlas company again on the street. They talked a few moments and then Sanderson said: "Oh, by the way, there may be a change after all in the plant site. One of the Board of Directors is awfully keen about the place on the other side of town, and he's rooting for it."

As if it made not the slightest difference to him one way or another, Applegate began to discuss again the various advantages and disadvantages of both sites. He took the Atlas vice president to lunch and so convinced him afresh that he promised to go back and do his best to swing the decision in favor of Big River. But Applegate did not mention his personal interest in the matter.

"I'll let you know right after the meeting, Ed. It will be day after tomorrow. And if I need you I may call on you to run over and give them a talk," he laughed.

"Fine," responded Applegate. "I'm sure I can make them see it!"

But it was this anxiety which had been in the back of his

mind as he watched his lovely daughter that bright morning in early summer. He had delighted in giving his children the best that this world could afford. He had taken great pleasure in the home he had built on Sherbrooke Avenue and was proud of the honored place he had earned in the life of the big city. It had all been accomplished by his own ingenuity and hard work. He had just been exulting in the beauty of their home and surroundings when he caught that glimpse of Joy as she blew him a kiss on her way out. A shade of apprehension disturbed him as he thought of what might happen to his home and his children and to the whole structure he had built up, if this present deal did not go through. But he had great confidence in his own powers of persuasion and if he received adverse news from Atlas the next day he still did not intend to let the matter rest. The whim of one member of a Board was not a sufficient obstacle to hinder a man like Edward Applegate.

Oh, he knew it was a risky thing he had done. A more cautious man would have waited until the decision was finally announced irrevocably. But then it would be sure to leak out and prices for land out there would soar.

He smiled again with a little lifting of his handsome black brows as he recalled the gasp of wonder his assistant had given when he had showed him what he was about to do. Harvey was an odd fellow, calculating and canny. That was one reason why Applegate had hired him. He could think a problem through in an instant. Applegate recognized admiration in that gasp and he could not help a little modest gloating over it.

On the whole, Edward Applegate was well pleased with himself that morning as he turned away from the window. He took a deep breath of excitement and anticipation as he thought of what the mail might bring him the next morning. Then he walked confidently toward his desk in the library. It was then, suddenly, that he felt that strange whirring in his head and everything became dark.

And the next morning when the postman brought his mail, it was Pembroke Harvey who opened the letter from the Atlas Corporation. Having received the message about his employer's illness, he had stopped at the hospital on his way to the office. It was vitally important that he know just what were the chances of Applegate's recovery.

He arrived at Room 309 just as a distinguished looking gray-haired man was leaving the room accompanied by a white-coated interne. He stopped the older man with: "Oh, Dr. MacKenzie!"—for all the world as if he were a fellow physician.

Patiently the tall man hesitated, stopped and seemed to question the rights of this young man who looked so smoothly confident.

"I am Mr. Applegate's assistant, you know," Harvey quickly assured him with his ready smile. "Can you tell me how he is? There are business matters that will have to be decided."

Dr. MacKenzie stopped then and drew Harvey to a quiet place in the corridor.

"Mr. Applegate is in a *very* serious condition, young man. He is still almost wholly paralyzed. He must not be disturbed for any reason whatever. Business must not be mentioned in his presence. He probably does not take in anything at all yet; it is hard to tell. But any mention of matters of a serious nature might be the end of him. There is still only the barest chance of his recovery."

Harvey looked impressed. "Oh! I see," he said. His face showed concern. "Could you tell me about how long this condition will last?" There was a great deal of anxiety in his tone.

"It is impossible to say, of course," responded the doctor. "If he lives through the next few days he may linger on for weeks or even months in a more or less paralyzed state. There is scarcely one chance in a thousand that he will recover entirely."

"Oh I see!" Harvey's tone was distressed. "Then even if he should, it would not be likely to be soon?"

"Not a chance in the world," the doctor said positively, looking curiously at the young man. "It will be a couple of months, I should say, before he recovers sufficiently to hear anything of business. Actually I doubt if he ever will, though I would not care to say that much to his daughter," MacKenzie warned, nodding his head toward the white room where Joy was seated again in a big chair, still waiting disconsolately.

Pembroke Harvey thanked the doctor who hurried away to his next patient. But Harvey went over and tapped lightly on the room door. He could see Joy's bright head bowed on her hand leaning on the arm of the chair. An eagerness stirred within him as he looked at her, a desire recurrent often of late, to possess that lovely thing for his own. She was a prize worth trying for.

The nurse came sternly to the door, shaking her head. She pointed wordlessly to the sign on the door "No Visitors."

But Harvey gave her his confidential smile and motioned that he would like to speak to the girl in there. He always counted on his smile winning a way for him and it generally did.

So Joy came out. Her lovely blue eyes were wet with tears hastily brushed away.

He smiled what he hoped was a sympathetic smile and said, "I called last night, Miss Joy." He wanted to make sure that she knew of the call, for that good-for-nothing old colored woman likely never thought of him again.

"Yes," Joy answered in a colorless tone. "It was good of you, Mr. Harvey."

"If there is anything that I can do, please remember that I am at your service, Miss Joy." He said it with a deferential bow.

"Thank you." Her voice was still dull.

"There may be some business matters that I should talk

over with you but I am sure you should not be burdened with
them now. May I call later this week?"

Joy nodded, more to get rid of him than because she cared
about what he said. She felt not the slightest interest in business. She knew nothing about it anyway and what did business matter now, while her father's life was in the balance?

Harvey went back to his office, entering by the side door
which led along a narrow corridor ending in the two doors to
his and Mr. Applegate's offices. As he passed his employer's
office he glanced at the gold lettering on the door. Then he
glanced at his own plain glass door. He narrowed his eyes
and then he smiled to himself as he went in, and the outer
ends of his eyebrows slanted up as he smiled. A new responsibility sat upon his shoulders. It was up to him to carry on in
Mr. Applegate's place. For the present at least, *he* was the
whole construction company. He wet his lips as if his new
power tasted good.

Before he sat down to his work he gave a glance at the big
outer office. That was *his* office force out there, *his* corps of
workers. They were responsible only to him now. He stood
watching their busyness a moment. Then he went into Mr.
Applegate's office and brought the pile of mail from his desk.
On the top of the pile was a letter from the Atlas Corporation.

Harvey sat down, picked it up eagerly and was about to
tear it open. Then he paused. It was addressed to his employer, of course.

Still, there was no one else to open the mail. He sat and
looked at the letter for some time. He was fully aware of the
great risk they had taken. He had been more apprehensive
about the whole thing than was the astonishing man whose
assistant he had been for the past two years. In fact he had
spent the greater part of the nights this week end trying to
work out a plan for his own future if this move of Applegate's should turn out to be a failure. He had already thought

of a way to get his own money out again without too much loss, and he had several other companies in mind to approach for a job immediately, should this be the case, for he had no notion of staying here if the man was going to have to cut expenses and pinch salaries for a time in order to remain in business. Harvey was determined to succeed whether other people did or not.

But now since his talk with the doctor there was a whole new aspect to the present affair. Applegate was out of the picture indefinitely. The situation might hold more for Pembroke Harvey than he had anticipated.

So he hesitated a long moment before unfolding the one sheet of paper the envelope contained. If this was an adverse decision, he would get out while the getting was good. It would be a blow to a lot of his plans, for he had hoped that before very long he might become a really intimate friend of the Applegate household. Then another increase or two in salary and the partnership that Applegate had hinted at, and the hand of his employer's beautiful daughter would be his for the asking. If only this proposition worked out Applegate would be a very rich man, a quality much to be desired in a father-in-law. But if this deal fell through he wanted no partnership. Even the beautiful daughter of a man who had failed would have no appeal. Failure did not figure in Pembroke Harvey's future. He had always envisioned for himself a long and colorful life in which he mounted from one pinnacle of success to another.

Just as he was about to open the letter, while the rosy glow of his ambitious dream was hovering in his mind, the drab figure of Tom Thorne, a stenographer and clerk in the office, appeared in the doorway. Annoyedly Harvey looked up. It was only a routine question that Thorne wanted answered, but Harvey spoke gruffly. For some reason he had never liked Thorne. He was a capable man, who lived a quiet middle-aged life behind his spectacles. Nobody seemed to know much about

him. It was not that he was intriguingly mysterious, but
Harvey always had the thwarted feeling that there was something in the little man which he could not understand or
master. Applegate had always set great store by Tom Thorne,
so Harvey never had openly expressed a dislike of him. But
now he dismissed him curtly and went back to his letter, stopping first to get up and close his office door. This letter might
require some serious consideration and he wanted to be alone
and undisturbed. It occurred to him in passing that that fellow
Thorne was aware of this real estate deal, for Applegate had
entrusted to him the stenographic work. The thought annoyed
Harvey subconsciously but he dismissed the thought of the
man as he had dismissed the man himself. He was just a
mousy little fellow, not worth bothering about.

Then he read the letter.

> Dear Ed:
> Your convincing logic won the day but starting
> date has been put off two months. See you later.
>                "Sandy"
>                   E. M. Sanderson

The world seemed suddenly to glow in a dizzying radiance
about Harvey as he read the note over and over.

Slowly his tongue crept out and carefully wet his full red
lips all the way around. The outer ends of his eyebrows turned
up. A gratified smile spread over his face. He had spent most
of the previous night in considering every angle of the whole
situation in the light of Mr. Applegate's illness. But now that
the real estate deal was a certainty he wanted to give it more
consideration.

For an hour he sat in deep thought, slowly twisting the gold
ring on his finger and watching the tiny ruby eyes of the tiger
face on it glint and gleam wickedly up at him. There were
great risks now for him to take, himself. But there was much
to gain. He pictured himself first as a business magnate well-

known and respected; then as the host at an elite gathering in the spacious Sherbrooke Avenue house; it seemed that he saw Joy as his bride, her exquisite face smiling adorably up at him. He took another deep breath and arose, committed to a plan that had gradually dared to take shape in his mind. He almost laughed aloud at the simplicity of it. Why, with Applegate out of the picture and his own signature already authorized, the thing was a natural! A man would be a fool not to walk through an open door like that. And it would all be under the guise of saving the business! What a break!

Only a slight frown disturbed his brow as he reflected that the working out of his plan might be a bit hard, for a time, on the girl he planned to marry. Then he shrugged. It was the best way, and she would be better off than ever in the end.

He went into the next office where Mr. Applegate's desk was and sat down at it. He spread his hands out on it. The polished mahogany felt good to his fingers. The wicked ruby eyes in his ring winked up at him again. This was a sunny office. It was handsomely furnished. It was a good place to work.

Pembroke Harvey wet his lips carefully and smiled at the eyes in the ring.

# ∽ Chapter 5 ∽

DAY AFTER DAY dragged on for Joy. She spent most of her time in that bare white hospital room. The doctor ordered her out now and then to get a walk and a breath of fresh air but she pled with him so that finally he gave up, telling her that any time now there would be some indication of change in her father's condition.

Emmy tried to feed her well at night, and she tucked her into bed with many a caress and a "Lor' bless yo', honey!" But Joy felt numb.

Now and then Mickey would appear at breakfast or dinner, and ask anxiously after their father. But he soon accepted the hiatus in family life and sought to divert his thoughts from their gloomy forebodings in pastimes with "the gang." Sometimes Joy would rouse to worry about him, but what could she do now? Wait till Daddy was better, and then she would try to interest him at home. It was depressing for him, of course. Once he had burst out at the dinner table with,

"Fer cat's sake, Sis, when are ya goin ta quit lookin' like a tomb? Gee! this is *some house* to live in!" And he had shoved back his chair and stamped out. That night he did not return until quite late, after midnight. Joy felt troubled and guilty about it, but try as she would to brighten up, her old merry smile would not come at her command.

It was Friday evening that the doctor suddenly turned toward her from his place by the bed and motioned to her to come near.

With a fluttering heart, she rose and went to the bedside.

Her father's eyes were open and there seemed to be recognition in them. She stifled a glad cry as the doctor warned her to be quiet.

Gently she took her father's hand, smoothing it and softly whispering, "Daddy! Daddy!"

Oh, what a relief to be able to speak his name to him and hope that perhaps he had heard.

The eyes seemed to smile, then there was a weak flutter of the lids and they closed again.

Dr. MacKenzie kept his hand on the patient's pulse for a long time.

Joy waited in agony. Her father looked so white and still again. Doctor MacKenzie's face was tense. Had he—*gone?* She wrung her hands silently in a terror of suspense.

At last the doctor raised his head with a calm confident look and nodded.

"I *think* he will live," he said soberly.

Joy gave a sobbing gasp.

"I only think so, child. We cannot know for sure. And it will probably be a long siege. More than a few days."

"Oh!" cried Joy. "It doesn't matter how long if only he comes back to us. I can wait, and I'll do anything you say. Nothing matters if only Daddy gets well!" Suddenly in her relief she buried her face in her hands and sank into the big chair sobbing silently.

The doctor came over and gently patted her shoulder. Those gray eyes had seen much suffering yet they had never lost their gentleness.

"Oh, thank you, thank you, Doctor," stammered Joy through her tears.

"You thank God, child," he said. "He has been very good to you."

Joy smiled weakly and nodded to him as he went out.

That night at dinner, after he had heard the good report, Mickey looked up at Joy several times as if he were going to speak, then he shut his lips grimly again. Her eyes were on her plate and she did not notice. Finally in the silence he blurted out, "The gang's comin' over tonight ta play ping-pong." He said it defiantly and then looked hard at Joy to see how she was going to take it.

An expression of dismay crossed her face and she put down her fork. Her brother's face hardened instantly.

"Oh, Mickey!" Joy exclaimed. "Couldn't you wait a little, till Dad's better?"

"I thought you said he *is* better!" retorted Mickey.

"The doctor said perhaps he will live, that's all, and we don't even know that for sure. Oh, I don't see how I could stand a party tonight."

"It's not a party," insisted Mickey, "just some o' the fellas, an' we'll stay down in the game room. But if you own the house now, all right, have it your own way."

He got up and shoved back his chair noisily and started to stamp out of the room again. But Joy quickly called after him.

"Oh, no, I didn't mean that, Mickey," she said, passing a hand over her aching forehead. "I suppose there's no reason why they shouldn't come. I'm just tired, I guess. Yes, let them come."

But Joy put her head down on her arms and groaned. How could she stand those boys tonight? It was Emmy's night out, too, and Joy was no cake baker. What could she serve them? She called Mickey and gave him a five dollar bill. "Run down on your bicycle to the drugstore," she told him, "and get what you can, kid. And you can keep the change."

Mickey growled his surprise at his sister's unexpected generosity and muttering, "Gee, thanks!" he rode off.

Joy sighed again and went upstairs to her room and lay down wondering when all this trouble would end.

She heard Mickey come in, and a few seconds later the door chime sounded. She listened. It was not his gang, for there was no noise.

"Mickey!" she called softly down the back stairs. "Will you answer that?"

"Heck!" came Mickey's gruff complaint from the kitchen. "I'm fixing the food. Oh, all right, I'll go," he grumbled. "Probably some stiff to see you, though."

A moment later she heard a murmur of voices. One was Mickey's; it kept breaking from high to low which always embarrassed him greatly. The other voice she did not recognize. It sounded suave and courteous.

Then Mickey came up scowling.

"It's fer you, just as I thought. It's Dad's assistant and he'll want to talk business. Gee! I'd hoped you would come down and play some. You can lick any o' the gang all hollow at ping-pong."

Joy smiled wanly at his compliment, attributing it accurately to the change from the five dollar bill. But she was glad to have an excuse not to play tonight, she felt so utterly worn out.

Wearily she dragged herself down to the living room, smoothing back a gold curl as she went.

Pembroke Harvey arose from the stiff chair where Mickey had rather unceremoniously seated him and made a low bow.

"Good evening, Miss Joy," he smiled. "It is good to meet again under better circumstances. The doctor assures me that there has been a change for the better."

Harvey seated her elaborately, his face sober. "I meant to say, that the circumstances are better as to your father's *physical* condition," he went on with a slight emphasis. Joy wished he would leave her father out of the conversation. It hurt her to have to discuss the details of his illness with one who was practically a stranger.

"But," he went on solemnly, "I regret that I have to be the bearer of unhappy tidings on another score. It grieves me especially because I can see that you have had so much to bear already. I could have wished that there were some other one to whom I could commit this telling, because, in the nature of it, it can connect me in your mind with trouble only and that is the last thing in the world that I would desire." He threw her a meaningful glance which she missed entirely. "But of course I was the obvious one to come. In fact, the only one who understands about it." He paused.

Joy had listened with only half her mind to his studied phrases and now as he paused she wondered what on earth he had been talking about. Had he asked her a question and was he now waiting for her to answer? How embarrassing! But almost immediately he continued, leaning toward her impressively. "Has the doctor ever suggested to you what may have brought on this illness of your father's?"

Oh, why would he keep going back to that? sighed Joy to herself.

"Why, no," she said absently, "not exactly."

"No?" Harvey cleared his throat sympathetically. "Has he never suggested it might have been from strain? Business worries, you know?"

"Well, no," responded Joy, wondering at this young man's questioning, feeling a sort of apprehension as he probed. "Of course he did ask if my father had been worried over anything especially."

"That's it," spoke up Harvey leaning forward. "I was sure that must be it. You see," he went on quickly now, "he was very anxious over a certain deal he was making. I don't know whether he had said anything to you about it?" Harvey looked keenly at Joy as she answered.

"Oh, you mean the big contract with Atlas? Yes, he mentioned it but," Joy gave a little shrug, "I don't pretend to know much about business."

"Well, I was sure he must have mentioned that," went on Harvey, "for it was most important. But more than that," he lowered his voice and spoke solemnly, "he had practically wagered his whole business and his own money besides on another deal in connection with that." Harvey paused to see what effect his words were having on Joy. She only looked bewildered.

Then he leaned close to her and spoke softly as if to a child. "May I ask whether you have any private income of your own, Miss Joy?"

"Why—why," she stammered confusedly. "I—what do you mean?"

Harvey, in his agitation and sympathy got up and came over to sit beside Joy. He considered taking her hand, as if he were comforting her.

But she still looked mystified. She was not yet thoroughly aware of the situation.

His face was sober and sorrowful and he laid his hand over hers. "You poor little girl," he purred. "You don't take it in, do you? You have had so much already! Do you know what it means for a man to lose everything he has?"

Joy's eyes grew wide with horror and something came up in her throat so that she could not utter a word.

"It is evidently that news which was too much for your father. I'm sorry!" soothed Harvey. "I regret, too, that *I* have had to be the one to tell you this."

Slowly the full import of his errand penetrated to Joy's stricken soul.

"You mean," she gasped, "you mean, that—my father has failed in his business?"

"That's what they call it," he said sadly, "when a man stakes all he has and loses." His head was bent low so that she could not see his face.

"And everything will be sold over our heads?" Joy found it hard to speak above a whisper.

"Well," ventured her caller, "you may be able to keep some few things that you prize. But usually when a business goes, everything goes. That is, if a man is honest and wants to pay all his debts. I am going to see what I can do for you," Harvey assured her magnanimously. "I shall keep for you what I can." He had told his conscience that that was the way it would work out in the end so it was not an untruth. He had not actually had to lie to her, he reasoned. She had played right into his hands.

"But tell me," he urged again, "do you have any private means? Of your own, I mean, that would not be in your father's name?"

In dismay Joy tried to think clearly. She suddenly realized that this young man was her only straw to clutch at. Her father had spoken of taking him into partnership some day. He was her father's trusted business assistant and as such was in a position of adviser to her. She supposed she must tell him these personal affairs if he were to help her, and he seemed to want to help her.

"Why, I have a few hundred in my own bank account. Would that have to go, too?" Her lips were cold and trembling.

He shook his head reassuringly. "Oh, no, of course not," he said. "It is good you have that ready cash for it looks as if everything in your father's private account as well as his business will have to go. I understand that your father gave you power of attorney anticipating that long trip he was expecting to make. Is that right?" He was looking at her keenly through narrowed eyelids.

Joy nodded. "Yes, but I don't understand much about it."

He smiled grimly and patted her knee. "Never mind that, child. I'll tell you all you need to know. It is going to be my business and my pleasure to look after you as well as I can. I will show you just what to do. You can simply sign a check to the company for the amount in his bank account. It may help considerably to overcome the deficit. But there! That is enough business tonight. I would like to try to cheer you up.

Is there anywhere you'd like to go? Anything you would like to do?" He drew up the flesh of his chin and tucked his lower lip comfortably over the upper.

But Joy was not noticing his face. She had just begun to take in the enormity of this calamity. She had been going on these few days since her father had been ill, ordering the best for him, secure in the thought that of course there would be money forthcoming to pay for everything. There had always been money. Now there was nothing! All at once it had vanished.

She looked despairingly at this young man who had come and devastated her life. Yet he seemed kind and no doubt was trying to help. In fact he was apparently the only one who could help.

"Oh no! No, thank you." She scarcely gave a thought to his offer of entertainment. "Do you mean that there is absolutely nothing between me and starvation except that bank account of mine?" she asked hoarsely.

Pembroke Harvey looked into her beautiful blue eyes that held such oceans of trouble in them, and he exulted in her loveliness. He put pity into his own eyes and hung his head sorrowfully. "That is what I came to tell you," he said mournfully. "But I shall do my best." He looked up encouragingly, conscious that he was her one bulwark. "I'm going to save what I can for you," he smiled. But it was not a pleasant smile. Joy did not even notice it. She suddenly had a feeling that she hated this young man who had dared to come into her lovely home and with one blow crush it to atoms. But that was ridiculous. He had had to come, of course. He was her father's assistant. It was kind of him. She would be able to see it that way some day. But now she felt she could not talk to this stranger and have him prying any more into her affairs. She must get away alone to her room and think this all out before she said anything more. She stood up.

"I thank you, Mr. Harvey, for coming to me with this. I

shall try to understand it, and my brother and I shall no doubt have to talk over further details later with you. It is a great blow, of course. But it is nothing to me as compared with my father's health."

She kept edging her caller toward the door. He would have been quite glad to stay and try to comfort her. He had rather hoped she would break down and cry on his shoulder. It would have given him a wonderful opportunity to get really well acquainted. But as it was, he had discovered a quality in her which he could not help but admire. Her courage was fairly formidable to him. What a girl!

As he was leaving he paused to say confidentially, "If I were you, Miss Joy, I would keep this illness of your father's as quiet as possible. Just tell people he is taking a rest, if you like, or that he is just under the weather for a time. It would be better for what business there is left if it is not generally known that he is out of the picture at present."

Joy was only half listening to what he said, but she had no desire to tell her affairs, so she simply nodded and said good night.

Harvey smiled triumphantly to himself as he took his way home. It had been a gratifying evening.

# Chapter 6

STEPHEN DONOVAN FIXED his mother a cup of hot strong coffee and a nice cream soup with crackers. The soup came out of a can he found in the cupboard, but he managed to make it taste good and the tray was attractive when he took it up to her. He roused her enough to make her eat it, went down to the little store and got her a new magazine he knew she liked and then, snatching a sandwich and a cup of the coffee himself, he started out on his quest for the girl he had met that fateful day.

He strode up to the corner with long eager steps, and turned the way he had seen the girl turn. He knew of course that she would not be there, for certainly she had not been hiding behind the corner house all morning waiting for him! Yet he had a sense of defeat and disappointment when he saw the long empty block ahead of him. His whole heart was set on finding her.

As he recalled the lovely picture of her standing before him looking up at him with that pure look of honest admiration, his heart turned over again with the sheer joy of being able to hug such a precious memory to him. How had such a thing ever come to him, Stephen Donovan? He had been so utterly discouraged and helpless in the past weeks since his return home that he had unconsciously grown to feel that nothing good would ever be in his life again. He lifted his head and straightened his shoulders just because that lovely girl had

offered him her homage. It was a sacred thing to him, to be
guarded in his thoughts, never to be viewed lightly, even in
his own mind.

He recalled the brightness of her yellow gown, although he
could not for the life of him have told what it was made of, or
that its simple classic lines had been born in a Parisian dress-
maker's studio. He remembered that gay little gold curl that
the June breeze had stirred until it frisked mischievously back
and forth around her dainty pink ear. He had a crazy wild
desire to put forth his hand and touch the softness of those
crowning golden waves. Oh, she was precious!

Stephen took a deep breath. He was going off his balance.
This was ridiculous. He must get himself on a steady keel
again. Who ever heard of a man meeting a girl once for half
a minute and acting like this about her? But if he could only
see her again, surely he would find whether she was real flesh
and blood or whether he had just dreamed her. He started on.

If she had actually been as well dressed as he remembered,
then she might have come from one of those fine houses up on
Sherbrooke Avenue. But surely a girl like that would not have
noticed him, nor cared to speak to him, clad as he was in old
working clothes. He walked on eagerly, scanning the yards
and windows of each house for a glimpse of a bright yellow
dress, or a golden head, but he saw none. Once he thought he
had found her, but when he reached the house where he had
seen a patch of yellow in the back yard, it was only a fluttering
dress on a clothes line.

On and on he walked, twice passing the Applegate house
unaware. The ambulance, with Joy in it, had long since come
and gone. Finally, discouraged and wondering whether he had
only dreamed the girl, he took his way back home but he
knew he would never cease to look for her.

He went into the house and turned on the radio to listen to
the ball game. Laurel had gone to the game with a fellow
Steve did not know. He had come for her while Steve was

fixing his mother's lunch. Laurel had defiantly introduced him as "My boy friend, Frank Ferroni." He had not liked the man's looks. He was dark and gay-mannered with his black hair cut low in front of his ears. Steve hated that in a man. It always looked as if he were trying to call attention to his own good looks. A man like that was sure to be a smart aleck, Steve thought. He wished he had been around when Laurel had started to go with boys seriously, the last year or two. He would have been able to steer her in her selection. For Laurel was a handsome girl, sure to be sought after, stunning to look at, with her very dark eyes and hair, and her look of flashing intensity. That look used to suggest an attitude of being fearlessly ready for any fun that offered, but it had altered since Stephen had been away. Now it was simply a devil-may-care look. He sighed. What *could* he do for his mother and sister?

Even the big league game did not hold his interest this afternoon. He found himself going over again in his mind that talk that his father had had with him before he died.

*God!* That was the one way his father had suggested that he try to steady the family. But how was a young man to know how to go about that? And if he did, why should he expect his mother and sister to listen to him? What did he know about God, anyway? His father had taught him very little. He knew only that his father had believed there was a God. Certainly his mother had never acted as if she took a God into consideration at all. In college his professors had discussed with patent condescension the possibility of a personal God, and almost without exception they had decided against Him. Steve had listened to their talk and watched their lives, and was not convinced that they knew what they were talking about. But he still had no notion of how to discover God himself.

He sat and stared at the radio knobs, scarcely aware of the announcer's voice calling the plays. Somewhere within him there was a conviction that there was a God, and that his father had been right, that in that God lay the answer to his problems. If this was not so, *there was no answer,* and Steve was not yet ready to admit that there wasn't. He was aware of a longing to know God. If he could get to know Him, surely He could do something for him. Yet how was he to go about it? It seemed that the search for an unknown God was something like the search for that girl he had seen, or thought he had seen. Would she turn out to be what he thought? Or would she prove as self-centred as most of the girls he had known? Perhaps God would not turn out to be what he hoped, either, if he ever found Him. But just as he had paused in his searching for the girl, knowing that it was not the end, that he would look for her as long as he lived, so he knew now that he had begun a search for God that could only end in finding Him, or finding that his father and his grandparents had been mistaken and there was no solution to a problem such as his.

He did not pray. He had never been taught to pray. But it was as if he entered into a covenant with himself, with his father, and with the God who might exist, to search until he found.

At last he heard his mother stirring, and with new patience born of his pity and his settled determination to find the way out he went up and cheerily urged her to get herself fixed up and they would go out to a nice little tearoom for supper.

They had a quiet time together, although it was hard these days for Steve to realize that this was really his mother, for she seemed so dull and colorless, when she had always been vividly alive and alert. He struggled to be cheerful. Some lovely music came in on the radio in the little restaurant and she brightened at that.

It was not a very lively party but at least Steve knew that his mother was all right as long as she was with him. He wished he could know the same of Laurel. They watched the traffic go by the big plate glass window beside them until dusk came on and they could no longer discern more than the shadows of cars passing. Joy's car was among them as she took her troubled way home from the hospital, but of that he was unaware. Rather drearily he got his mother home and finally to bed.

As soon as he was sure she was asleep he went out again to walk the streets. It had occurred to him that in the evening when the lights were lit in the houses, it was barely possible that he might catch a glimpse of the girl he was searching for. If he did discover where she lived, that house would be singled out for him as if it were a holy place.

So he walked and walked, condemning himself for a fool but still searching eagerly, hungrily. He covered every block within reasonable walking distance of that store where she had bought her loaf of bread. But he saw no sign of her.

It was midnight before he came back. Laurel was not home, so he took a book and read a while. Finally at two he went upstairs. Then he heard a car draw up in front of the house. He waited. It was nearly half an hour more before Laurel came in. He stepped out into the tiny hall to speak to her. But she must have caught a glimpse of the disapproval in his face. She looked him boldly in the eye and flaunted into her own room without a word. But her glance said, "I'll do as I please, and it's none of your business!"

Steve sighed again and went to bed.

Evening after evening he walked many blocks in the vicinity after he got home from work. Still he saw no sign of the golden-haired girl who had walked so sweetly into his heart that holiday.

It was about a week after he had first seen her that he turned back after going all the way to the end of Sherbrooke Avenue. One large stone house on the block was lit up and he could hear young eager boyish voices laughing and calling out to each other.

Suddenly the front door of the house opened and there she

stood, in the doorway! She was taking leave of a young man who bowed courteously and walked down to his sleek gray coupe that waited in the street. Then the front door closed and Steve could see no more. The light that had shown dim in what must be the living room went out and there was no further sign of her, although the boys' voices still sounded out on the quiet summer air.

Steve stood still, thrilling anew at the sight of her. There was no doubt in his mind that it was she. Her image was so clear in his mind that he felt he could not have mistaken her slender graceful figure. To think that he had found her! He stood a long time, watching the house. He felt as if he would like to stand guard over it all night lest harm should come to it before he could see her again. He exulted in the beauty of the place, even though its very elegance set her far apart from him. Their ways would probably never cross, yet Steve felt he had a small right in her. Had she not honored him with her glance and her smile, and her words? And all unsought by him?

He had a passing feeling of enmity for the well-tailored young man who had walked so confidently down those steps and taken his satisfied way. No doubt he was a friend, perhaps more than that. The thought suddenly· stung Steve in the heart. He had not gone so far in his thoughts of her before. Of course such a girl would have men friends. No doubt she was much sought after. What a fool he was even to dare to look at her! Yet he knew he would never give up seeking her until she herself refused to see him. He did not go so far yet as to hope to win her for himself. She seemed too sacred, too precious, to think of as a possession. But he found himself so guarding the very thought of her that he felt he would like to thrash the very daylights out of that other young man if in the slightest degree he did not measure up to what such a girl deserved. He went home at last telling himself that he was crazy, but exulting in the thought that at last he had found her.

If he could have seen her after that front door closed he might not have left the place all night.

Joy had turned from the door and stumbled to the couch, switching off the light as she went. She had a feeling that she must get off to herself where nobody could see her distress, to take in alone the awfulness of this thing that had happened.

This dear home! Her wild eyes stared through the shadows at the familiar chairs and tables, the handsome rugs that her father and she had chosen together. These things were not theirs any longer! Some hard faced creditor would soon be in there and snatch them all away. Joy got up and paced desperately up and down the room. She looked out the window at the elm-shaded lawn and down toward the swimming pool. What good times they had always had.

Their lives had been one long dream of luxury and pleasure. Oh, little troubles had come up from time to time. That time Mickey had had the mumps he had been very sick. There had been a fire, too, in one wing of the lovely house. But they were such small things, compared to this trouble! Now where would they go? If her father was sick a long time, who would find them a place to live? Who would earn their livelihood? The ghastly overwhelming realization came to her at last that she was the head of their household now. Mickey could help some time, perhaps, but then what would become of his schooling? She had had two years at college, she could do without more. But it was she who must make decisions, earn the money, find a place to live, and then take care of the place and feed them all. A terror came upon her. With an awful groan she flung herself upon the couch and buried her face in the pillows, shaken from head to foot with trembling and dry sobs. She felt as if she were being beaten blow after blow by great hammers as she quailed beneath each fresh realization of what would be expected of her.

After some time, through the dark billows of her thoughts, she became aware of Mickey's voice calling her, impatiently, angrily, then anxiously. He was out in the hall and saw the dark room and knew the visitor must have gone. Probably he thought she had gone off and left her brother in the lurch. Weakly, hoarsely, she tried to answer him.

"What's the matter, Sis?" he cried.

He rushed in and switched on the light trying to hide the panic in his voice, remembering too well, no doubt, the shock of what had happened last week. Quick pity brought Joy to herself again and she sat up and made an attempt to smile.

Mickey looked at her woebegone face and burst out again gruffly, "Fer cat's sake, whatsa matter?" Then caught his breath with, "Is Dad—worse?"

Poor Mickey! She must remember that his gruffness probably covered a terror as great as her own.

She spoke gently. "Come here a minute, kid," she said in a low voice, motioning to a seat beside her on the couch.

"No, it's not Daddy. But it's bad news, Mickey. You'll have to know it. Shall I tell you now or do you want to go ahead with the party downstairs first?"

Apprehension crept into Mickey's eyes. Almost fiercely he said, "Let's have it now. Get it over with! Business, I s'pose, since that guy Harvey was here."

"Yes, it's business, Mickey. Daddy's lost everything!" Joy's voice broke and her gold head went down against Mickey's shoulder.

Mickey put an arm about his sister, and responded lightly, "Oh, is that all? Gee! Well, we'll make out, I guess. Come on, let's get down there. The fellas 'll wonder where the deuce I am."

He got up, dragging Joy to her feet with him.

"Snap out of it now, kid. All tamorra to get used to the idea. C'mon down now an' forget it." And he sailed off waving her to follow.

Joy stood looking after him aghast. Of course he didn't take it in. He was young, and had never wanted for a thing.

And the responsibility would not be upon him anyway. It was hers. Slowly, with the feeling that she was carrying the whole weight of the big stone house upon her shoulder, Joy forced herself to go down the stairs and meet the boys there. Perhaps it was best after all to pretend to look cheerful, whether you felt so or not. Perhaps that was the way brave people carried off things like this. But Joy could not rouse to play her usual brilliant game of ping-pong and she seemed to see the boys as in a fog. Nothing about any of them attracted her and she wondered what Mickey saw in them. All the time she kept thinking, "This time next week, perhaps, we won't be here! This place won't belong to us! We won't own a ping-pong table. There won't be money to buy refreshments, even if I should feel like having a party."

One thing after another, little personal belongings, came before her and seemed to look her in the face pitifully as if they were saying good-bye to her and reproaching her for letting them go. But what could she do?

By and by Emmy came in from her "day off." Joy and Mickey had been wont through the years to take their childish grievances to her, and Joy excused herself and went to her at once with the news.

The old woman looked compassionately at Joy's drooping desolate little figure there in the middle of the kitchen and swept her into her arms comfortingly.

"Don' you never min', honey chile," she said soothingly. "Hard things often does come in big lots, an' it seems as if there'd be nothing else fer a while. But they does clear up in time. You need to git down on yore knees and trus' in the good Lawd, honey chile. Looks like a hard way to go, but He's he'ped many a one outa hard places. There'll be an end to it some day. Jes' you be brave now."

The good old faithful woman smoothed her honey child's hair and tried to comfort, but when Joy finally got the boys out the front door and went to bed she was far from being com-

forted. Emmy's words seemed unreal to her. Perhaps there
was a God who could help, but if there was, why didn't He?
Anyway, she didn't know Him. Maybe if she did—well, she
must try to think this thing out. *What* could she do to earn a
living?

But her thoughts were tangled and she found herself floun-
dering in darkness, when all at once she thought she saw a tall
knight in shining armor come riding toward her through the
darkness. But he had not reached her yet when she awoke to
daylight again, and her problems were all there in a phalanx
challenging her.

# Chapter 7

Gradually the office force at Main Street and First Avenue began to realize that the atmosphere had altered. A rumor floated about that all was not well, though who started it and whether there was truth in it was hard to say. No one took the responsibility of having stated as much.

There was a good deal of dissatisfaction among them all. Nobody liked the new boss and everyone hoped that it would not be long before Mr. Applegate was back. Any one of them would have worked long hours overtime for him gladly, without extra pay. But this Harvey man was a different matter.

"He's too bossy!" sniffed a streamlined upswept blonde who worked fast and thereby was able to spend many marginal minutes during every working day inspecting her very long, very red fingernails.

Miss Kerr, the woman who sat at the desk opposite agreed dully. She was older than the blonde and had been with Mr. Applegate for some years. Her work was accurate but she was slow.

"I never could see why the boss got a guy like Harvey anyhow," went on the young stenographer sociably. "There's plenty o' fellows right here in the office that had been with him fer years and deserved the job. Take Sellers. I'd like to uv seen him get it." The older woman restrained a grim smile. Everyone in the office knew that the girl was enamored of Mr. Sellers. Still the red lips rattled on. "But I heard that old

Apples was tickled to death to get Harvey away from National. They say he had made a brilliant record there. But heck, I can't see anything he's done in his two years here that's so brilliant." She got out her lipstick and mirror to see what needed to be done to her face, but she hastily whipped them out of sight as the door of Mr. Harvey's office opened.

But it was only Tom Thorne who came out of the office. He had evidently been receiving some sort of reprimand, for there was a troubled look on his face, and his usually peaceful brown eyes behind his thick lenses were unwontedly disturbed.

Tom Thorne had been with Mr. Applegate ever since he started the business. Mr. Applegate had always considered him his right-hand man. He was quite a bit older than his employer. In spite of the fact that he was only a clerk Mr. Applegate had sometimes taken him into his confidence and asked for his judgment on certain minor matters. He respected Tom Thorne as a man, and his integrity was beyond reproach. If only he had had more education and a good deal more self-assertiveness Applegate would have been able to give him a much better job. But he was far too self-effacing to make a real success of himself.

This morning, as he walked down the aisle of desks, Tom Thorne had a ridiculous desire to burst into tears. Of course he didn't. But he had not felt like this since he was a small boy and ran to his mother for comfort. He had just received notice that he was to be laid off, and it was something like being told that he had only two more weeks to live.

He had come to work for Mr. Applegate straight from business school and had been faithful and efficient ever since. Many were the long hours he had put in overtime when the business was first starting and he was the only helper. And he had weathered many storms along with his employer. Even in Mr. Applegate's personal life he had found ways to show his faithfulness to the man whom he honored greatly. When little Joy was born it had been Tom Thorne who was on hand to call his employer from a near-by city and then drive Mrs. Applegate to the hospital. When a few years later she passed away it was again Tom Thorne who attended to everything for Mr. Applegate. And many a time while Mr. Applegate was still struggling with his grief he had taken Joy and Michael on some delightful excursion.

He had never married himself, and, loving children, he had enjoyed showering affection on the motherless children. Tom lived with his maiden sister. His was a quiet, unambitious life. He put in a faithful efficient day at the office and then came home to spend nearly every evening making the little garden around their brown cottage a thing of riotous beauty.

But it seemed to Tom this morning as if his whole quiet existence had been shattered by a bombshell. It had never occurred to him that such a thing could take place. His heart had swelled with admiration and pride in Mr. Applegate's business ability. He had never considered for one moment that he might fail. Of course, Mr. Harvey did not actually say that the business had failed. Merely that it was going to be necessary to cut down expenses.

Harvey had figured closely and decided that if he laid off enough workers, their salaries, together with the big rent he could get for Applegate's house, would pay the interest on the monies that he and Applegate had borrowed until the Atlas money began to come in. He had discovered that Applegate's private account was not as large as he had expected, probably because he had milked it to put all he had into the real estate deal. Still, it would help and he had had Joy sign it over to the business. If Applegate remained out of the picture, as the doctor seemed to expect, and Harvey could carry the deal through to success, Harvey would be the sole one to profit, with Joy in on it as his wife, of course. If Applegate did improve, what could anyone say except that he had carried on nobly and wisely for his employer? Of course there was a shady side to his dealings with Applegate's daughter. But he felt that that was necessary in order to squeeze every possible penny from every source, and also to bring Joy Applegate to a place where she would accept his offer of marriage from sheer desperation if for no other reason. He had little doubt, however, that he could easily win her. By the time Applegate was on deck again to ask questions, if he ever was, they would be married and the whole thing would have blown over.

So Harvey had said nothing about the real estate deal to anyone, least of all to Tom Thorne. It was not to be expected that he would. Thorne was only a clerk. Mr. Applegate, now, he was different, mused Tom. He had spoken to Tom about it enjoining him to secrecy, and Tom had beamed with pride in the trust. No word of it should ever pass his lips, he determined. But now things must not be going well, for Mr. Harvey had said that there would only be a skeleton force left for the present.

When Tom saw the elderly Miss Kerr receive her summons and go tremblingly into Mr. Harvey's office he sighed. Then he began to wonder about Mr. Applegate and his family. Was this thing going to affect Joy and Michael? He made up his mind to find out just how Mr. Applegate really was. In his retiring, timid way he had never ventured to pass the crisp person at the desk who always gave her formal report and warned him, "No visitors."

He had called up the house and Emmy had given him only discouraging reports. He had not so far been able to speak to Joy herself.

For a time even his own shock at his dismissal was forgotten in his worry over Mr. Applegate's condition and his business.

He went straight to the hospital from the office. As he approached the desk an elevator opened its door and Joy stepped out. Tom was shocked to see how pale and troubled she looked.

Joy brightened at sight of him. She and Michael had

both been fond of him since childhood. They called him "Uncle Tom."

"Oh, Daddy's just about the same," she answered his question mournfully as they walked to the street door. "No, I don't suppose there's anything anyone can do," she responded hopelessly again. "I'm just about at the end of my rope." She looked so like the motherless little girl that Tom remembered comforting years ago that he had an impulse to take her in his arms and let her cry it out. He seemed so sympathetic that Joy felt as if it would be a relief to talk to him, just as she used to do when she was small.

"I'm just going home," she said. "Ride out with me and I'll drop you on the way."

Tom listened to the whole sad story, and his own part in the crash sank into insignificance. Joy did not go into details or mention the real estate deal, so Tom did not feel free to speak of it. He, with a fair bank account and his house clear, was in a secure financial position, compared to this poor child. He could get another job without too much trouble. It might not be as good, but it would feed him and his sister. This lovely girl was not equipped to meet her situation.

"Every day that I stay in that big house makes me feel more desperate," Joy said with tears behind the words. "I *must* get out and begin to save, and earn something! I have called two or three real estate men and they have promised to try to find something for us to rent, but that was three days ago and I haven't heard from one of them. The way things are these days I probably won't. There just aren't any cheap houses for rent. I suppose I could sell my car and get enough from it for a down payment on one of those new little boxes they are putting up in a development somewhere, but I don't know what work I may find I have to do, and I might need the car for it. I think I ought to just rent, don't you? Yet the only house I've heard of is two hundred dollars a month. In a few months what I have would be gone."

"Renting would be better just now," he agreed in his quiet gentle voice that made Joy feel as if this whole problem were just a sum in arithmetic, or geometry, that could be worked out with proper care and time. "I'll see what I can find you," he said. "Real estate men are not the ones who have rental properties these days. It is the bread man and the milk man who know that a family is going to move, and they put their special customers onto a house before it ever gets to a real estate office."

"Oh," said Joy, realizing suddenly how much there was for her to learn of the ways of human living, "I'll try that. I'll speak to them."

As she let Tom out at his neat little cottage, he took off his old felt hat and stopped a moment looking at her seriously and hesitating in embarrassment. He looked back at his little house and then at her mournful blue eyes again.

"I—" he turned his hat round and round—"this isn't much, of course," he waved toward the house, "but I want you to know that if we can't find you any better, there will always be a place for you and Mike with us, and of course your father." His gentle brown eyes were down and his voice was very low as he said this. It was hard for Tom Thorne to presume to offer his poor little refuge to this girl who had always had everything.

But Joy smiled. The tears were in her eyes as she put out her hand and felt it grasped warmly in the thin fingers of her old friend.

"Oh, *dear* Uncle Tom!" she cried. "That is just like you! And it is a precious thought to me that there is such a place for us to come to. But I must try to be independent, you know, and for your sake I hope I can soon find something. But I shall never forget your kindness! Oh, if only Daddy would get well, I feel as if I could do anything!"

"Perhaps he will, child. We'll be—" he grew red and em-

barrassed again. "That is, my sister and I—will—be praying
for him, you know!"

"Thank you, Uncle Tom!"

But Joy wondered as she drove on home why it was that
quiet faithful people like Emmy, and Tom Thorne, were the
ones who seemed to depend a lot on praying. At any rate, she
felt a little less forlorn now that someone whom she knew and
trusted was aware of her difficulties and had promised to help.
She had no great faith that timid little Tom Thorne could do
much in the way of finding her family a place to live, but her
heart warmed again as she remembered his bashful offer of a
home in his own cottage. How like him! How loyal he had
always been to her father. How pleased her father would be
to know that Tom had said that.

But Tom, walking alone a few moments among his roses
before going in to face his sister with the dreadful news he had
to tell, was wondering how it could be that as fine a business-
man as Mr. Applegate could have allowed his affairs to come
to such a pass that his own son and daughter were practically
penniless. There must have been more at stake than he realized in that deal that evidently did not go through. With a
heavy sigh he went into the house to find his sister.

The next two or three days were much alike to Joy. She
spent them in anxious planning and fruitless waiting. One
evening she drove into the garage, wondering for the hundredth time whether she ought to try to sell her car. She went
into the house through the kitchen. Emmy was not there. She
could hear her voice at the telephone. It held a note of distress.
Joy's heart froze.

"Yes, nurse, thank you. Her car's jes' come in. I'll send her
right away."

Emmy hurried out to the kitchen wiping her eyes with her
apron.

"Oh, Miss Joy, honey chile!" She went to Joy and put her

arms about her. "Dey's called you back, honey. They want you should come right away."

Fear clutched Joy. She took a deep hoarse sobbing breath. "Oh Emmy!" she almost screamed. "Has Daddy—*gone?*" Fiercely she grasped the woman's arms to force her to tell the truth.

"I don't b'lieve so, dearie," trembled the old woman. "They said he was took worse, that's all. Oh, honey chile! You want I should go with you?"

Joy straightened up.

"No, Emmy, there isn't time. But you can—pray!" And Joy rushed out the back door to the garage. Her car tore down the driveway as Emmy dropped to her knees. Then she heard it stop and Joy let in her brother who had just turned in the gate on his bicycle. Thankful the poor girl had some one with her, Emmy poured out desperate cries to her Father in Heaven.

Joy's tires scraped the gravel as she slid out into the street with Mickey at her side, tightlipped and grave. Neither of them noticed a tall young man walking past their house who stopped and gazed wonderingly after them.

Steve Donovan had formed the habit, since the night he had discovered where the lovely girl lived, of walking past her house on his way home. It was off the bus line, and took him three blocks out of his way, but he looked forward every evening to the chance of seeing her again. This was the first time he had caught even a glimpse of her since that first evening when she had stood silhouetted in the doorway saying good night to that other young man.

He could see that she was disturbed. He caught his breath at the reckless way she had raced down the driveway, for he was near enough to see her start. He could not catch what she said to the boy she picked up but he guessed it must be a brother from the way they met. He saw that she was white and worn, and his heart stood still with horror when he saw

her veer out into the street and tear down to the highway.
Yet he could not restrain a bit of a smile at her fearless skillful
driving. What a girl she was! He wondered what had upset
her so. How he wished that he dared to ask, and try to help.
He decided to come back after supper and see whether she had
returned. He hastened home, to be able to come back and take
up his watch the sooner.

But it was very late, past midnight, when Joy and her
brother came home. They drove wearily to the garage and
went into the house, turning out the dim light in the kitchen
almost instantly, and in just a few minutes all the lights were
out and the house was still. But there seemed to be a sense of
trouble hovering about the place and Steve lingered quite a
while before he took his puzzled way home, uneasy and distressed, although he told himself that he was playing the part
of a fool, worrying over someone else's troubles when he had
already enough of his own.

# ～ *Chapter 8* ～

Joy and Michael spoke very little on that ride to the hospital. Joy, tense and alert, drove at fierce speed. On the way up in the elevator she and her brother glanced at each other word-lessly. It was a sort of desperate reaching out each to the other in their common need.

Dr. MacKenzie was there in the room, with his hand on the patient's pulse, watching keenly for any sign of change. The nurse was on the far side of the bed. Joy and Michael saw that at least they were not too late, and took up their stand at the foot of the bed, steeling themselves for another siege of suspense.

After a while the doctor went out for a time on other calls, leaving orders with the nurse. Joy and Michael from sheer exhaustion sat down to wait, but Joy scarcely took her eyes from her father's face.

It was just ten days since she had come into the house and found him lying so still. Ten days that seemed like an age to her. She had not known that life could stand still as it had during this week.

Michael fidgeted restlessly, glancing now and then at his father, and then ducking his head into his hands for a long time.

For two hours they sat thus. Dr. MacKenzie came back twice. Once he called Joy out into the hall and motioned to Michael to come too.

"I scarcely thought your father would last until you got back here this afternoon," he said gently. "It is hard for you both to sit here, and yet I hardly dare to let you go even yet.

"But the pulse has rallied somewhat and if it remains steady I want you both to go home and get some sleep. He may surprise us." The doctor laid a kindly hand on Michael's shoulder. "You look out for your sister, won't you, boy! She needs you. This is hard on you both, I know."

Gruffly Michael murmured assent, sweeping his long copper lashes upward just for an instant in appreciation of the fact that the doctor was treating him like a man.

Just then a nurse tiptoed down the corridor with a summons for Joy to the telephone.

Joy picked up the receiver. It was Tom Thorne.

He apologized for bothering her at the hospital.

"Oh, I'm glad you called, Uncle Tom," said Joy in a sad little voice. "I would rather talk to you just now than 'most anyone. You are sort of family, you know."

"I don't forget you, be sure of that, Joy," said the mild man, rather embarrassed by Joy's words. "I think I have found a house that might do. It's not far from your present home. The people are moving out tomorrow, and the ones who were to rent it have suddenly been transferred to California with almost no notice. You have to sign the lease tonight if you want it. Would you feel like looking at it? It is not even a single, but it has three small bedrooms, and it is only fifty dollars a month."

"Oh, I couldn't go to look at anything, Uncle Tom. Not now. If you say it's all right, I'll take it. I don't care much what it is. I can trust your judgment, I'm sure. I'm so grateful, Uncle Tom."

"Well, then I'll put a down payment on it for you and bring you the lease to sign. That's the only way to keep a house overnight these days. I'm afraid maybe you will think it's pretty poor when you see it."

"Oh *any*thing will do, Uncle Tom. It's wonderful that you found one at all. Thank you, Uncle Tom. Now I must hurry back. And, Uncle Tom, you keep on—doing—what you said the other day. Will you?"

"I surely will, little girl. You can count on me."

Somehow it was comforting to have that quiet voice in her ear, so steady, so reassuring. Dear old Uncle Tom. He would never do any great things in the world, but he was a good friend. And to think that he had found her a house. She gave little or no thought to what it might look like. Tonight her mind was all on her father.

Another hour her brother and she sat waiting and watching. Tom came and she signed her name hastily and thanked him. Then at last Dr. MacKenzie came again and sent them home, although his face was still serious.

# ᔓ *Chapter* 9 ᔓ

THE APPLEGATE HOUSEHOLD slept late the next morning, all but
Emmy. She answered the phone when it rang about nine
o'clock.

It awakened Joy whose nerves had been on vigil all night
waiting for a call from the hospital. She jumped up with apprehension and ran to the upstairs phone. She broke in anxiously. "Who is it, please? This is Miss Applegate."

The suave voice of Pembroke Harvey answered, inquiring
solicitously first as to her health, then adding, "And your
father? Is he any better?"

"No, Mr. Harvey. He was worse last night. I thought it
was the hospital calling just now." Joy's voice broke as she
spoke. The days of suspense were telling on her control.

"Oh, now that is *too bad*. I am *so sorry*." Mr. Harvey was
all sympathy. "Do let me help you, Miss Joy! I called to ask
if you would like me to get a mover for you. Have you found
a house yet?"

Joy wished she did not have to discuss her affairs with this
man. He was not a person on whom she cared to lean. She
wished she could say, "Oh yes, it's all arranged, Mr. Harvey."
But she couldn't. There was a vague house, but nothing was
arranged. There was still darkness and confusion. Strange
how gladly she had told her troubles to old Tom Thorne.

But Harvey caught at her murmured assent. "Oh then, let
me get a mover for you. And I thought you might like me to

bring a friend of mine who is an auctioneer. We could go over some of your things and suggest what you might hope to get for them."

Joy's heart sank. How terrible that this man, practically a stranger, should have any right to suggest such a thing as his going over her precious belongings. But she suddenly realized that she was not familiar enough with values to be able to set a price on the lovely pieces of furniture and bric-a-brac. Wildly she rummaged through her thoughts for some way out of this. She found that she had been hoping against hope that they would not have to be sold, after all.

"Why," she hesitated. She felt as if this *must* be put off until she could get her bearings. If her father did not live it might be that she and her brother would not be able to have a real home any more. With tears frighteningly near she went on, "I think I shall have to wait until Father is better again even if it does cost me a little more. I must be at the hospital to-day. I—I have a mover in mind, but I appreciate your offer, and I suppose it would be better for me to have an expert value the things. Call me again in a day or two and I will let you know. Thank you, Mr. Harvey. I must go now."

The next few days seemed all alike. Joy hovered over her father constantly, and grew more pale and frail-looking. As she sat through the long hours she forced herself to meet and wrestle with the problem of what to sell.

She knew she ought to go and look at the house she was renting, but she shrank from doing so. She was putting off as long as possible the reality of this move. She knew that as soon as she saw the other house and began to picture their dear belongings in it she would break down completely. It would seem as if all her life were smashed to atoms.

She tried to be practical. She thought if she sold her mother's grand piano and the handsome big carved mahogany desk that belonged to her father, with perhaps a few of the larger oriental rugs and an antique vase or two, that the proceeds from those would provide enough to go on for some time. But she knew she had very little idea of just what those things would bring. Oh, how confusing the way was! That suggestion of Pembroke Harvey's, distasteful as it was to her, was probably the best one.

So when Mr. Harvey called again she told him she was ready to see his friend. That was the day the first bill came to her from the hospital and she was in a panic. Also, the first of the month had arrived and household bills began to swarm in. The electric light bill alone was staggering. It had never occurred to her to be careful to turn off lights. She set her pretty lips in a firm, desperate line and paid out of her pitiful hundreds the bills that she felt must be taken care of immediately; the rest she fastened together to be considered later.

Then she put her mind to the problem of what to sell and what she might reasonably expect to keep. She made a careful list of them.

There were some fine antique oriental rugs which her father and mother had bought when they were first married, and some which her father and she had selected when he built the house on Sherbrooke Avenue. She remembered how proud and pleased she had been that her father had taken her with him, and allowed her a voice in choosing them. She had listened attentively as the dark-skinned salesman had explained, in his exotically foreign accent, the mysteries of their art. He had showed them the difference between the valuable antiques, glossy from weather and wear, and the modern orientals which had been treated with chemicals to imitate that sheen. Then he had assured them that a fine antique increased in value with age. Yes, her rugs should bring a good deal.

But how could she bear to part with them when they held such precious memories? There was the time when she had spilled ink on the beautiful big blue one in her father's room. She had been just a little girl then. She had cried and cried

over it, but when her father came home and she confessed her
part in the disaster, he had been so comforting! He had taken
her in his arms in his big chair and stroked her gold curls and
told her how pleased he was that she had not tried to hide her
misdeed. He told her not to worry, that it was only a stained
rug, not a broken heart, and that it was washable ink anyway,
and would come out. The cleaners had done wonders with it.
*That* rug she intended to keep!

She sighed. Of course rugs were merely works of art and
did not compare with food and shelter and health and loved
ones. But they had become an integral part of her life; they
seemed like friends. They represented a great deal that made
up home, to her.

All that was before she found that she was not even to get
the money from them.

Pembroke Harvey had soon disabused her mind of the idea
that she would have the proceeds from the sale herself. He
made very plain that everything possible should go in order
to satisfy creditors. Life looked very dark to Joy the day she
learned that. She felt as if she scarcely had a right to consider
her breath her own any more.

Where would she get enough to live on? Even if her father
recovered sufficiently to be brought home, he would probably
need a nurse for a while. How was she ever to earn enough
to afford that? She felt as if a thick fog full of nameless
terrors were pressing on her, choking her.

Then the door chime sounded and she went downstairs.

## ~ *Chapter 10* ~

PEMBROKE HARVEY AND his auctioneer friend had arrived.

Harvey was all sympathy, and courtesy itself. He introduced the man with him as a Mr. Thibault. The stranger scarcely glanced at Joy in acknowledgment of the introduction. His black eyes were darting about the luxurious rooms, already appraising everything he saw. She could not tell from his expression whether he was impressed with their value. He seemed to have his thoughts well cloaked by a pale flaccid countenance. A huge diamond sparkled on his left hand, another on his tie. His manner was all business.

It was torture to Joy to have his bold black eyes sorting out her treasures, assaying them as if they had been so many head of cattle.

When they went upstairs Joy marched ahead and quietly but firmly closed the doors of her bedroom and her father's and Mickey's. "There is nothing in those rooms to be sold," she stated with finality.

After all, there must be some sort of a home to be made for Mickey, if not for her father. Besides the minimum bedroom furnishings, she was keeping a few comfortable chairs and a couch, and the pretty maple breakfast room suite. The new dining room would not take one half of their big mahogany suite anyway. No large pieces would be practicable in so tiny a house.

Once while Mr. Thibault was in the library going over some

handsomely bound sets of books, Harvey drew Joy aside into a corner. He spoke in a low voice, beaming down on her confidentially. "I have something good to tell you, I believe," he smiled into her eyes.

Joy looked up dully.

"I think most of your lovely things can be kept right here in the house, and you can think of them as being where they belong! You can even visit them!" he went on eagerly. "I have some friends," he said, "who are rolling in money. They are moving to our city and I told them about this place. They have seen the outside and they want it. They have come from an apartment so they haven't much furniture and they will take what you leave. Can you think of any better luck?"

Harvey gave a nervous little laugh, and reaching out held Joy's arms a moment as if he were rejoicing with her.

"Isn't it wonderful?" he asked her looking straight into her face.

Joy drew away a little, saying sadly, "I suppose it is," and thanked him, although she wondered why it was so wonderful for her, as she would have no part of it and could not bear the thought of coming back here where someone else would be using their things. But then, he had thought he was doing her a kindness. It probably seemed to him a nice way to settle the problem.

"I always loved this place, you know," he went on, still looking down into her eyes, or trying to, for she kept them turned away wishing he would let go of her.

"It was the first home I visited when I came to this city two years ago. I didn't know a soul here, and your father was so kind to me. It was wonderful to me, meeting you. You made me feel less lonesome." He smiled and reached for her hands but Joy merely sent a fleeting look of recognition of his appreciation across her white face, and turned definitely toward the library.

They sat down while Mr. Thibault did some figuring. Occasionally he would mention a rug or a piece of furniture, and remind Joy that there was a worn place in it, or he would question the authenticity of an oil painting. Gradually Joy began to wonder whether her father really had been fooled as to values, as this man seemed to think he had. She was aware, of course, that that could easily happen, when a clever sales- man found a customer whom he knew had plenty of money.

Joy gave a little gasp when Mr. Thibault announced the amount her things should bring as two thousand dollars.

"Oh!" she cried in dismay. "My father paid ten times that for less than the things I am selling." Her hands went up to her throat as if she felt it hard to get her breath. She did not know what a pretty, pathetic picture she made but Pembroke Harvey was watching her.

"Oh, of course, my dear," soothed the suave voice of Mr. Thibault. As if he were talking to a little child he patiently began to explain to her. "That piano, for instance, was a very fine piano when it was new. But you must realize that it is a good many years old now." He smiled deprecatingly and shrugged, spreading out his pudgy fingers on which that gorgeous diamond gleamed. "And another thing," he went on, "popular as oriental rugs *used* to be the style now is carpet, in keeping with modern furniture. Oriental rugs date a house, these days." He spoke sneeringly and Joy was conscious of a sense of resentment at his tone, but she was too well bred and too disheartened to show anger. Besides, what good would it do her to get angry at this man. She was at his mercy.

Pembroke Harvey was watching them both keenly. He saw that it was time to put in a peaceable word to Joy. "Don't you worry too much about the price, Joy." He had never pre- sumed to call her that before. An indignant shudder went through her. Joy was not snobbish, yet the familiarity seemed ill-timed. Was this part of the humiliation of losing one's money, too? Oh well, it was a small thing. He had spoken gently as if he really wanted to help her. She even felt glad of his presence there. He seemed to take her side against this stranger. "I think I may be able to work up the price a little with the people who expect to take your things. I'll see what I can do. We are going to see that *you* come out as well as possible in the end," he promised. He spoke confidently as if he had ways of making things come out right that others did not know.

Joy did not answer. She wondered whether she ought not to get another man to come and give his estimate, but there was real need for speed. So at last she gave a halfhearted assent to their plans and saw them out the door. Then she went sadly off to find Emmy. Emmy was one of the two real confidants she had, Emmy and Tom Thorne.

Good old Uncle Tom. He had found her a mover, though she did not mention that to Harvey, and he had sketched for her a plan of the little house, giving dimensions of rooms and even the sizes of windows. It had saved her from traipsing back and forth to measure and see what she could use. It did not occur to her to take the slightest interest in seeing the house.

Mickey, however, had asked for the address two days ago and he had come home from reconnoitering with a thoroughly disgusted look on his face.

"Well, it's a swell dump we're getting, isn't it!" he gloomed. "Where did you ever manage to find such a palace?"

"Oh, is it so bad, Mickey? I haven't seen it. Uncle Tom discovered it for us. There just weren't any houses at all to rent, kid," Joy said pathetically. "The prices are out of sight and there aren't any anyway. Won't it do?"

"I s'pose it'll have to," grumbled Mickey. "Some dump, though," and he stumped off to pack up his baseball things. In a moment he reappeared in the dining room where Joy and Emmy were on their knees packing dishes and kitchen things. Joy could not think of affording professional packers, and she had immediately dismissed their other help after she learned of the business collapse. "I don't s'pose there will be any use in taking the ping-pong table," he growled.

Joy looked up wearily. Her lovely gold curls were rumpled and there was a smear of dust across her white face. She tried to speak cheerily.

"Why, I guess you might, kid. I don't think it would bring much if we sold it." She made a feeble attempt at a laugh.

Her pitiful appearance softened her brother's tone somewhat. "Gee, you look fierce, Sis," he said gruffly. "Here, you go lie down and I'll do this." Clumsily he pulled her up and gave her a little shove toward the couch. His unwonted thoughtfulness almost unnerved Joy. She wanted to burst into tears at the little kindness. But she knew that that sort of weakness would disgust a brother of fourteen so she controlled herself and gave a trembly little giggle instead. She felt suddenly nearer to him than she had since that night they had rushed back to the hospital together. She wondered whether trouble always did that, brought people who went through it nearer together. Could that perhaps be a reason for trouble? Her tired mind stowed the question away to take out later and ponder over.

She had a passing thought that if she could only get a really close relationship established with her brother she might be able to have some influence over him. So far, if she made the slightest remonstrance about his impudence or his friends he would scowl and leave the house.

Joy was glad of Mickey's help just now for she had begun to feel panicky about the enormous task ahead of her. Besides, she begrudged every minute spent away from her father. He was conscious now quite often, but he was still locked in that awful stillness. Only his eyes would try to follow her whenever she moved.

So she worked feverishly, rushing off every now and then to the hospital then rushing home again as soon as the patient seemed to fall asleep. If Emmy had not helped a great deal with the packing she would have been utterly swamped.

And now when Mickey tried to make her pause for rest, she found herself keyed up to such a pitch that it was physically impossible for her to lie still. She did stretch out on the couch, to let Mickey know that she appreciated his offer, but she was continually remembering something that should be looked after, or written down on a list to be attended to, and she would jump up every minute or so, until finally Mickey scolded:

"Fer cat's sake, Sis, lie down and take it easy. The whole world doesn't depend on you. We'll get moved somehow. No need in you actin' like a one-armed paper hanger with the itch."

"Mickey!" reprimanded Joy, but nevertheless she gave a little giggle and tried to settle down.

Finally they reckoned up what there was left to be done and decided that they could finish it on the morrow, and all three dragged themselves wearily to bed.

# ⌐ *Chapter 11* ⌐

STEVE DONOVAN ROUSED enough to reach over and turn off his alarm clock. He felt dog weary. He had had only a very few hours' sleep. For one thing, his mother had been so cross the evening before, and he had thought and worried and thought about what to do for her until quite late, while he sat up wishing his sister would come home from her date. She was out with that fellow Frank Ferroni again, and Steve did not trust him.

He found himself thinking ironically that it was a strange situation for him to find himself in. Usually things were the other way round: the son was the prodigal and kept his mother and sister worrying about him. Steve did not take the slightest credit to himself that he was not the black sheep, he only accepted the fact and laid it all to the topsy-turvy condition of everything in the world. He didn't pretend to understand any of it.

He was unusually distressed about his sister for when she finally did come in, toward three o'clock, she would not speak to him, and as she passed him on the stairs a strong odor of liquor struck him. His heart sank. Not Laurel too! Oh, God! What could he do?

Laurel fairly hissed at him when he followed her up the stairs to try to have a talk, and she went into her room and slammed the door.

Steve stood and stared at the blank door. His big shoulders

slumped and he looked as if his sister had struck him in the face. Slowly he turned and went into his own room.

If he only had someone to whom to go for advice. He thought over the men he had known whom he respected. There were one or two whom he liked very much and whose business judgment he would take, but Steve knew that both of them had trouble in their own homes. How could a man be expected to know the answer to some other man's problem if he could not solve his own?

Perhaps a woman would be better fitted to deal with this thing. There was a social worker, pretty and hygienic looking, whom Steve had seen a couple of times going into the house two doors below Donovan's, where the father drank and the seven children were ill-fed and sick half the time. Steve shuddered. She seemed so brutally competent! It was good, of course, that those poor children had some help, but the problem itself in that house had not been so much as touched. Anyway, Steve would never humiliate his family by appealing to a welfare worker. This was not a case for a person like that.

No, he would have to find someone who knew just what his mother was up against, who understood her from the inside. And Laurel too. It was beyond Steve to understand why Laurel was attracted by that conceited nitwit, Frank Ferroni.

Steve walked to the window and looked out. His room was at the back of the house and overlooked dozens of houses just like theirs. Did each one of them hold a tragedy something like his? The thought overwhelmed him. He groaned within himself. Was there no help, anywhere?

He looked up at the steady stars, *so* far away, caring not at all about these bitter woes down on little Earth. Was God up there beyond those stars? Did He care? If He did, why did He not do something about it?

As Steve tried to think out that old old question it suddenly came to him to wonder whether the people who were living in trouble had ever appealed for His help. He hadn't, himself.

Perhaps by some unknown law help from on high was withheld until it was called for.

"All of us are ready to blame Him for not doing anything for us, when it may be that He has wanted to and we wouldn't let Him," mused Steve. "Dad admitted as much. He said he never had 'tried God.' Well," he said aloud with sudden decision, "I will then! I don't know exactly how, but I'll try."

He got down on his knees and looked up to the vast space above him. The summer heat poured in through the tiny window in waves but Steve did not notice it.

"Oh, God!" he said softly. "If You're there, help me!"

In the prime of his strong young manhood Steve felt weak, utterly beaten. A great sob shuddered up through his choking throat. "I'm at the end of my rope, God. I don't know what to do!"

Several minutes he knelt there, knowing no more to say, but crying out in his soul to the One whom he believed to be the only One who could help. At last he felt quieter and climbed into bed. But there was only an hour or two left for sleep before that alarm clock went off.

By sheer force of will he struggled out of bed. As he dressed he wondered whether Laurel was awake yet. She had to leave the house very soon after he did in the mornings. He knocked on her door. No answer. He knocked again, louder. Finally at the third knock he heard a murmur and a groan. He opened the door. "Time to get goin', kid," he urged, cheerfully.

Laurel turned over and opened her eyes part way. Then she gave another groan. "Oh hell!" she broke out. "Let me alone, will you? I've got a fierce headache. I can't go to work today. Get out of here."

Stunned, Steve stood and looked at her. He had never before heard his sister use such language. His father had been most particular about their manners and the way they spoke. Laurel had indeed gone far on the road away from the family standards of right and wrong. Oh, Steve was accustomed to hearing cursing, of course. He swore himself on occasion, but he had been trained to think of a girl as a little finer than a rough boy, and it went through him like a sword to hear his sister talking "like any common brat," as he put it. For an instant he stood looking at her, sorrow and chagrin in his level gaze.

Then she flung herself over in bed and almost screamed at him, "GET OUT, I say!"

Sadly he turned and went out, closing the door.

He knocked on his mother's door, roused her enough to go in to see if she could help Laurel and then went downstairs and set about preparing a nice breakfast for both of them. A good hot cup of strong coffee might straighten Laurel out. Probably she would feel better after she was wide awake.

Just as he got the tray ready his mother came down, her hair still untidy. She had slid into a soiled housecoat that had one sleeve half torn out. She said she would take the tray up.

Steve gulped down a cup of the coffee himself and started off to his work. But he had little heart for it or for anything.

He was a little later than usual and had to run to catch his bus, so he did not have time to walk the three blocks around to pass the house on Sherbrooke Avenue, and he failed to see the moving van that was drawn up close to the house in the driveway.

It was while he was eating lunch in a little dreary drugstore a block or two from the lumber company's office that he heard a voice he thought he recognized.

He did not usually go to this drugstore for lunch. Usually some of the men in the office sought him out to go to lunch with them at the restaurant near by, but today he avoided them. Then he walked on till he found the little drugstore. It was not clean, and the food was not good, but he was not hungry in spite of his meager breakfast.

He sat in the last booth facing the rear of the store so he had not seen two young men who came and took the booth directly behind him. He could hear their voices but he paid no attention to them at first. The radio in the store was blaring and there was heavy traffic going by. But Steve in his weariness had leaned his head against the wall and their words came to him clearly.

It was not until he heard the name Laurel that he suddenly became alert. Then he realized that he knew one of the voices. It was Frank Ferroni, the boy of the flashy clothes and smart-aleck haircut. He mentioned having been out with Laurel the night before.

"Boy, is she some baby!" he boasted to the other fellow. His voice was high and rasping and he ended every sentence with a vulgar sort of giggle, silly in the extreme, it seemed to Steve. He was irritated that this coarse fellow should have the effrontery even to mention the name of Laurel. Why should she go out with such a sap!

"Ever take her out?" queried Frank again, boastfully, evidently assured of the reply of the other boy whose voice sounded younger and full of awe at Frank's superior experience. "No? Well, when I get done with her you oughta try her. Maybe she isn't a gal! Just give her a little drink or two and oh my!"

Then the voice was lowered confidentially, but Steve could still hear every word. Suddenly the blood came up in his head and he gritted his teeth. His great fists were knotted and he sat in tense rage.

All at once Stephen arose to his full height and taking one stride to the other booth towered in terrible wrath above the slick black-haired young fellow whose tongue was still rattling on.

The boy looked up impudently. His bold black eyes still held lewd laughter. Then he saw the righteous rage in the face of the giant who had suddenly appeared from nowhere. Cautiously he rose from his seat shrinking into the corner of the booth as he did so. His eyes darted about fearfully, cannily, searching for a good spot to make a getaway.

In a voice fierce with controlled rage Stephen said to him: "My name is Stephen Donovan. Come outside in the alley and have your teeth knocked down your throat."

The talker took one look at the huge clenched fists that hung in easy power at Steve's sides, and at the great broad shoulders, then spread his hands in an insolently conciliatory manner, saying blandly, "Okay, okay, okay. Take it easy, brother. Just let me explain."

"I'm not your brother and God help me I never will be!" spoke Steve fiercely. "Will you come out or shall I take you out?"

He grasped the other's arm in an awful grip and propelled him out the back door of the store into the dirty alley. The fellow strained and struggled. He had a lot of bull strength under his debonair manner, but that iron grip was too much for him.

Steve gave him a shake as he stood him against the wall outside. "Get set!" ordered Steve.

But the words were not out of his mouth before the round bull head shot like a bullet at Steve's stomach. But Steve had not spent his days in college and in the service acquiring merely book learning.

Like lightning he dodged and caught the other on the shoulder as he passed him, spinning him around staggeringly. Before the fellow had scarcely got his bearings again Steve's right landed with an ugly crash directly on the man's foul mouth and his left in the pit of his stomach. Ferroni crumpled up and lay groaning.

Steve stood over him. There were several onlookers by now, in spite of Stephen's efficient manner of getting the man out of the store.

Steve spat out his ultimatum. "That will be all for *this*

*time!*" He warned. "If ever I find you have come within a mile of my sister again you will be *very sorry*."

Steve straightened up and walked sternly away. Some guffaws at the expense of the fallen man sounded out, and some faint cheers. Evidently he was not a favorite among that crowd, at least.

Steve heard a girl's voice among the others, from some office window, perhaps. She sang out raucously: "Oh-oh, Frankie! Wait till Laurel hears about her hero!" Steve whirled but not a face was in sight at any window. He went on again, grinding his teeth in impotence. To think that his sister should have let herself in for a thing like this. What had ever started her going with such a low-down crowd?

But Stephen was marching back to his work feeling not at all like a victor. He had never been so stunned and shamed. His sister! The subject of licentious chatter! Oh, God! Help! Now! He began to realize that a good deal of the fellow's talk had been mere boasting, improvised for the occasion to produce amazement, but it was horrible enough that the words had been spoken.

The rest of the day went by for Steve as if he were stumbling in the dark. It had been a little relief to his tortured soul to have the outlet of knocking that fellow down. But there was no real satisfaction in it. Steve knew he could beat up practically anybody he wanted to. He had a powerful build and he knew how to fight. He wished all his problems could be solved by a mere fight. How easy that would be. But to win two strong-willed women from their ways, that was beyond him.

On the way home he did not even walk around by Sherbrooke Avenue as he usually did. He felt his humiliation too keenly. His face burned with shame as he imagined for a moment what that other lovely girl would think if she met his sister and knew what had been said about her.

As Steve came to Emerson Street and started to turn down

the incline where the row of houses began he felt as if it would be more than he could stand, to go home and into the bright light of the dining room where he would have to face his sister with those words about her hammering at his ears. It was not that he loved her less than before, but that he felt so keenly the shame that had come to them all by this thing.

So he kept straight on instead of turning, and walked and walked. Before long he found himself out in the country. He climbed a hill where a wooden fence ran along the road, enclosing a field. Worn out and faint from lack of food, he swung himself up on it and sat on the top rail for a long time, gazing out over the darkening valley.

It seemed to him as if there was not the slightest use in going back to the city. He would have been glad if dark oblivion could have come and wiped out the life that was called Stephen Donovan. How futile it was! Yet he was too brave to resort to wiping out that life himself. There was some reason for him to go on, surely. To feed and care for the two poor wandering ones that were his family if for nothing else. Though why *their* lives should be prolonged was a mystery to him. Life! It was inexplicable. What was it for? If one lived nobly, well and good; perhaps that was worthwhile, but if not, why was there some unspoken law that a life must continue?

At last after a long time, when the cool quietness of the evening and the steadiness of the hills and the stars had somewhat calmed his spirit, Steve looked up again at the sky. "Oh, God," he said again, aloud, "I've asked You to help. I thought last night that the worst had come. But now—Oh God! I'm licked! You will have to help if You are going to!"

The others were already in bed when Steve got home. With little ceremony he got himself into bed and immediately dropped into exhausted heavy sleep.

The next morning at breakfast Laurel would not speak to him. When he tried to be pleasant to her she flared up in a fury and walked out of the room.

Their mother looked sadly from one to another. "Laurel says you didn't treat her friend right," she said hesitatingly. She fairly adored Stephen and could not bear to think ill of him.

Steve looked at his mother. That stern look came into his eyes that always made her a little afraid of him. "No," he said in measured tones, "I did not. I should have strangled him. If Laurel knew what he said about her she would understand. But I don't think he will be around here again!"

Mrs. Donovan looked worried, and said nothing. Steve went out to work and soon Laurel went out, too, without speaking again.

That evening on the way home Steve remembered something his mother had asked him to get at the grocery, so he went on toward the little corner store. As he passed the house at the end of the row, he suddenly became aware that he smelled smoke. He glanced around. Most people were getting their suppers ready at this hour. Perhaps someone had burned something. No, it was wood smoke, and strong.

Then he saw a gray haze pushing its way in curling wisps from the rear of the last house. He ran toward it.

# ⤳ *Chapter* 12 ⤳

THE DAY BEFORE the move Joy went to see the other house. She had sent Emmy over several days before to clean, and Emmy had returned, fuming at the dirt and rubbish that she had found there, so Joy was having some misgivings.

Mickey went along. "Tisn't so far but we can walk," he said. "And it sure isn't worth it when you get there!"

"But I'm just too tired to take an extra step," said Joy wearily, climbing into her little coupe and taking the wheel.

As she pushed the starter she glanced at her hands that had always been kept so immaculately. They were grayish now from the dust of her packing. Two nails were broken, and she looked ruefully at them. She had often wondered at people who did not keep their hands well groomed. She had always considered them slovenly. Was there a chance, perhaps, that she had misjudged them? At least some of them? Was it hard work, not carelessness, that took away that exquisite-as-a-seashell look? Her standards were being changed in many ways these days.

Joy brought the car to a stop in front of the house that Mickey pointed out, and her heart sank. The house she had rented was the dreary brick one at the end of the row that she had passed those few short days before on her way to the little corner grocery!

There was the grimy store, as dingy and illkept as ever, waiting, it seemed to Joy, in shabby persistence to gobble up the few dollars she would have left after the movers were paid.

"Oh-h-h-h!" she groaned, and put her head down on her arms across the steering wheel.

Mickey watched her a moment, astonished to see his sister collapse, since she had been the one all through their trouble who had stood steady and brave, meeting one blow after another. Suddenly he burst out roughly with, "Well, what's eatin' you? I *told* ya, didn't I? Didn't I *say* it was a stinkin' lousy dump?"

Joy raised her head.

"Oh, Mickey, don't use such vulgar words, *please!*" she reproached him. "If we *have* to live in a place like this, *do* let's keep our own decent standards, at least."

"Yeah!" roared Mickey, thoroughly angry now. "Okay, if I don't suit you I can get out! All I hear any more is 'don't.' I guess if you don't like my ways, nor my friends, I can make out by myself. There can't be many worse places to live than this dive anyway."

He started out of the car in his fury, but Joy was filled with remorse. She grasped his arm. "No, please! Mickey. I'm sorry I scolded you. I know it's going to be just as hard on you as on me to try to live here. Please stay and help me. You have been a wonderful help these last days. Please, Mickey!"

The boy looked sullenly into his sister's pleading blue eyes, saw the stark despair there, and then the courage. Reluctantly he allowed himself to relax, saying grumpily, "Oh, all right! have it your way. But for Pete's sake let's get in and get this over with. I promised to play in the twilight game tonight."

Joy said nothing to that, although she failed to see how a boy with a spark of affection or concern for his sister and sick father could go out and *play baseball* when there was so much that he could do to help. However, ball games seemed to be the panacea for most males, she concluded, and after all, Mickey was not much more than a little boy.

She tried to put some vigor and cheer into her voice as she walked up to the house, saying, "Come on, you help me decide where things are to go." But it was a pretty gloomy pair who having made the rounds of the pathetic little dwelling, got into the car again to drive home.

Home! No, this place would never be home, decided Joy as she glanced back at it from the corner, and noted the papers and rubbish cluttering that vacant lot. There was an abandoned pushcart bent over with its chin on the ground like a camel tired of its load. Its battered sides were stove in and one wheel was off. It seemed to Joy to epitomize the whole discouraged-looking block. Well, she must try as well as she could to clean up their house and make it cheery. This brother of hers simply *must* have some helpful guidance. He was growing bitter.

She made another desperate effort at cheer. "Well, it's all you said and more, kid," she smiled at him. "A pretty sad spectacle, isn't it? Bad enough to laugh at. Remember how Daddy always used to make us laugh when we were faced with anything hard? I'll never forget the time you had to take some cough medicine. Daddy got down on the floor and howled with you and you burst out laughing."

But her pleasantry fell flat. Mickey refused to respond with more than a grumpy snort of disgust. Joy sighed. Why wasn't it enough to have all this trouble without having to carry Mickey on her heart too, like a big naughty child?

In silence they drove home and still silently they ate their supper, although Joy tried several times to say something cheerful. She was glad when Mickey bolted down his last bite and excused himself. She had no appetite herself and choked on the nice chicken sandwiches that Emmy had fixed.

Joy had had a talk with Emmy as soon as she heard that they would have to move. "I'll have to let you go, too, Emmy," she said mournfully. "You won't have any trouble finding another place, of course. But I don't know what I'm going to do without you!" The tears came into her eyes as she imagined herself struggling through all the intricacies of housekeeping, about which she knew almost nothing.

"You pore dear chile," soothed Emmy. "You'll make out all right, I ain't afraid o' that. You got enough o' yore daddy in you ta get on somehow. But I hates to leave ya. If 'tweren't that I'm still having to take keer o' that sister o' mine what's been sick so long, and he'p with her chilluns, an' she a widda, I'd jes' stay on anyhow. But you'll make out, honey chile! You'll make out!"

"I'm sure I don't know how, Emmy. I won't be able to afford to have the laundry do our things any more, not even the sheets and big things. And as for ironing, you know I made a mess of things the few times I've tried it. Shirts! How can I ever learn to iron *shirts!* Although," she caught her breath in a sob, "I don't suppose Daddy will be using starched shirts for a long time and Mickey hates them."

"Yes, you'll find that things will work out slowly, honey chile. De Lawd nevah lets us have mo' than we can stan' at a time. I done foun' that out long ago."

"Maybe so, Emmy," said Joy unbelievingly, "but it looks as if He had this time."

Emmy shook her head. "Wait till you looks back on it, an' then you'll see. It's all come fer some good reason, honey chile," she insisted gently.

"I can't see it, Emmy. It doesn't seem to me as if there could be any God who cares at all."

Emmy caught the note of wistfulness beneath the bitter words and if her trusting soul was shocked she gave no sign of it. In a voice that was still gentle she reminded: "An' how about all the years when you was took keer of? Din you nevah think o' the millions o' chilluns what nevah had no ease at all? Life *all* hard fer 'em?"

"Yes, I have, Emmy, and that doesn't seem fair either. Besides, if something like this came to *them,* they would be more ready for it than I am."

Emmy smiled indulgently. "Now it's words what you says. Fust you says tain't fair to 'em and then you says 'tis. Now which is it?"

"Oh, I don't know, Emmy," said Joy half laughing and half tearful. "Things are all so mixed up in this world. Everything's all wrong."

"Well honey chile, I admits they *seems* mixed up, and I admits dey is plenty o' wrong. But de wrong is from ever'body's sin, honey chile. We is all pore sinners, every one of us. But that's whut we got a Saviour fer! An' the sooner somep'n happens to get us down on our knees to say we're sinners, the better off we are. Now I got to get these pots an' pans puck up."

Joy had wondered vaguely several times about what Emmy had said. She wished that she had a faith that could trust through hard times. How did one acquire it, she wondered? All she could do was to stiffen her courage and push ahead with all that she had in her, but she was beginning to realize that there was not much courage left.

And when moving day came, with its overpowering multiplicity of details to be attended to, she began to feel as if she too would finish up in a hospital somewhere.

Emmy stayed at home and told the movers what to take, as Joy was fearful lest some one of the pieces that were to be sold to the new occupants would be taken by mistake. The tenants had not yet materialized, but Mr. Harvey seemed quite certain that they would.

Joy went over to the house on Emerson Street and directed the movers there, having already planned for most of the things on the basis of the sketch which Tom Thorne had given her. But she was aghast as she saw one thing after another being brought in for which she had made no provision. She had thought that she was going to be so efficient, and that by night everything would be in its place. But she was not aware of the way in which boxes of china and boxes of books could overflow all bounds, and she had forgotten to figure on the thickness of some of the large pieces of furniture—she had measured only wall space—so that when they were placed they jutted out so far that there was scarcely room to walk between. Oh, there were innumerable problems that she was called upon to meet that trying day. She had thought she would get a chance to run over to the hospital, perhaps while the men were at lunch. But the day flew by and she was breathless and exhausted when at last the van had gone and she could sit down and look around at the formidable piles of boxes and cartons; pictures leaning precariously against tables; blankets towering on the beds; beautiful linens sprawled on the dusty floor, having fallen out of their cardboard box that had broken in transit. It seemed a horrible havoc.

Mickey came in in the late afternoon, took a look around, and saw that no supper was in evidence or seemed likely to be. He swore crossly and went out again slamming the screen door, making it shiver and send a shower of rusty particles all over the floor, leaving in their place several ragged holes for mosquitoes to come in.

Emmy arrived soon after that, and found Joy dragging herself around in bewildered circles, moving one pile of things from a bed to a table and then putting them back again to make room for another pile of something else on the table. She was doggedly hunting sheets and pillows so that they would have at least some decent beds to sleep in. That was all that Joy could think of by that time, a place to lie down and rest.

Emmy capably produced the pillows, slipped some fresh covers on them, whisked the sheets over one bed, and then another. Then she drew Joy down on the big old couch, and while she rested Emmy heated some water and made her a cup of tea.

Somehow they got through the confusion enough to eat something and go up to bed. But Joy had no sooner gone into her room and yanked on the old-fashioned unshaded pull-cord light, then she gave a little squeal of horror.

"Emmy!" she cried in despair. "*What* are *these?*"

Emmy came, took one look and gave a snort of disgust. "Them's roaches," she said scornfully.

"Will they bite?" asked Joy more in discouragement than fear.

"No honey chile. They don' bite." Emmy sighed. "They's jes' dirty. We'll hafta get us some roach powder. Might as well fergit 'em tonight."

But Joy could not forget them. She lay down in her own bed but she had a feeling that even that was alien and that those bugs were about to swarm upon her and crawl all over her if she fell asleep. It was a long time before she could relax. Then it began to rain, dismally.

Mickey came in about nine-thirty and Emmy gave him the soup and sandwiches she had saved for him. He ate them sullenly and climbing over a pile of boxes he made his way upstairs and to bed.

Emmy stayed down a few minutes to wash up Mickey's few dishes, and Joy lay listening for her to come up, realizing how tired the poor woman must be. As she listened she became aware of a slow plunk, plunk, plunk in her room over by the dresser. She turned on the light again, half fearing that the army of bugs had organized against her.

She saw a wet place on her polished walnut bureau. She looked up and sure enough there was a steady drip of water. The roof leaked! Joy called wearily to Emmy to bring up a bucket from the kitchen, and then, utterly disheartened, she crawled back to bed again.

Joy had insisted that Emmy sleep in the third bedroom until she found her new job and had to move. So at last even Emmy thankfully lay down and fell asleep.

The next morning, however, she was up long before the two young people. She had built a fire in the little bucket-a-day stove, gathered up all the towels and clothes that she could find and was washing them, so that she would be able to leave Joy with everything clean to start her housekeeping.

She had a good hot cup of coffee and a nice breakfast ready when Joy came down. In spite of her loneliness and distress, Joy had slept well and had a little fresh confidence to start the day.

She took a quick run down to the hospital while Emmy was straightening up the kitchen and hanging out the wash, but when she returned she found Emmy ready to go out.

"I hates ta leave ya, honey chile, but I got a message fum Mis' Landreth ta come see her 'bout wukkin', this noon time. She's a good lady to work fer, I hear, an' I better go get me the job. I'll come back after lunch soon's I kin."

"Oh, I want you to go, of course, Emmy," agreed Joy. "I must learn to get on without you now." She smiled pitifully.

Emmy betook herself to the new mistress and Joy was left in her own kitchen alone. She gazed around helplessly, a choking feeling coming up in her throat. What should she do first? She felt as if it were useless for her, unskilled as she was, to try to cope with any of them. She was more at a loss than if she had suddenly been set down in a foreign land where the language and customs were all unfamiliar.

How good of Emmy to wash up everything. The tears started as she thought of the kind old woman. She had been like a dear old grandmother, all her life, thought Joy.

She walked into the tiny dining room, stepping carefully over piles of boxes and cartons. There was excelsior and paper everywhere. Where was she to put all the china she had brought? She sighed heavily.

Then she went into the living room. The overstuffed chairs that had looked so handsome on Sherbrooke Avenue filled up the room here. There was no way to place them so that each was not elbowing the other for more space.

There were piles of boxes here, too, books, and vases and lamps, all waiting in heaps to be unpacked and given their own niches in the economy of the household. Where was she to put the books? At home they had had three walls of the library lined with books from top to bottom: handsomely bound sets of classics, all the new novels, biography, history. She had not been willing to leave them for the new occupant, for she felt that if her father recovered, they would be the one thing that he would want. Then the shudder of fear that he might not need them clutched her again.

She tied on the big apron that Emmy had left and went to work on the dishes first. Hour after hour she worked, unpacking and washing and putting away. She started out putting up the pretty dishes artistically but as she went on, growing more and more weary, she saw that space was more important than art and she stacked them where she could. A great many of them she repacked in barrels to be stored in the cellar.

Finally she reached the last pile of plates she planned to keep out for use. She stood at the sink, first on one aching foot and then on the other. She turned on the hot water and tossed in some soap powder. But, dabbling her fingers in to foam up the suds, she found that the water would no longer run hot. What could be wrong? Where did hot water originate in this house, she wondered. All at once it came to her that Emmy had said she must watch a stove in the cellar and not let it go out. She had never once thought of it all day! She rushed downstairs.

## ↪ *Chapter 13* ↩

HALFWAY DOWN THE cellar stairs Joy stopped and caught her breath in a quick gasp. She thought she had heard a scuffling noise. She remembered that Emmy had seen a rat in the cellar when she built up the fire in that laundry stove. Joy was not a timid girl, and had always despised girls who made a great show of squealing and running from a mouse. But a rat was another thing. She was not sure how she should deal with rats. A long moment she stood, waiting, peering apprehensively into the cobwebby corners of the little basement. At last, hearing nothing more, she gingerly took her way over to the dusty little stove.

There was no warmth coming from it, and it was with many misgivings that she grasped a rusty tool on the floor. It was made with a peculiar little tongue on its end, which looked as if it should fit into the hole of the stove lid. She tried it and lifted the lid. There was nothing inside but black clinkers and ashes. Now what was she to do? She had not the slightest idea how to build up a fire in a stove, and Mickey wasn't there.

She took a deep breath and set her little chin. There was nothing to it, of course. Just put in some sticks, or perhaps paper first, and then light them. When they got to burning well, pile on coal. She cast her eye about for some kindling wood. There were only two or three thin sticks lying there on the floor. Perhaps if she had enough paper to get them going they would do. She went upstairs for some newspapers. There were certainly plenty of those, after the unpacking of all the china.

She took a pile of papers down and began to crumple them up as she had seen others do, feeling quite competent as she poked three or four sheets of the paper into the stove's round black maw. Then she laid the little sticks on the top of the paper. She had forgotten to bring matches and went upstairs once more to hunt them. On her way down this time she thought she heard again that scraping scuffling noise, but having made the nearer acquaintance of the cellar during the past few minutes and found it not too formidable she resolutely made herself walk straight on down. Nevertheless there was a little nervous glancing around as she made her way to the waiting stove.

She looked in at the few sticks she had placed so neatly. Perhaps there might be more outdoors. She lifted her skirts from the dust and cautiously made her way over to the slanting old-fashioned cellar door. As she put her foot on the lowest step of the outdoor stairs, in order to reach the wooden bolt that fastened the door, she heard the scuffling noise again, and this time it was directly under her. A shiver went up her spine. But realizing that the thing whatever it was, was probably more afraid of her than she of it, she set her pretty lips firmly, tugged at the bolt and finally pushed up the cellar door. It was good to have a little more light. But the sunshine was stiflingly hot, the view was scarcely more inviting than the dirty cellar, and not a piece of kindling could she find. She hurried back. She must get that fire lit. Mickey would soon come in and grumble if there was no supper and no hot water for a bath.

Frantically she struck her match and touched off the paper. It soared up eagerly into flame. In no time at all it was burned, and the wooden splinters were only charred. She saw that there must be more paper. She pushed the hot sticks aside and stuffed a lot of paper in. Then she poked around to get the sticks on top but they wouldn't stay as she wanted them. They would likely burn, though, no matter where they were.

They burned. This time they burned up completely while she was putting a few coals on top of them. The coals did not catch and soon she had nothing left but more ashes, and some black fresh coal in her stove. Its open mouth yawned jeeringly up at her as if it were tired of all this fussing. It seemed a most uncooperative stove. Joy stood and hated it.

Well, there was nothing for it but to get more wood somewhere. She looked at the packing boxes. It should not be too difficult to chop some of those apart. So she went in search of the hatchet. But all she could find was a hammer and screw driver. Her dainty hands were unaccustomed to the tools, but she was full of determination. She chose the smallest, most flimsy-looking box and gave it a tentative blow. The box simply bounced on the floor. She held it down and struck harder. That caved in one side board. Encouraged, she hacked away. Once she missed the box entirely and gave herself a bad bruise. She wanted to stop and nurse it but she would not give in. So she worked away, though the tears sometimes threatened to overflow.

At last, with splinters in both hands and bruises on her shin bones, she looked down at the pile of kindling she had managed to achieve and decided that there was enough to start another fire.

She went up for more newspapers, and hurrying back hastily stuffed them in. Then she put all her kindling on top and lit the paper. It blazed up with gratifying briskness. Quickly she grabbed the bucket of coal to take advantage of the blaze. She poured on a lot of the coal this time. The blaze died down suddenly. Panic-stricken she poked at the mass to pull off some of the coal and allow the sticks to burn again. But the sullen fire was pouting. She frantically reached for another box, and pried off another board or two, thrusting them in among the coal. But the mean little stove only smoked. It would not burst into flame again.

Joy was not aware of the existence of drafts in a coal stove. She looked down at the obstinate thing and spied the door at the bottom. Maybe that should be open! She reached down and opened it but a small avalanche of ashes fell out on the cellar floor and she quickly shut it again, deciding that that had been the wrong thing to do.

The room was filled with smoke now and she was coughing. Her eyes smarted. She rubbed them with the back of her hand and made a black streak across her cheek but was unaware of it. She was past caring about her looks.

Suddenly the thought of all the confusion and disorder upstairs, the frustration down in the cellar, and the heavy load of fear for her father, all rose up together and descended crushingly upon her. She felt as if she had come to the end. There was no help anywhere. Emmy had not come back all the afternoon. Mickey was gone she knew not where. She dared not leave all this mess to take care of itself as she had done with so many things all her life, for she simply *must* get out on Monday morning and begin to look for a job. The little she had in the bank would soon be gone and then where would she be, to say nothing of Mickey, and her father? Who would pay the hospital bills if she had no work? Oh God! would this night of darkness and terror never end?

She sank down on one of the packing boxes and put her pitiful streaked face in her dirty little hands and sobbed, with great long shuddering sobs. All the anxiety and heartbreak of the past weeks seemed to rise up within her in awful insurrection, pushing desperately past her self-control. She thought she was losing her mind.

Joy did not hear footsteps running around the house and down the cellar stairs. She was utterly unaware that a handsome young man had stopped stock still in front of her with amazement and sorrow mingled in his eyes. It was not until she felt a strong kind arm around her and a big hand smoothing her hair that her sobbing ceased. For an instant she thought she had fallen asleep and was dreaming that her father had come home, so loving and tender was the touch of those hands. She dared not open her eyes and break the trance she was sure she was in. Even though it was unreal, it was sweet, like soothing music to a tired soul, as comforting as a mother's hand to a baby in the dark.

Still dazed, and still pretending for the moment, Joy dropped her hands and let her head rest back against that wonderful strong arm. It was like the arm of God, only Joy had never thought of God in that way before. Emmy had told her God would meet her need if she would ask Him, but she had not considered that her feeble cries could be appraised as suitable prayer. She had only a deep sense of need; could that be prayer? Prayer a God would answer?

Just an instant she yielded to the comfort, then she came to herself, for a soft bit of linen was wiping away her tears, as gently as a mother could have done. Where had she heard something about God wiping away tears? Didn't they read that at funeral services? Was she *dying,* then? Where was she? With an effort she forced herself to open her eyes.

She was looking up into the face of a man, a man she did not know, although there was about the face something vaguely familiar. She was not frightened, for there was such tenderness and deep reverence in that face. Where had she seen those eyes before? They held a sympathy that asked nothing for itself, only a wish to comfort and strengthen her.

And then he smiled. It was such a smile as a mother might have given to her most precious little child, a smile of gentleness, of selfless love and understanding, a smile that seemed to enwrap Joy's poor tired little soul in its great depths and rest her, through and through.

She closed her eyes again to clear her vision and once more she looked. She felt as if she had come home at last after weary wanderings in uncharted lands. Home was in that smile. Then gently, very gently, those firm, clean smiling lips leaned over and touched her forehead, in a kiss that was like a sacrament. Then the man released her and stood straight and tall before her, and she knew him.

She smiled back at him and knew not what a lovely piteous picture she made, with her blue eyes still bathed in her tears, her gold hair tossed like a child's, the grime on her cheeks serving only to accentuate the delicate roseleaf whiteness of her skin. Her smile seemed like a morning after storm. But the young man had no words to offer. To him it was as if he had come unannounced into a shrine. The dirty cellar was a holy place.

"Oh!" she breathed, "it's you!" and smiled again in wonder.

"Yes," he said in awe, "and I have *found you!*" His voice was exultant. The very cobwebs on the grimy rafters hung in solemn silence as if they had been wrought and draped especially to clothe the hallowed scene. And the scuffling creatures of the darkness must have slunk back into their corners before the light of glory in the young man's eyes.

As he continued to gaze at her with tender homage, all unconscious that he was still watching her, she began at last to come to herself; the soft pink stole up in her cheeks and her lashes drooped. She cast about for some casual remark to break the embarrassment that had suddenly overwhelmed her.

And Stephen, seeing her sweet confusion, suddenly realized that he was the cause of it. Instantly he turned his eyes away and spoke, joyously taking command of the situation. For he had become aware of new strength, new vigor that seemed to have flooded through him at the moment when their eyes met.

"Can I help you here?" he offered. He had already taken in the smoking stove, the almost empty box of matches, and the pitiful little sticks that straggled beside it on the floor. Skillfully he manipulated the stove and its dampers. She watched him in admiration as he crushed a packing box with a few

deft blows, broke a heavy board or two over his knee and soon
had the stove blazing away again.

As he worked she was so filled with the wonder of how he
came to be there, and how marvelous it was to have him lift
the burden from her, that she had not yet a word to say to him.
More than all, she was thrilling again to the tender strength
of his arm about her. It did not occur to her to question his
right to do what he had done. She had been in need and he
had met her need.

Swiftly he worked, and then opened the front window of the
cellar to let the smoke blow out. When the fire was content-
edly munching on its meal of coal, he came over and sat down
near Joy on another wooden crate.

"We'll let it burn a bit before I bank it down," he said in a
pleasant matter-of-fact tone. But he noticed that she still had
nothing to say, and he fell silent a moment, a troubled look
on his brow. Then he said in a low tone,

"I suppose I ought to ask your pardon for what I did. I
really meant no disrespect. I—I saw—you were in trouble and
—I—just—didn't think what I was doing. I hope you will forgive me," he finished with a rush.

Joy lifted her sweet blue eyes to his trustfully.

"*Forgive* you!" she cried softly. "I think it was the *nicest*
thing anyone ever did for me! Oh, how can I thank you
enough for coming just when you did? I was—well, I guess I
was just about ready to give up!" she ended with a little helpless gesture.

"I understand." He said it tenderly. "I don't know just
what you're up against right now, but I know the feeling!"

"Oh-h-h!" Her tone was gentle and full of sympathy.
"Well," she hesitated, with a smile that was mischievous and
yet sad, "if you tell me your story, I'll tell you mine!"

Joy wondered at herself as she made the remark. She had
met this young man only once before, for scarcely more than
a moment. She did not even know his name. All she knew

was that there was shame in his home. Or no! she did know more than that. She knew that he was courteous and thoughtful, even to his mother who had brought that shame upon him. She knew that he was tender and gentle, full of sympathy and understanding. She knew that he was strong and skillful. And she felt as if she had known him for years. There was no doubt in her mind that he was a man to be trusted. She was not sorry that she had said what she had.

He smiled back sorrowfully. "That's a bargain," he agreed. "I guess you know most of mine, though." His eyes were down, as if he would still like to hide his shame. But her own eyes seemed to draw him and almost against his will he looked up and met her gaze. Again that deep sympathy was there, the same that he had seen that day on the street. There was comfort in that look. It suddenly seemed as if the trouble were a little less now that there was another who knew and shared it with him. He returned her look with his own and they felt as if they had talked it all over although so few words had been spoken.

"You don't know my sister, though," he went on as she waited. "She has grown hard and bitter since I have been away at college and in the army. She is going with a tough crowd, and she won't listen to me. I don't know what to do and I keep thinking it's too late." He almost groaned as the horror came over him again, the awful feeling he had had as Laurel passed him on the stairs.

Joy longed to be able to say something that would help him. But what help did she have for him?

"I know a little of what that is," she said slowly. In the face of his grief and what seemed his greater trouble it seemed like an affront to mention her own worries. But she had agreed to. "I have a kid brother who is going with a tough gang. He is getting more and more fresh and hard every day and I have failed to manage him. I worry a lot about him, but I can't do anything, and Daddy—" her voice broke a little

—"I don't know whether he will ever be able to take charge of things again."

Stephen looked up with a troubled face, inquiringly.

"Daddy had a stroke." She said the words as if they hurt her. "It was that same day I met you on the street. I went home and he was lying on the floor." The horror of that scene came over her again and showed in her eyes.

Steve shook his head in perplexity at the strange ways of catastrophes.

"That was in the house on Sherbrooke Avenue?" he questioned.

"Yes. Why—how did you know?" she asked in amazement.

He smiled. "I searched for you for days. I went up one street and down another. Finally last week I caught a glimpse of you. You were standing in the doorway saying good night to a man who went down to his car at the curb."

Joy thought a moment. "Oh, that must have been Mr. Harvey. That was the terrible night he brought me the news of Daddy's failing in business. That's why we're here now. And Daddy's still in the hospital! We just moved in yesterday and everything's an awful mess, everywhere, with roaches and rats, and the roof leaks and I just *couldn't* make this old stove work!" The tears brimmed up into her blue eyes again but she managed a little giggle.

"Gosh!" he exclaimed. "You poor kid! And you can *laugh!*"

The admiration in his voice made Joy feel as if he had showered the greatest compliments upon her. And the look in his eyes brought the rosy color up to her pale cheeks in a sudden glow once more. She almost burst into tears again, it seemed so good to have him care.

Steve got up and went over to the fire to nurse it along a little more, and Joy did not see the trembling of his hands as he lifted the bucket of coal. She did not know how strongly he was tempted to put his arms about her again and try to comfort

her. But he would not take advantage of her now, not for anything. That other time when he came in, he had acted impulsively in the shock and amazement of the moment. And
anyway she had not been quite herself. But he would never
forget the sweetness of that moment, the soft touch of her
gold hair under his hand, her lovely face turned up to his in
glad recognition as she opened her eyes. No, he would have
that to remember all his days, but he would never presume
upon it or even seek to recall it to her.

He straightened up and stood before her, and once more Joy
took in his manly height, his easy grace, his strength of
physique and character. He stood humbly as if he were offering to her a small thing of little worth.

"Whenever I can help, in *any* way, I want you to know that
it will be the greatest pleasure to me." He waited as if to
ascertain whether his gift of service would be acceptable.

Her beautiful face lit up. "Oh, how wonderful that will be!"
she said. "Just to know that there will be a friend at hand to
call on when I'm in a jam sometimes! You know, it's funny,"
she paused, "I have lots of friends, and I suppose some of
them *might* know how to build a fire in a mean little laundry
stove or—or—kill a rat for me—" her laugh rang out—"but I
don't know one of them I could call on to help with Mickey,
for instance, and I'm sure not one of them could have come in
and known how to comfort me as you did." She lifted her
eyes and gave him a friendly straightforward look that told
him that she did not resent what he had done, now that she
was clear in her mind again.

Suddenly she glanced at her wrist watch. "Oh, my!" she
cried. "It's after six o'clock. I've kept you here working for
me and you're probably hungry as a bear. Will they be waiting dinner for you at home?"

Steve shook his head gloomily. "Not likely," he said. "Half
the time I get dinner myself, not that I'm much of a cook," he
added with a wry smile.

"Oh!" exclaimed Joy, trying to hide the shock of his words as she had a revelation of what a home would be without someone to order it. She had had no mother, but there had always been Emmy.

"Don't worry about me," he said. "You go ahead and do what you have to do. I'll stay a little longer if you don't mind and see that this fire is okay before I bank it for the night."

"If I don't *mind!*" echoed Joy. "Well, I can't think of anything I'd like better. And I hope you will give me some lessons in taking care of the thing. Wait a minute. I know you're hungry and so am I. I'll bring a bite down here and you tell me how to treat the stove so that it won't go out on me again."

Joy was no cook, but she had had plenty of practice in college at fixing up snacks in a short time. She whisked out the butter and a loaf of fresh bread that she had bought that morning. She laid delicate slices of ham on the bread and spread a dash of mustard over it. She opened a jar of Emmy's homemade pickles and tucked some on the edge of the sandwich plate. There was some coffee left from morning in the glass coffee pot. She reached for two of the tall frosty glasses she had washed that day and slid some ice cubes into them, filling them up with coffee and rich cream. The tray was just large enough to hold the little silver sugar bowl. She was back in the cellar before Steve had finished chopping up another box, which he said he would leave for kindling in case the fire went out again.

"But I'll stop around in the morning before I go to work," he promised, "if seven-thirty is not too early for you, and I'll make sure that you have all the hot water you want for tomorrow!"

"Oh, that will be wonderful," said Joy, placing the tray carefully on a third packing box. "You don't know how that relieves my mind. I got to thinking that *everything* was going to go wrong, this afternoon before you came."

"I know the feeling!" he said. "Boy, does this taste good! I didn't eat much lunch today, nor yesterday either." A stern look came into his face as he recalled the drugstore experience of the day before. He sighed. "I wish there were some way to get hold of my sister Laurel."

"Laurel! What a lovely name," cried Joy. "By the way, I don't know your name. Introduce me, please."

Steve laughed. "Stephen Michael Donovan. Only please make it just Steve."

"Oh! Michael is my brother's name. How *I* wish there were some way to get hold of my brother!"

Steve was silent for several minutes. "I'd like to ask you something," he said at last, helping himself to another sandwich. "There's one thing I haven't tried, and I don't know how to go about it. Do *you* know God? Do you know how to get next to Him, and maybe get some help from Him?"

Joy looked up, surprised. No boy had ever spoken like that to her before. But Steve's nice brown eyes were serious. There was a sweet humility on his fine brow that somehow belied the sorrow about his mouth.

Joy thought a moment, wondering what to say. She was not embarrassed. She did not feel that she must be reserved before this boy. They had looked into each other's eyes and found something in common.

Thoughtfully Joy answered, "No, I don't know God. I've sometimes wished I did. I think I believe there is a God."

"Yes, I do too. And my father told me just before he died that I ought to try God. He said my grandfather and grandmother *knew* Him. But Dad died and I never got a chance to ask him what he meant by knowing God. I've put a question now and then, to a professor or two at college, and I tried out the chaplain in our unit, but none of them seemed to know Him any better than I did."

"I don't believe I know anyone who does," mused Joy. "Or —yes, I do. I think perhaps Emmy, our colored cook knows

Him. She has had trouble and seems to lean on Him. She used to teach me some songs when I was little, and she made me learn the twenty-third Psalm. I don't remember much of it now. I sort of think a friend of ours, a Mr. Thorne, may know something about things like this too. I don't know why I never asked him about it. I guess I never thought of God much. I was having a wonderful time just living and I didn't feel any particular need of a God. I just supposed if there was one He was nice to keep things going so well for us." Joy laughed apologetically.

Steve nodded with understanding. "Maybe it's only when people get in a jam that they think much about Him. Sort of a raw deal to give Him, when you come to think of it. I wouldn't be surprised if He considers our attitude sin, more so than lots of crimes. I never saw it that way before, though."

"Could be," said Joy thoughtfully.

"Dad and I used to go to church sometimes," she went on. "I never got much out of it, though. Of course the music was lovely, but when the sermon was going on it was always so boring I just amused myself thinking out what I was going to do during the week." Joy laughed a little again, nervously. She wondered what this nice boy would think of her. She sounded like a heathen.

But Steve was not hunting flaws. His face was serious and his dark brows were drawn. She could see that this subject was not one that had just recently come into his mind. He was in earnest. He sat holding his empty glass and twirling the few drops of coffee at the bottom of it.

"You will think I'm crazy, I guess, if I say this," he said slowly, "but I think God sent *you* here as an answer to my prayer!" He looked up to see how she took that. She was not laughing at him. She only looked amazed and puzzled.

"You see," he went on, "I had about got to the end of my rope, too. I felt I had to have somebody to help me. Last night I talked to God as if He were there, and I asked Him to do *some*thing. And today I find you. Of course you don't realize what it means to me, but I've been looking for you. And now it sort of seems as if I'm not alone any more."

"Oh!" breathed Joy in a small voice. "But I can't solve my own problems. *I* couldn't be any help, though I'd love to."

"It isn't that so much," explained Steve. "Of course you don't know how hard I've been looking for you since I met you that day. To find you here seems like a miracle. And now you are in trouble too. Not that I'm glad about that, of course. It seems inexplicable that anybody like you should have any trouble at all!"

"Oh, don't say that!" exclaimed Joy. "I guess I'm pretty much of a sinner, though I never realized it before. I don't know why I would deserve anything else."

"Oh, but," he said suddenly, looking straight at her, *"you* are *lovely!"*

He stated it as a fact, almost impersonally. But Joy felt the color rush to her cheeks again and she caught her breath.

"No, don't ever be afraid that I shall take advantage of your speaking to me that day, or of—this," he waved his hand around the cellar, at the stove, and the dishes, and the packing box where she had sat when he first came in.

"I would never be afraid of *you!"* she said in a low tone.

After a moment he went on: "What I'm trying to say is that a great thing has happened in my life. I prayed last night, desperately. And this came today. You may not have anything to do with my prayer, but I can't help thinking you do. Anyway it has made me feel as if God cares. And I know I'm going to make it my business to find out how to know God, somehow. I'll keep on till I do!" He spoke with a quiet determination that gave Joy the feeling that whatever this young man set out to do, he would do, and woe betide anyone who tried to stop him. She had never met anyone like him. She could not imagine any of the boys of her acquaintance speaking as this young man had just spoken, taking God seriously like that. Again she saw herself as very small, in spite of the compliments this boy had given her. She recognized that he was setting his feet this afternoon on an unknown path with high purpose. And she suddenly felt that she would suffer inestimable loss unless she also took that path with him.

"I would like to know Him, too," she said, very shyly but with utmost seriousness. A long moment he studied her, and at last, seeing she was sincere, he put out his hand and clasped hers.

"Let's!" he said.

Then as if the question were settled without need for further discussion, he turned to the little black stove, which had been quietly doing its duty all the time they talked, gave it a look and a poke and closed its drafts, then he turned and smiled brilliantly.

"I sure do appreciate the supper," he said, "and—everything! I'll see you in the morning!" Then he sprang up the cellar steps three at a time.

But no sooner had he reached the top than he started down again. "Do you know you haven't told me your name yet? Or don't you want to? It's all right if you don't," he assured her.

She laughed. "Of course I do," she said. "It's Joy. Joy Applegate."

A look of wonder came into his eyes. "Joy!" he repeated. "Joy! Yes, it would be Joy! I'll see you in the morning, *Joy!*"

He clasped her hand again and was gone.

# Chapter 14

Joy stood at the foot of the cellar steps gazing up at the square of light from which the tall figure of Steve Donovan had just vanished. The past hour or two seemed like a dream. She could still see his form silhouetted there against the sky as he had stood looking down at her saying her name over and over: "Joy! Joy!"

Then she closed her eyes and felt again the strength of his comforting arm about her and the gentle touch of his lips on her forehead. If any of her other friends, even the boys she had known all her life, had dared such intimacy she would have resented it and shaken them off in short order. She was not a girl to pawn caresses carelessly. But this boy's touch had been simply tender and comforting, like an angel's, she thought wonderingly. The old lilting smile that upturned the corners of her mouth stole back to her lips.

But just then she heard footsteps, weary ones, shuffling up to the back door. And at the same time, loud stamping steps on the front porch and a bang as the front screen door slammed. Emmy and Mickey were both back. She had no dinner ready for them and those dishes were still in the sink! Swiftly she gathered up the plates and glasses from the packing box and hastened up to the kitchen.

She whisked the dishes in her hands into the sink with the rest, suddenly at a loss how to explain the presence of *two* sets of them. She saw that Emmy had already noted them, and she stammered, "Oh! I meant to have supper ready! I had—a little bit myself a while ago, with a—a—neighbor who came in to help me." Her cheeks were blushing furiously as she finished and Emmy glanced curiously at her out of the tail of her eye, as she tied on her apron and went patiently to work again, apologizing,

"Sorry ta leave you so long, honey chile. I found Mis' Landreth was havin' unexpected comp'ny tonight an' she asked me could I stay and get her dinner ready. I'm ta start in there Monday. Seems a good place, but I shore hates ta leave you."

"Don't you worry, Emmy. I'll make out somehow," said Joy more brightly than she had spoken for many a day. And again Emmy gave her a keen look, noting the upturned corners of her mouth.

Mickey sauntered in and watched Joy getting eggs and sliced ham out of the refrigerator.

"Hunh! Gointa have *breakfast* again, are we?" he growled. "Gee! When if ever do we get settled in this dump so we can have a real meal again?"

Joy's heart sank. If only Mickey would be reasonable and not sulk all the time.

She looked up sharply and retorted, "Real meals cost real money, young fellow, as well as time and effort and that's a scarce article now, get that straight."

Mickey's brows drew down in a heavy scowl and he turned on his heel snarling, "Oh, yeah? Well, I guess I can take care of myself all right." And he stamped out of the house again, slamming the door harder than ever.

Joy almost dropped the eggs in her dismay. "Oh!" she cried despairingly, *"why* did I have to say that to him?"

Even Emmy sighed. "Tain't no use talkin' to a man, big ner little, when his stummick's empty," she sagely remarked as she emptied the dishpan and took a clean tea towel to attack the pile of clean dishes.

Joy glanced at her tired back and was filled with remorse.

"Emmy, I'll bet *you* haven't had a thing to eat, either, have you!" she challenged.

"Wall, no'm, but it's different with a man. I'm used ta waitin', er goin' without."

"You're going to stop and eat dinner right away, Emmy," ordered Joy. "And *I'm* going to cook for *you* this time," she laughed.

Emmy smiled wearily. "You'll make a right good cook some day, honey chile, don' you worry none. All it takes is hunger and a man to cook fer, after a little time of tryin'. Ya don' have ta start out with fancy food, you know."

Joy giggled and felt her cheeks growing pink again as she remembered how quickly and easily she had prepared the simple repast that she and Steve had had together down cellar a little while ago. She had really enjoyed getting that, and it had not seemed difficult.

But later, when she and Emmy went to work again at the packing boxes, Joy was rather silent, for she had begun to feel that she was definitely at fault in the case of Mickey. She wondered where he was finding food, or if he was going without. She knew he had little or no money of his own. Perhaps he was trying to earn a little. Poor boy. There wasn't much he knew how to do. Her heart softened toward him as she thought he might possibly have been working all day, mowing lawns or something, and had come home tired and hungry, only to have his sister preach at him. The tears came into her eyes as she worked. Poor Mickey. He was probably just as lonesome as she was herself, or as she had been until this afternoon when that wonderful friend came to help her. The thrill of his coming went over her again in a happy flood. Well, perhaps Mickey had gone to the house of one of his friends and would have a good dinner there. She tried to convince herself that he had, but she forgot that he was an Applegate, as she was, and nothing on earth would have induced him to lower his pride enough to beg a dinner from one of the gang.

Joy was in the dining room after supper, deep in the inward parts of a packing box when the doorbell rang. It was an old-fashioned bell, not a soft-toned chime such as they had had on Sherbrooke Avenue, and its harsh chattering clang startled her worn-out nerves.

She peered up from the edge of the box, dishevelled as she was, and saw a young man standing at the open front door. It was growing dusk but she recognized Pembroke Harvey. Now why did he have to come at a time like this? He was always so impeccable, so immaculate. Joy had a feeling that she looked worse than she did.

He smiled confidently, his lips showing wet and red beneath his little well-trimmed mustache.

"Well, how's our little housekeeper tonight?" he said debonairly, with just the least shade of condescension, Joy thought. But he must understand her situation. Who else, if not he? He was only trying to be pleasant.

Wearily she wiped the damp hair back from her forehead with the back of her hand. Harvey noted the grace in her gesture and was gratified to realize that this girl, *his* choice of a girl, was enticingly well poised and attractive even in the midst of her work. Generally she was as fresh looking as if she had just come out of a bandbox.

She tried to smile and appear cordial. "Won't you come in?" she offered. "There *may* be some place we can find for you to sit!" She removed an armful of books from an easy chair and stool helplessly looking for a place to put them.

"Oh, don't disturb anything for me!" he said, seizing the books from her and efficiently placing them in a row in the one small bookcase Joy had brought. His help would have been welcome except that they were not books she had planned to put in there; she was going to pack them again and store them in the attic. However, he seemed to take for granted that he knew just where they went and he continued his work aggressively until the whole pile was in, filling the bookcase tightly. Joy was too tired to correct him, even though she would have to take them out again after he was gone.

She sank down on the couch and he was glad to settle down cosily beside her.

He patted her little soiled hand, but his touch did not thrill her. He looked down at it and said, "These pretty hands ought not to have to do this dirty work. They look best scampering up and down the piano keys, as I saw them do one day when I came to see your father."

Joy caught her breath in a little gasp of memory that hurt. It had cost her many pangs to part with her mother's lovely grand piano.

"I guess it will be many a day before I have a piano again," she said wistfully.

"You miss it, don't you?" he said as if he were speaking to a little child. Joy wished he would not treat her like that. She was not complaining about her misfortunes. It made her seem so silly and weak. She bit her lip, trying to conquer her foolish feeling of vexation.

"I know," he went on in a low voice, almost too full of sympathy. "But I don't want you to have to miss it. That was one of the things I came to tell you. Those friends of mine have arrived and they insist that I come there to stay with them at least for a time. They say the house is too big for just the two of them. And as I have had only one miserable room to stay in I am only too glad. And just think! You can come any time you like and play *your* old piano. They adore music and they want what they call 'young life' around them. So you will see, they'll give gay parties and you shall be there often, just as you used to be. Why, the house doesn't seem right without you!" he finished flatteringly.

Something in Joy cringed at the thought of going back to their dear old home and having other people there managing everything and using the things that still seemed like hers. Whoever the people were she would have difficulty not to hate them. Why didn't this young man know that? Yet Mr. Harvey seemed so cordial. He was evidently trying to make things easier.

"That's very nice of them," Joy managed to say, "but I think I shall probably be too busy for either piano playing or parties for some time to come."

"Oh, no!" he remonstrated. His voice had a compelling quality that surrounded and threatened to swallow her up. "Every girl needs some fun, you know, just as every lassie needs a laddie," he quoted playfully. Then as he saw she was not in a responsive mood he arose saying, "I know you are tired tonight, my girl, and I will not keep you up. You get plenty of rest and when you are straightened out here you will feel like having some fun, I'm sure. I shall be back in a few days and spirit you away for a frolic somewhere!" He flashed his eyes straight into hers and smiled his red smile beneath the little mustache, as he leaned over and took both her hands and drew her to her feet with a laugh.

"You will hear from me!" he promised as he left.

Joy was glad when he was gone and she could get back to her work. Of course it was nice to have people care to look her up, but she had a feeling that Harvey considered himself above this place, and was daintily walking through mire to get to her. Well, she couldn't blame him much. He was used to nicer things and so was she. But Steve Donovan was too. She could tell that from his speech and his manner, and the grace of his whole demeanor. Yet Steve had not made her ashamed of this house, even though she fed him in the cellar!

And as for *ever* going back to the house on Sherbrooke Avenue, as long as someone else was in it, that she would never do! So she set her lips and worked on until midnight, sending Emmy to bed with the excuse that she wanted to wait up for Mickey and have a talk with him when he came in.

When Mickey did come in there was a frown on his hard young face, a hunted look. He stamped toward the stairs angrily, throwing something from his pocket at her feet as he passed her, and snarling, "There! Maybe that'll buy some decent food for a day or two."

Joy reached over and picked it up. It was a five dollar bill. Her heart smote her. He *had* been working and was too proud to tell her!

"Oh, Mickey, *dear!*" she cried, running up the stairs after him. "Thank you, but you ought to keep this. You will need it. That's grand of you to go to work! Where did you get a job?" She spoke exultantly. If Mickey were going to dig in and help it would be so much easier.

But Mickey reached the top of the stairs and slammed his door with only an angry, "Aw, *shut up,* can't ya? It's none of your business."

And Joy's heart sank again. If he was going to be cross all the time it was no help. She would rather have him cheery the way he used to be, even if she had to spoil him to get him to smile! No, that wasn't right either. Of course he was spoiled already or he wouldn't act like this. Perhaps he was still hurt by what she had said.

She spoke gently through the door.

"Mickey, I'm terribly sorry I jumped on you the way I did. I guess I was just tired and discouraged."

No answer.

"Will you forgive me, Mickey?" she urged.

But all she heard was a snarl of anger and a shoe thrown at the closed door.

Joy felt like bursting into tears. But she knew Mickey hated tears. A crying sister would never win him.

She went into her room but she did not turn on the light. She stood looking out on the dreary street which managed to look dismal and dirty even under the soft starlight. She wondered whether perhaps that grand boy up the street was looking out his window, too, and whether he was just as discouraged as she was. The thought that he might be sharing these night hours with her, even the despair of them, was comforting. She fell to recalling their talk together and the agreement they had made. She wondered how he planned to go about getting acquainted with God, well enough acquainted to ask Him to help them. Some people prayed. Joy didn't know any prayers except the little poems her mother had taught her when she was tiny. They seemed not to suit the occasion. They were precious, but like the dear little dolls and toys that she cherished from that happy babyhood with her mother.

Well, if she was taking for granted that there was a God, there was only one thing to do, and that was to talk to Him as as well as she knew how. With a strangely warm feeling at her heart at the thought that Stephen Donovan might even now be kneeling at the same Throne, Joy knelt beside the open window looking up beyond the stars, and spoke softly.

"O God, we are in trouble and need help." Unconsciously she had said "we," for it was as if Stephen were kneeling there beside her.

"It may be our own fault somehow. I don't suppose I've ever really been good. I've never worshipped You in all my life. That is a great deal to ask You to forgive, but we need help. Please help me to help Mickey. And oh! *do* help Steve. He has worse trouble than I have. Amen."

With a sense that she had made a feeble step toward establishing contact with the Almighty, Joy crept into bed.

And over on Sherbrooke Avenue in Joy's old room, lay Pembroke Harvey, sound asleep. He had gone home well satisfied with the way his plans were working out. It would not take long for a girl raised to luxury as Joy Applegate had been, to tire of her poverty and be more than willing to run back to ease, especially when ease should be offered in the person of such an altogether desirable young man as Harvey considered himself to be.

Joy had swallowed his first pill of explanation about the business submissively. It was bitter, no doubt, and it was too bad that she had to leave her lovely home, but it was only a temporary move, he reasoned. As soon as they were married she would be back. And he could not hope to succeed with his plan of swinging the deal alone if he had to allow enough from the business to support Joy in the big house; he needed the rent from it, too. He had arranged with his friends to pay it directly to Applegate's business account. Neither party had desired a formal lease.

Meantime, he planned to send flowers twice a week to Joy. He wanted her to learn to look to him as her one source of luxury. He had figured closely and felt he could afford to do it. The flowers could be reckoned into his business accounts very easily as—well, say advertising expenses. Yes, that was it, advertising Pembroke Harvey!

There were not many young men who had such an opportunity offered to them, a door open to success, unlocked and swung wide by another's gold. He would be a fool not to enter it, even though it did mean a little time of hardship and inconvenience to some of those concerned. Think how well off Joy would be in the end! She would come into all that her father would have made, and what her clever husband would have, besides.

Harvey's red tongue stole out and wet his lips in a gratified way as if the luscious plum that was hanging on the Applegate tree for him was almost within reach.

He had gone over the situation from every possible angle and as far as he could see there was absolutely no point at which he was actually overstepping the bounds of the law. That was good. In case of the recovery of the owner of the business, improbable though that was, everything must be found to be in good shape, handled with wisdom and good judgment, otherwise he might be found to be out in the cold when the time came for sharing the profits.

Already Harvey could picture Joy in a stunning evening gown down in the big reception room of the Applegate house, standing with him to receive some of the elite of the city. What a girl she was! Gracious and beautiful, just the one to match his own good looks and brilliance. He could fairly hear people now, whispering about what a splendid couple they made. Oh, the dish of success he planned tasted good. He gave a sigh of anticipation and fell asleep to dream of it over and over again.

# Chapter 15

Steve had gone home with a leap and a bound. He found his mother and sister sitting forlornly at the clothless table in the dining room, with the remnants of a warmed up stew on their plates. Neither had eaten much, obviously.

When Steve came in, his eyes alight with eager joy over the girl he had found, his mother looked up with sodden interest. But Laurel lifted her sullen eyes under their beautiful black arched brows and stared at him.

"Well, what's on your chest?" she inquired insolently. "The boss has given you a raise, I s'pose, since he's heard you can lick somebody smaller than you!" Her hard eyes blazed with smouldering resentment. "Or is it that you are going into the prize ring and be a great big hero?" She said it so sneeringly that even her mother looked reproachfully at her.

Steve's eagerness faded, but he managed a fairly good-natured smile, determined to go more than halfway with his sister.

"Oh, nothing so spectacular," he said. "There's a new family moved in at the end of the row," he explained, "and they seem nice. That is, the girl—I—I've met her before," he finished lamely.

"Oh, a girl!" jeered Laurel. "At last! 'How are the mighty fallen!' I thought you were above anything like that."

Steve tried to grin again.

"Take it easy, Sis. This is a *nice* girl. No kidding. You

130

will like her. Only she's not *my* girl," he insisted. "She's way above us socially, or has been. She's really tops."

"Yeah? You can keep her. I can imagine what your idea of tops in a girl is! Since you came home from the service you have certainly become one awful priss. Some fellows pep up when they get with the gang in the army. But it sure did take the pep all *out* of you. I s'pose this delectable female doesn't drink, smoke, or swear, and she thinks a rhumba is some wicked kind of a drink?"

Laurel's tone was too full of contempt to be mere sisterly teasing, but Steve chose to continue to pretend that it was.

"Oh, sure," he agreed with a twinkle, "and she wears long black cotton stockings and high-buttoned shoes! Just my ideal girl exactly."

Steve's good nature was so spontaneous that Laurel let a little grin appear at one corner of her mouth in spite of herself. And even Steve's mother laughed a sad shadow of a laugh.

"Have you had any dinner, Stevie?" Mrs. Donovan roused to ask him. But Laurel was not ready to give up her taunting yet.

"And I suppose you will soon be getting out your black gloves and your prayer book and going to church with this model specimen?" she prodded.

Steve looked serious a moment. Then he smiled, a nice frank wide smile.

"I don't know just where my gloves and prayer book are at the moment, but yes, I believe I will go to church this Sunday. How about going with me?" He looked at both women and spoke with as much courtesy and eagerness as if he had been asking them to go to a top notch entertainment.

His mother looked up at him indulgently. "That's nice, Stevie, do go. No, I don't feel up to it this week and I don't have the clothes. Maybe some other time. But you take your girl and go. It'll be a good thing to have one member of the family a little religious!" She gave a hard laugh.

But Laurel pushed back her chair with a harsh scrape and

stood up. "You can count me *out!* Definitely!" She said with a sneer. "Take your paragon and go. There's too many hypocrites in the churches to suit me."

Steve frowned a little. Then he said thoughtfully,

"Well, I've been wondering lately whether there aren't more and worse hypocrites *outside* the churches than there are in them. We outside think we are pretty smart, trying to get along without God. I'm beginning to think we're off the beam."

Laurel's eyes blazed. "So your girl friend thinks we're hypocrites, does she?" she stormed. "I thought something funny was eating you. Okay, we aren't good enough for her to associate with. Well, she needn't worry, she won't be bothered with *me!*"

Laurel picked up the two plates from the table and marched with them to the dismal little kitchen. She would not admit to herself that she missed the fellowship of her brother, that companionship that had meant so much to her in her younger days. She recognized that he had kept to some of the standards they had both been taught, and that she had not. But she intended to fight out her right to live her life as she chose.

Steve felt his new eagerness, that he had brought from the Applegate cellar, waning away. He had tried his best to be pleasant and had met every rebuff of Laurel's with good humor. But what was the use, if she insisted upon putting the wrong meaning on everything he said? He sighed heavily.

His mother heard him sigh and roused to the sense of something wrong. She tried to make up for Laurel's bitter words.

"That's nice that you have found a girl, Stevie. Bring her around. I'd like to meet her."

"Yes, do bring her around!" echoed Laurel. "And be sure to give me an advance notice so that I can be out. I'm really not up to her class, you know."

"Oh, Laurel, don't be so cross," weakly remonstrated her mother.

But Steve just sighed again and patted his mother's shoulder. "Thanks, muth," he said. "I will. I'd like you to meet her."

Then Stephen looked around the desolate little dining room and into the living room where last week's newspapers still lay crumpled on the worn cushions of the couch. Someone had been sleeping on them just as they were. One lace curtain, that had been handsome in its day, was torn and hanging in two long tatters. It had been hanging like that ever since Steve came home from the service. Dust filmed the furniture. All the lovely little figurines and bric-a-brac that his father and mother had picked up here and there through their years together were waiting forlornly for some attention in the very spots where they had stood since the Donovans had moved in last winter. The whole place reminded Steve of a neglected orphan on a poster he had seen during a drive for charity, a picture of the forgotten child, who needed a haircut, a new suit, shoestrings and a shine, besides a good thorough scrubbing, and underneath the picture was the caption "Suppose nobody cared?" Unconsciously Steve shook his head sorrowfully over the state of things. It was not that he was too proud to bring a girl like Joy into his home; she was not one who would think less of him because of it. But it seemed so unnecessary to have home like this. He decided to take a plunge and see what he could accomplish.

"Mother," he said hesitatingly, "do you suppose we could cheer this place up a little? Tomorrow is Saturday and I'll be home at noon. If you would tell me what you want done I could help."

Mrs. Donovan looked around the rooms unenthusiastically. Then she looked back at Stephen. Her beautiful dark eyes, so like Laurel's, held a smoldering contempt.

"It's not good enough to bring your friends to, is that it?" she blazed out.

Steve's heart sank. He might have known. She was just like Laurel. Both of them had to be handled with kid gloves because of their fierce pride. What could he say now to smooth his mother's ruffled feelings and make her realize that he was really only trying to help? He decided to laugh it off gently.

"You should see where I was entertained this afternoon, and you'd have no more worry about that! The young lady fed me in a dirty basement!" His fine face lit up again with the memory of the precious time they had had at that cellar repast.

His mother looked at him in astonishment, and even Laurel came to the kitchen door wiping a plate. She quickly made a show of putting the single plate away in the china closet to cover the fact that she had come to hear what Steve was saying.

Steve saw that he had his audience and he went on making what he could of the little incident, without of course, telling them the preamble to their meeting on the street some weeks before, and of how he had hunted for Joy.

"Yes," he went on gaily, "she was having the dickens of a time with the laundry stove down there. She had never even seen one of the beastly things before. She was practically smoked out. In fact that is how I came to stop there. I saw a lot of smoke coming out of the back of the house and went to be a hero by putting out the fire. Instead I put the fire in, and we ate sandwiches while I waited to bank it."

Mrs. Donovan smiled in interest.

"I don't blame her for not being able to make the stove work. I had an awful time when I tried one the first time. Your father had to build it up regularly for me every night when he came home. I just couldn't learn to manage it." She gave a little reminiscent laugh. As she did so it suddenly seemed to Steve that she looked more like herself than she had since his father died. He decided to play up Joy's troubles a little more. If he could get his mother to take an interest in helping someone else it might do her a world of good.

"I feel sorry for the poor kid," he said. "Her father had a

stroke, and his business has failed—the stroke was the result of that, I suppose. He is still in the hospital. The name is Applegate. I wonder if it could be Edward Applegate, the contractor?" The name had not registered in his consciousness when Joy had first mentioned it. All he had thought of at the time was her own lovely name, Joy.

Laurel had been listening in the kitchen, going about silently that she might not miss what her brother was saying, although she would not for the world have admitted even to herself that that was why she would not run the water in the sink yet. Now she came to the door and spoke, still acidly.

"I suppose she just couldn't bear to soil her lily white hands building up a dirty fire," she put in contemptuously.

It took several moments for Steve to swallow his anger over that remark, then he answered in an even voice, "Well, they weren't lily white when I saw 'em. They were filthy!" he laughed. "She had tried and tried to light the fire, chopped kindling and all, but she didn't know enough to open the drafts and the thing just smoked. She was all alone there. She has a kid brother but he doesn't seem to be much help."

"Probably a spoiled rich man's son, like they all are!" sniffed Laurel. "Wait until we get capitalism licked in this country and then everybody will learn to do their part!" she announced in a declamatory tone.

Steve turned away to hide his sudden horror. Laurel's words had revealed a new angle to the problem of what ailed his sister. That gang she had been going with were feeding her communistic ideas! Oh God, what next! But it would never do to show her he was shocked. He thought an instant and then suggested casually, "And in the meantime, perhaps we as neighbors might fill in and pinch hit for the kid brother and the paralyzed father. That's what I had in mind."

His persistent mildness was wearing down Laurel's antagonism somewhat, so that she had no smart remark to make in answer to that.

But Mrs. Donovan was intrigued. "Does the girl know how to cook?" she asked. Mrs. Donovan was herself an excellent cook on occasion; her trouble was that she was not dependable.

"I don't suppose she does," answered Steve, hoping that he could detect a spark of interest in his mother's tone. "She would probably be glad of a little coaching now and then," he suggested.

But his mother had already sunk back into her listless state probably having decided that it would be too much trouble, or that the girl would not welcome a stranger's offer of help.

Still Steve felt somewhat encouraged as he started upstairs to bed that night. This was the first time since he had come home that the family had had what might be called a real little chat together. Before this, either Laurel wouldn't speak to him or she had been rushing to go out, or else his mother was not quite herself and there was no use trying to make conversation.

She had promised to wash the curtains in the morning if Steve would take them down, and he considered that a real step toward some kind of rehabilitation. Perhaps when she put up the clean curtains she would notice that the rest of the room needed attention and get to work on that. If she didn't, he intended to do it himself.

So it was with a much lighter heart that he started off to work in the morning, with the curtains already in the washer, and his mother fussing about the living room with cleaning rags in her hand. He took long eager strides to the house at the end of the row, and could scarcely keep from running as he went to the cellar door. He would not presume to ring at the front door. He was deliberately taking the place of a worker rather than a friend.

The cellar door was already open, and there was Joy, running gaily down the stairs from the kitchen, looking lovely and fresh in her little yellow gown with the white ruffles. The dainty little corners of her mouth were curled up and that eager light was in her eyes.

The admiration in his look met her like a fragrant wafting of sweet perfume, and she found her breath coming short, and the telltale pink coming up in her cheeks again. She was annoyed with herself for the blushes that would come. She had had compliments all her life, about her eyes, her gold hair, her manner and her clothes. They had always flowed over her and passed off like a pleasant part of her pleasant existence. She had laughingly held off the boys from time to time who had tried to be a little more intimate with her, tossing back witticisms and keeping them at bay, reducing their fond sentiments to foolishness by her teasing. Why was it that just the sight of this young man made the thrills go racing through her, and she found herself stammering and blushing like a child?

She gave him a lilting good morning, and did not guess that Steve's own heart was pounding with the sheer joy of seeing her. That picture she made for him, and the musical sound of her voice, he intended to keep safely in his memory forever.

And when he smiled good by after a few moments and sprinted up the street she stood wondering what there was about this young man that so warmed her heart and brought comfort and courage for the day? She gave herself a little sensible shake and started up the cellar stairs. It must be that all the trouble she had had lately had shaken her nerves. That was it, of course.

But that *was* a nice young man!

# ᴐ *Chapter 16* ᴐ

Iᴛ ᴡᴀs sᴜʀᴘʀɪsɪɴɢ how quickly the Applegate's little cramped living room took on an air of cosy cheer as soon as the packing boxes were out of the way, and the Persian rug was spread down. Joy placed a colorful vase or two, and laid a new magazine on the little end table beside her father's big chair. A shivering sob went through her as she wondered if he would ever sit in that chair again, but she forced herself to go on with her work.

She made sure that there was a nice breakfast for Mickey when he came down, late, to be sure, but willing after much coaxing to condescend to drive some picture nails for her. He stomped out again as soon as he could extricate himself from her demands. He would not tell her where he was going or when he planned to return. She had to be content to trudge on through the dark way set for her feet, still worrying.

In the middle of the afternoon Pembroke Harvey's sheaf of American Beauty roses arrived, bringing an air of luxury that fairly choked the tiny house. Joy arranged them as best she could, though there were few places to put them where they would not look ostentatious.

Later Steve stopped in again to see to the little stove that was now cheery and submissive. She was glad he did not go upstairs, she felt so conscious of those roses.

He tried to plan how he could win her brother Michael.

"Perhaps a big league game sometime would help," he suggested. Joy's face lit up with hope.

"We will try for next Saturday afternoon. I'll take pains to get acquainted somehow before then," he promised as he went whistling up the street.

Joy smiled her thanks and went back to her work.

Mickey did not come in that night until long after midnight. In the morning Joy found a ten dollar bill under her door, but Mickey slept late so that she put off again asking him what he had been doing. He evidently wanted to keep it secret to enjoy surprising her with the money.

She had decided during the night that if she was to follow the way that Steve suggested and try to find out how to approach God, the first most sensible step would be to go to church. So she made up her mind that, work or no work, she would take time out Sunday morning and go to church. There surely must be one in the neighborhood. She realized that she must begin to economize on such things as gasoline and car upkeep, so she planned to walk.

She put on her pretty white tailored suitdress, with the bands of blue that matched her eyes, nestled a scrap of a white hat on her gold curls, and found thankfulness in her heart that at least she was provided with plenty of good clothes. She would not have that expense to worry about for some time to come. Her father had always given her a fairly lavish clothing allowance, and she was well stocked.

She started out quite early, with the thought that she might have some distance to walk before she found a church. She must get used to walking as the time might come when she would have to sell her car in order to buy food. She went up the block past the Donovan house, trying not to cast more than one glance that way as she passed it.

She had scarcely turned the corner when she heard footsteps behind her, and a low whistle. The footsteps quickly overtook her, and there was Stephen Donovan, freshly groomed and well tailored in a light summer suit.

"Hi!" he greeted her as he fell into step with her. "I'm on my way to find a church. Where are you headed?"

She smiled. "The same place! Do you know of one around here?"

"I am ashamed to say I don't. I haven't been near one since I have been home, or long before that, either. Do you care what brand you go to?"

"No, not really," she said. "I'm afraid I am too ignorant to know the fine points of difference between them. I know I don't care for the taste of the one Daddy and I tried a few times. It was cold and formal, and horribly boring. Although maybe I wouldn't feel that way about it now," she added puckering her pretty brow. "All I used to think about was fun and a good time. I wasn't trying to get any help out of it. That might make a difference."

"I suppose it might," agreed Steve. "I think some people criticize churches the way they do restaurants; because they have no appetite they think the food isn't good. But here's a little tyke that might give us a cue. He looks as though he were on his way to or from a church."

Ahead of them trudged a small boy with a large Bible under his arm. Steve hastened his steps and called, "Hi there, Skipper, wait a minute."

The boy turned and surveyed them solemnly from large soft brown eyes. He was thin and wiry, and his short curly brown hair was slicked down wet and smooth on his head. His clothes were clean, but they had been much mended.

He waited politely to see what was wanted of him.

"We are looking for a church to go to," explained Steve. "Could you give us a steer, young fella?"

The child surveyed them a moment as if he were sizing them up. "Yes, I could," he answered seriously. "There are two near here. But God is in one of them and not in the other! Which kind of church do you want?"

He faced them calmly after this amazing statement, awaiting their decision with evident interest.

Joy glanced up at Steve and saw that her own astonishment was mirrored in his expression. "We want the one where God is, by all means!" answered Steve seriously, without a trace of amusement, but he threw Joy a twinkling glance of wonder when the child was not looking.

With obvious relief the boy nodded his head.

"I *thought* you were like that, Mr. Donovan," he assured him. "Well, I'm going to that one now. It's only two blocks away. My sister left her Bible at home and sent me after it."

"How do you know my name, son?" asked Steve kindly.

"Oh, I've seen you before," answered the child. "You've been in the army till a little while ago, haven't you?"

"Yes," responded Steve. "You seem to know quite a bit about me."

"I get around," explained the boy with perfect poise. "And I only live around the corner from you, back there," he jerked his thumb the way they had come.

"Oh, I see," said Steve. "And what is your name?"

"Timmy Taylor. Say, I'm glad you're a Christian, Mr. Donovan. If you go to our church maybe they'll make you teach our boys' class in Sunday school. Gee, that would be swell! We don't have any teacher right now and we hafta go in with a *gir*-rul's class. Gee!" His voice expressed utmost scorn.

Steve and Joy smiled amusedly again at each other over the boy's head as he walked a little in front of them.

"How old are you, Timmy?" put in Joy.

"Six goin' on seven," he stated humbly.

"You seem to know quite a bit, though, for a six-year-old," complimented Steve.

The youngster gave a skip and a shrug. Then he said,

"Well, I know I'm saved, an' that's the most important thing in the world to know, isn't it?"

"I guess maybe it is," agreed Steve, studying again the sweet face of this most astonishing child. Suddenly Timmy turned in at a plain brown-stained clapboard building, and said, "This is it."

As politely as a grown man might have done it, he introduced Steve to a genial-faced white-haired man who stood at the door and then he skipped off down a short corridor to another room.

The older man took Steve's hand in a friendly clasp. "We are glad to have you here, brother," he said warmly. "The Bible School is in session just now. I'm sure you will enjoy it."

Joy and Steve were ushered into a pleasant room where twenty-five or thirty young people were seated informally. A youngish man was seated in the circle with them, evidently about to start his talk. He looked up and gave a wide welcoming smile. There was a twinkle in his eyes and eagerness in his manner. His name was Peter Rockland.

Joy glanced around at the group. They looked like a happy, intelligent crowd, from various classes of society. They showed by their eager expressions that they were there by glad choice, not because they were performing a duty.

Steve was struggling to find the place in the Bible which someone had handed him. A young man sitting next him reached over unobtrusively, flicking the pages of Steve's Bible, and found the place. Steve threw him a grateful look.

"We have just started the study of Genesis," said the young teacher by way of explanation to the two new members. "This class has only recently been formed, and we thought we would start to study right where the Spirit of God started to write: 'In the beginning.'" He smiled.

"Yes," broke in an eager young man, "and there's more in those first few verses than I ever knew there was in the whole Bible!"

A murmur of assent came from several others. Steve glanced around. The easy air of informality surprised him. It was not what his idea of church or Sunday school had ever been. There was no attitude of piety, no undue solemnity. Of course he realized that this was not the regular church service. He and Joy had evidently come in too early for that.

The teacher smiled delightedly. "Yes," he said, "the whole Bible is wrapped up in the book of Genesis! In fact, we are going to see, or start to see, this morning how the very first chapter tells God's whole plan of salvation. But let's have a word with the Lord before we start our study."

In the same conversational tone, as if he had merely turned his head to speak to Another, the young man said,

"Our loving Lord, we have come here to learn more this morning of the great salvation which Thou hast wrought for us. We are rejoicing in it, but we don't understand all about it yet. Open this Book to our hearts. Let Thy Spirit be our teacher. Set aside any human ideas we may have had and let this living Word of Thine take root in our hearts and grow, for Thy glory. Amen."

Joy and Steve were fascinated, studying this young man who seemed to be on such intimate terms with the God they had been seeking.

" 'In the beginning, God created the heavens and the earth,' " read Rockland. "Now we haven't exhausted all there is in that first verse," he smiled broadly, "but we won't stop to review much this morning. Just remember that when God created this earth it was perfect, ready to be lived in. You recall from last week's verses that sin in the heart of Lucifer, whom God had made ruler of the earth originally, caused a great catastrophe, and 'the earth *became* without form and void,' shapeless, empty, coated with ice at the poles and surrounded with fog, for perhaps millions or billions of years."

Steve listened attentively. He had never heard of such an explanation of earth's early ages before. He wanted to ask more about it. But he was a newcomer; these people had all heard it before. Perhaps he could see this young man later and find out what it was all about. Or perhaps he would not want to. He might decide before this was over that the teacher was a mere fanatic. But as he studied the steady gray eyes, the firm chin, the broad smile of Peter Rockland, it was difficult to think of him as unbalanced.

"Then came the time," went on Rockland, "when God began to re-create the earth. First He commanded light to shine.

"Let's take just a minute for the scientific end of this. That light may have been merely the earth's radiation or it may be that at God's command there was a lessening of the blanket of fog about the earth, permitting some rays of the sun to penetrate. The full light of the sun itself was not visible to the earth till four days later, according to verse fourteen. Notice that that verse does not say that God *created* the sun, moon and stars the fourth day. He had created them millions of years before, 'in the beginning.' "

Stephen was intrigued. He had never noticed that before, although he had read the book of Genesis in college.

"Now," went on Rockland, "what we want to see is how all this touches our own lives! We shall find that whatever God did back there in that seven days of the re-creation of nature He does again in the same manner now in the 'new creation' which is spiritual."

He glanced around at his listeners, and then grinned. "I see that that is about as clear as mud to most of you so far. Let's get it straight. Turn to Second Corinthians the fourth chapter, the sixth verse."

There was a rustling of pages, and again Steve's neighbor found the place for him quietly. Joy had already given up the hunt and shared Steve's Bible with him. Somewhere deep within him Stephen was aware that he was sitting in sweet companionship with the most wonderful girl in the world. He was thrilling to the nearness of her little hand on the Book, and from time to time he would smile down at her and hold for an instant the sweetness of the look in her blue eyes upturned to his.

"Bob, read that verse," Rockland called on one of the boys, a husky fellow with russet hair and a big voice.

With some little fumbling and embarrassment Bob's voice boomed out in the little room: "For God, who commanded the light to shine out of darkness hath shined in our hearts, to give the light of the knowledge of the glory of God in the face of Jesus Christ."

"Thank you," said Rockland. "Now let's see what that really says. The writer is evidently referring to the time of re-creation in Genesis that we just read about. He is telling us that the same God who brought forth light to banish darkness then, does it now, only now He does it in hearts, not in the sky. Turn to Ephesians four, eighteen."

Once more the flutter of pages, and Rockland read, " 'Having the understanding darkened.' This, and lots of other verses, show that since Adam's sin, all men are born into the world with hearts that are dark because of sin. But—get this!—God did not create man that way! He created him in His own image. It was man's choosing to sin that darkened his mind, and separated him from the life of God that had been in him.

"Now, here is the picture: God created the earth perfect; sin came in and spoiled it. Then He sent light and re-created it.

"Correspondingly God created man perfect; sin came in and spoiled man; but God sent light, in the person of His Son Jesus Christ, and 'If any man be in Christ he is a new creation.' You see? The New Testament tells us in so many words that the new creation made up of those who accept Jesus Christ as their Saviour, is the counterpart of the old physical creation.

"There is one important difference, however. The earth had no will of its own to accept or reject the light. Human beings do. They may go on in confusion and darkness if they choose to." Rockland looked up with a grin. "That would be sensible, wouldn't it?" They all laughed appreciatively.

"People do it, though! But do you see," he added earnestly, "how vital it is to accept Jesus Christ as your Saviour?"

Steve and Joy were listening in deep concentration, realizing that they had never before been faced with this question.

"Well," the young man resumed, "to go on from there, let's look at the next thing God did and does, after giving light. It says 'He divided the light from the darkness.' And as we look on down through the story we find that there was a continuing work of dividing. Now, that separating of things that don't belong together is what we commonly call 'clearing up', isn't it? Have any of you fellows a desk that needs it? Or how about a top bureau drawer?"

Several grinned self-consciously.

"How do you clear up? Isn't it done by putting together the things that belong together? Separating the things that don't belong? Well, that's just what God did. And He does it in lives now. He works to separate from His newborn child the things that do not belong in the life of a child of God. You ask why are there inconsistent Christians, then? Well, be patient. He hasn't finished with us yet!" Rockland smiled a tender understanding smile. "If a Christian resists God's working in him God sometimes has to deal with him pretty drastically until that one will say, "All right, Lord. Anything You say goes!

"You see," he explained earnestly, "God gave His own Son to die for our sins and that makes us very precious to Him. He is not going to stop until He makes every believer in Jesus just what He wants us to be. It may mean suffering for a time, but glory will come out of it.

"Now one more thought in this verse before we have to stop," went on the teacher glancing at his watch hastily. "And it's the best of all." Everybody looked up attentively.

"Have you ever noticed that when God speaks of a day He calls it 'the evening and the morning'? He puts evening first!"

A murmur of surprised assent went through the room.

"That is not a mistake. And it is not simply a quaint old-fashioned way of putting it. The Spirit of God who wrote this Book knew what He wanted to say! The reason for it is that that is always God's order!

"It is not man's, for man says, 'morning and evening.' Isn't that so?" They nodded, wonderingly.

"Do you realize," said Rockland, "that God's purpose has always been to have the hard things first, then the joy? First the darkness, then the light; first the suffering, then the glory. 'Weeping may endure for a night,' says the Psalmist, 'but joy cometh in the morning.'"

There was a satisfied ring of triumph in the voice of the young man, a ring of conviction, of authority.

"I've never known it to fail!" he said. "So if you are going through a pretty dark time in your life right now, just wait and trust. Morning is sure to come with its joy, if you are a child of God."

Steve felt his glance drawn to the girl beside him and he found her blue eyes swimming with unshed tears. She was looking up at him with a great longing and wistfulness, as if she were wondering whether she might trust the words of this strange teacher. Steve smiled down at her reassuringly and slid his big hand quietly over hers under cover of the Book and gave it a comforting little squeeze.

Suddenly the subdued sound of a bell was heard from somewhere in the building. The members of the class all sighed disappointedly and closed their Bibles.

"The time always seems so short!" said the boy next to Steve regretfully.

Two or three couples came up to Steve and Joy introducing themselves, and shaking hands warmly.

Steve smiled back, the wonder of what he had just heard still in his eyes.

"We are so glad to have you with us," greeted a Mr. and Mrs. Chatfield, an attractive young couple. "We are having a picnic, the bunch of us, next Friday. Couldn't you come? We would love to have you. We have such good times among ourselves—we are mostly all young married couples, you know."

Joy blushed and Steve grinned.

"Well, we'd like to come, I'm sure," he said, glancing down at Joy and taking note of her pink cheeks, "but I'm afraid we wouldn't qualify. We are just, well—friends!" he finished lamely.

Mrs. Chatfield laughed her apology, and her shiny brown eyes twinkled as she repeated her invitation. Joy answered this time.

"It would be fun, I know," she said wistfully. "I'll have to see how my father is. He is in the hospital, very ill."

"Oh-h!" sympathized Mrs. Chatfield. "We'll be praying for him. And I hope he will be well enough for you to join us. Please try!" She was so cordial that Joy had a feeling as if warm loving arms were reaching out to her. It was a new experience, and most comforting.

"Do you want to stay to church?" asked Steve in a low voice as he and Joy started down the hallway again.

He hoped Joy would say yes. He was anxious to hear more, to see whether he had really been missing something all his life, or whether there was a catch in it all somewhere.

"Oh, yes, I do," breathed Joy earnestly. "Did you ever hear all that before—what he was teaching?"

"I never did. I admit I'm somewhat confused, but I am going to stay with it till I find out what it's all about. They certainly are a cordial bunch, whatever they are. Did you notice what kind of a church this is?"

"No, and I don't care much, if all this turns out to be true."

"Same here," agreed Steve.

So they entered the cool pleasant little auditorium.

The service was simple. There was no vested choir, but a group of young voices, beautifully trained, sang a simple gospel hymn. The minister was just under middle age, spare and homely, with deep lines in his face, but with a gentleness born of understanding written on his brow.

He spoke in a conversational tone of voice as he read the story of Nicodemus.

"Nicodemus was a good man, you know," he reminded. "He was not conscious of being a great sinner. But Jesus told him that even he could not get to heaven the way he was. 'You must be born again,' He told him. 'Born from above' is what He was saying, literally. Born into the heavenly sphere by receiving heavenly life. You receive it as a gift, just as you received your physical life."

The minister looked earnestly from one face to another in his congregation.

"Have any of you been trying to live a Christian life?" he asked. "You can't, you know, until you have received the Christian life to live."

On the way home Joy and Steve discussed what they had heard.

"I wonder if those people are right," said Joy. "It seems too good to be true, doesn't it?"

"Well," answered Steve thoughtfully, "if God is as great as He is supposed to be, I'm beginning to think that perhaps we have had things all backwards. Perhaps the best things are the true ones. Maybe it's good *enough* to be true."

He flashed a brilliant smile at her and it seemed as if already the light that those people had spoken of was beginning to shine in their hearts.

# ~ *Chapter 17* ~

MONDAY MORNING Joy started out to find work.

She had spent an hour or two at the hospital the afternoon before and was just a little encouraged by her father's improvement.

Mickey had brought her another five dollar bill, too, although he still would not tell where he was working. She had searched through the want ads of the newspaper and found two or three places that she thought she might have the courage to try for.

One position was receptionist in a dentist's office. That seemed as if it would not be too difficult. Surely she could answer the phone and keep track of appointments.

But the cold eyes of the dentist looked her over, took account of her youthfulness, approved sternly of her looks, then asked, "How much experience have you had?"

She summoned all her dignity. With a smile she answered brightly, "Oh, I'm just starting."

He frowned. "Can you type?"

"Oh, ah, well, a little."

He frowned again. "Are you familiar with medical terms used in dentistry? I need someone who could take shorthand notes and type my lectures for the dental college."

It seemed to Joy that the man's long thin face grew much longer and thinner as she gazed at him in dismay. A double

set of teeth that he held in his hand were grinning horribly
up at her as she answered in a very small voice,

"I could learn them, I think." But she did not dare to mention that she could not take shorthand. She could write very
fast and if he would only let her try perhaps he would not
notice that she was writing longhand. But she had no chance
to offer that suggestion.

"You won't do," he decided frostily, and went back into his
office.

Outside the building she bit her lip to keep it from trembling. She must not be discouraged. There were other places
to try.

There was that ultra exclusive shop for women's apparel.
From the wording of the advertisement she judged that it was
a saleswoman that was needed. Surely there was no special
trick to selling lovely garments. She had been to the shop once
or twice, and had felt very luxurious in what she had bought
there. Thankful that she was well dressed herself, she went to
the address.

She walked confidently to the back of the salon and asked
for Madame Blanc herself. She was conscious of the admiring
stares of a paunchy gentleman who had entered just ahead of
her. He had taken a lounging position on one of Madame
Blanc's modernesque chairs in an alcove at the back of the
shop. He was smoking a fat cigar that showed very wet on
the end he took from his mouth. His thick pale lips sagged
above a double chin which lay folded over an expensive gaily
colored tie. His little finger flashed two huge rubies as he re-
placed the wet cigar between his lips, keeping his eyes on Joy's
pretty figure all the time.

Joy met the same kind of cold stare from Madame Blanc that
she had found in the dentist's face. Why did all employers
have to put on that icy stare as if to dare anyone to have the
courage to work for them?

Joy smiled her prettiest and stated her errand.

"Good morning, Madame Blanc," she said with sweet dignity. "I have been into your shop several times, and I have just loved the beautiful things that I bought here. Now that I find I am to earn my own living, I thought I would enjoy selling some of them to other people."

Joy had composed that little speech while she was walking up and down waiting for the store to open.

Madame Blanc had begun a smoothly groomed gracious smile until Joy came to the part about earning her living. Then her face froze again.

"We have no need of a salesperson!" She clipped off the sentence and turned away.

Crestfallen, Joy started down the length of the showroom again. She was conscious of the beady eyes of that fat man, and of the two or three perfectly coiffed salesladies who were hovering about. But Joy walked with easy grace and poise though she was trembling within from disappointment and chagrin. Just as she reached the door one of the saleswomen hastened after her and touched her arm.

"Madame would like to see you again a moment," she announced as if the queen had condescended to notice a little beggar girl.

With renewed hope, Joy traversed again the long velvet-carpeted salon.

She did not notice a slight nod that the jewelled gentleman gave toward the desk.

But Madame Blanc still spoke coldly. "There may be an opening for a girl to model lingerie," she vouchsafed, as if it were a top secret government position which she was offering to Joy. "If you would care to try out for it you may."

"Oh!" gasped Joy. "What—what would I have to do?"

Madame Blanc looked completely through her; scorn seemed to drench Joy's soul. The woman did not even make any attempt to explain to her. She simply turned away, leaving

Joy facing another woman, only a little less cold, who said in a scared sort of voice, "Come this way."

Joy followed, to an inner sanctum made of mirrors. The woman produced an outfit of the thinnest of thin gauzy undergarments.

"Come out when you are ready," she ordered, and walked away.

Joy picked up the filmy things, trying to grasp the situation. Was she actually expected to appear in these wisps and parade herself up and down for inspection? The thought appalled her. Where was she to come? Not out there as long as that man sat there, surely. She could not bring herself to don the things. Yet she desperately needed work, and here was a job offered. Her mind was in a tumult. She thought of all the bills that were piling up in the hospital, and she started to take off her dress. Then she suddenly wondered what she would tell her father if she ever had to let him know she was working. He would want to hear all about it.

And her friends. Stephen Donovan, for instance. Her cheeks grew red with shame and she laid down the flimsy garments and fastened her dress again.

But the thought of her need came back to prod her. What if she found nothing else? Couldn't she tell people she was "just working" in this shop? She need not say what she was doing. She hesitated again, wondering what was the right way for her to go. She wished she had someone to guide her. Suddenly she thought of those people she had met at the little brown church yesterday, and their God, whom she was seeking to know. *He* would know what she should do, if He cared as they said He did. Her heart threw a quick cry heavenward. "Oh, God, please show me!"

The saleslady appeared again at the curtain of her booth. Her eyebrows went high when she saw that Joy was not ready. Her words stung like bits of ice.

"Madame wishes you to come at once. The gentleman is anxious to see the things and go."

The gentleman! Joy's hand flew to her throat as if she were choking. She was expected to put on those chiffons and walk in front of that horrid looking man! Never! She had heard that men sometimes went to women's shops to have things modeled which they wished to buy to please some woman of their fancy, but she had found it hard to believe that any girl would be willing to show them. She drew herself up to her small height and looked the cold-faced woman straight in the eye.

"I cannot do that," she said. "I prefer to keep my decency, even though I do have to earn my living!"

With her head held high she marched out of the booth and down the long agonizing way of the salon once more, and just as she reached the door she heard a sneering titter from the saleswomen. Her cheeks were flaming by the time she got outside. That unspeakable man had kept his unclean eyes upon her every step of the way down the room.

She walked rapidly away from the place, breathing fast with the relief of her escape. How had she ever thought that it was a glamorous thing to buy clothes in such a place? Never again would she set foot in it, even though she had millions to spend.

She climbed into her car and closed the door, putting her head down on the wheel and sobbing away the shock she had received. Then she raised her head and looked up, beyond the roof of the little coupe. Her eyes were wet and her lips were still trembling.

"Thank you, oh God," she said, "for showing me. *And how* you showed me!" The tears broke forth again and it was several minutes before she got control of herself enough to dry her eyes and drive on.

She wondered whether she dared go to another place. She saw that there was much for her to learn. How her father had sheltered her! And now she must shelter herself and him too.

What a strange thing life was! Yet she felt as if she were not completely unsheltered, after all, for there was God now. He had answered her prayer. He was caring and guiding. With far less confidence in herself, she drove on to the next address she had on her list.

But she still had no success and was weary and heartsick when she finally drove to the hospital to spend a little time with her father.

Dr. MacKenzie was there, and he threw her an encouraging smile as she came into the room.

"If your father improves as much as he has lately," he said, "I think we can have him home in a couple of weeks."

Joy smiled at her father who seemed to try to smile back with one side of his mouth. His eyes looked his love for her and she bent and kissed him. But she hid the terror at her heart as she thought of the awful hole the hospital bill would make in her slim bank account. What if nothing were coming in by the time he came home? Would they have to ask for *charity*? Oh, God, I *still* need your help!

But she chatted gaily to her father, scraping together all the little amusing events of the day that she might leave a cheerful impression with the sick man without revealing any of the trouble.

It was a bright moment when she came home at last and found Steve there at the cellar door. He had just come home from work and had stopped to see that the little stove was still on its good behavior.

It was only a few words they had together, for Steve had promised to take his mother downtown that evening. But it seemed to rest Joy's tired soul just to be with him those short moments, and feel his strength and courage as if they were enfolding her. She felt as if she wanted to store away in some holy place the look he gave her.

She went into the kitchen and fixed the nicest supper she knew how to make. She had stopped on her way home and bought lamb chops because Mickey loved them, although she had been aghast at their price. She had never thought of how much they cost before.

But no Mickey came. Finally, after waiting until the chops were almost cold, and the baked potatoes were limp and soggy, she sat down alone and drearily poked down some food, putting a plate into the still warm oven for Mickey when he should arrive. His job, whatever it was, was probably keeping him.

She straightened up the kitchen with unaccustomed hands that took longer than necessary to the task. Then she emptied more cartons, studied the want ads in the evening paper, and crept forlornly into bed.

The next two or three days were spent in much the same way as Monday. Mickey came in late every night and slept late every morning. Joy felt too tired and troubled to start any questioning.

Tom Thorne stopped in to see if Joy needed any help, and she was grateful. None of her other friends had looked her up. But that was not surprising; most of them were away.

Some of the places where she applied for work that week told her to come back later, but most of them required some skill which she did not have and she began to have a very poor opinion of herself indeed.

The little glimpses of Steve were the only bright spots in her days. Even the time spent with her father was so one-sided that it tired her; she had to try to talk cheerily without bringing in some subject that would require explanation to banish the puzzled bewilderment in his dear suffering eyes.

Thursday morning as Joy was starting out a little earlier than usual she saw a beautiful dark-haired girl come out of Donovan's house and start up to the corner. She knew it must be Steve's sister Laurel. Joy jumped into her car and hastened after her. She reached Laurel at the corner. Slowing up she called to her.

"Laurel!" The girl stopped in surprise. Joy smiled disarmingly. "Aren't you Laurel?" She asked. "I saw you come out of Donovan's house."

The girl nodded, rather coldly. She had guessed who this must be, the girl Steve had raved about. She was not going to be condescended to, she decided.

But Joy smiled again. "Are you going downtown? Won't you ride with me? I get terribly lonely!"

Laurel hesitated. The girl was certainly pretty. And her navy dress and hat were stunning. Nothing tacky about her, anyway. Joy had opened the door of her little car and was waiting. Well, it would do no harm to find out what she was like, reasoned Laurel. Rather ungraciously she climbed in.

Joy began to chat pleasantly, and Laurel soon forgot her prejudice and talked vivaciously. Somehow the subject of horseback riding came up and when Laurel discovered that Joy loved it and had even tried a little indoor polo once, Laurel's estimation of Joy rose considerably. She couldn't be such a priss if she liked to ride.

"Oh, I love horses!" cried Laurel enthusiastically. "I've only had a few chances to ride, but I love it better than anything next to music!" Her dark eyes shone with longing.

"Oh, do you play or sing?" questioned Joy.

Embarrassed that she had given herself away, Laurel blushed a little and stammered, "Oh I sing, a little. I wish I could play, really well! We have a piano and I thump away on it some but I never had any lessons. I've always thought that would be all I'd ever ask—if I could have some *good* lessons. I did start two years ago to take singing lessons. The teacher wanted me to train for opera," she said wistfully, "but I couldn't afford to go on, he charged so much."

"Opera! Well, you *must* have a lovely voice!" exclaimed Joy. "How I'd love to hear you sing! May I come and play for you to sing some time? I love to accompany. And I had to sell my piano. I miss it. I'll be glad to teach you all I can on the piano, though I'm no genius."

Laurel turned toward her, her eyes gleaming with eagerness.

"Would you really?" she cried. "Oh, that would be marvelous! Mother used to play for me to sing, but she doesn't seem to take any interest now that Daddy is gone. Oh, I'm so *thrilled!* I would rather sing than anything in the world. Somehow it feels so good!"

Joy looked at the lovely girl with pity. Here was somebody who might turn out to have real talent. Joy thought regretfully of the ease with which all things used to come her way, and how lightly she had taken them. She suddenly felt infinitely older than the other girl. If she could interest Laurel by playing for her, and perhaps teaching her a little on the piano, that might be helping Steve to solve his problem.

"Mother used to sing a lot," chatted Laurel, in a friendly way now. "She has the most gorgeous contralto voice that goes way down deep and tangles up your heart. But," she added sadly, "we can't get her to sing any more. She hasn't sung a note since Daddy died."

Joy's heart went out to the girl, she seemed so eager for life, and so much that she longed for was being denied her by her mother's failing to meet the need. She was not naturally hard and bitter, that was plain to be seen; she was only disappointed and hurt. No wonder Steve was troubled over his sister, knowing how talented and charming she could be.

"Where am I to drop you?" Joy asked suddenly, as they neared the downtown business district.

"Oh, anywhere it's convenient for you," responded Laurel. "I'm used to footing it from the bus, and this ride has been nice. Where are *you* going?"

Joy gave a little shrug. "I don't know, exactly," she said distressedly. "I am trying to find some work to do that people will pay me for! I'm finding out that I can't do *any*thing that seems important." She gave a little laugh, but Laurel, young

as she was, caught the note of desperation behind it. She
studied Joy a moment.

"Have you tried in the music line?" she suggested. "If you
play you might get a job doing that."

"Why, I never even thought of that," said Joy, brightening.
"Perhaps I could. But I wouldn't know where to go."

"Well, I work at Wolfe Brothers' Department Store and I
heard the other day that the pianist in the tearoom orchestra
was going to leave. Maybe you could get that, unless," the
tinge of scorn crept into her voice again tentatively, "unless it's
not highbrow enough for you."

"Oh, I'm not looking for a highbrow job," Joy assured her.
"I'm way beyond that now if I ever was!" She laughed. "I
play popular stuff now and then, only I must admit I like the
other better. There's more in it, it seems to me."

"I like the long-haired kind, myself," confessed Laurel, "but
they don't go for it much in tearooms. I just thought maybe
you wouldn't want to take a job like that."

"I'll take anything!" said Joy vehemently. "Anything that's
decent," she added, remembering her experience at Madame
Blanc's.

"Okay, then, park back of the store here and let's try now,"
said Laurel. "I'll introduce you to the manager."

Cheered and hopeful Joy parked her car and the two girls
walked chummily into the enormous store building. Wolfe's
was the finest department store in the city, and its tearoom
was a popular spot. Joy would no doubt be seen by many of
her old friends, and it might be embarrassing, but she was
beyond reckoning on such obstacles now. She *must* get a job.

Mr. Timmins, the manager, was pleasant at least. He obviously admired Laurel, and that helped. He looked Joy over
with evident approval.

"The piano job is already taken," he said, and Joy's heart
sank. "I don't know whether the man will turn out to be

good enough, though. You could give us your name and we'll be glad to give you a tryout if he doesn't make it."

Oh, another delay, thought Joy in despair.

"But," he went on, "we have an opening now for a clerk in the glove department, if you would care to try that."

Laurel glanced at Joy quickly to see if she would consider herself too fine to work as a salesgirl. But Joy answered gratefully.

"I'd be glad to try it," she said.

And so it was that a half-hour later she found herself behind the counter, being instructed in the various styles, makes, and prices of gloves, and the correct way to fit them on the customers.

The day seemed very long to her, as she was unaccustomed to being on her feet constantly. But the excitement of trying to learn so much all at once, and the elation of really having some work, kept her going. She had arranged to have lunch with Laurel, and they planned to ride home together.

"It will be so nice to have someone to ride down with every morning," said Joy on the way home. "That is, if you will go with me?"

Laurel cast her a glance testing her sincerity. "Gee! I'd love to. But I won't unless you let me buy half the gas."

Joy's normal disregard for expenses made her exclaim, "Oh, no! Why should you? I'd be going anyway, and it costs no more for the car to take two. You're not a heavyweight!" She laughed.

But Laurel insisted and Joy gave in.

"If you really meant that about the music lessons, too, I'll take you up on it," said Laurel. "But not unless you let me pay for them."

"Pay!" cried Joy. "I'm not a music teacher. It will be a pleasure just to have a chance at a piano."

"Well, I'm only a beginner, but beginners have to pay for lessons."

So they finally agreed and the two girls parted at Donovan's door planning to get together Friday evening for some music. Laurel wished she dared ask Joy to come for dinner but no telling what state her mother would be in.

Steve met Joy at her back door a few minutes later, as he had insisted on taking the regular responsibility of the laundry stove. She told him of her day with Laurel and his face shone.

He tried to thank her but no words would come and his eyes only devoured her, speaking more than he knew to her tired heart. Her lashes dropped and the pink stole up again into her cheeks.

Then she looked up shyly and said, "I sort of think God is answering, don't you?"

"I sure do!" he agreed heartily.

"Now if only we could get Mickey on the right track," said Joy puckering her brow again. "He seems to be working but he won't tell me where."

She looked so little and so troubled that Steve had a great longing to take her in his arms again and comfort her. But he fought back the desire to embrace her. That would be taking advantage of her confidence in him.

"I'll try to watch for him tonight and get acquainted," he promised.

But that night Mickey was later than ever, so Steve did not see him.

# ～ Chapter 18 ～

PEMBROKE HARVEY HAD been keeping in touch with Dr. Mac-Kenzie pretty regularly. It would not pay him to be ignorant of any change in his employer's condition. Harvey seldom thought of Applegate any more as his employer, however. The office force had become Harvey's office force, and the business Harvey's business to guard and to nourish. He dismissed any qualms his conscience stirred in him with the thought that of course he was going to do the best for the business that was possible. But the sudden accession of power over so much money had made him greedy for more. He could not get out of his mind the thought of some enormous blocks of stock which he had learned that Applegate held. It would give him a feeling of greater security if he could get Joy to sign transfers of those to the business. From time to time he toyed with the idea.

When the report was given that the patient might be expected to be taken home in a few weeks Harvey bestirred himself. Things were progressing fairly well, but just in case Mr. Applegate should recover sufficiently to talk business it would be as well for the whole situation to be thoroughly sewed up with the tender thread of matrimony between himself and his employer's daughter. No doubt then about a partnership! And there would be no need of detailed explanations.

Except for his semi-weekly roses, Harvey had left Joy pretty much to herself for the first week after she had moved to the dreary little house. His plan had been to let her get a good big dose of poverty, and drink of discouragement deeply, so that she would be all the more ready to accept release when he offered it. He had thought his reasoning in this was extremely clever, psychologically. He felt that this line fitted in with the reaction of girls as he had observed them.

So it was with a good deal of confidence that he drove up to the tiny house on Emerson Street, on the evening of the day that Joy had signed on to clerk at Wolfe's glove counter. The first thing he saw from the porch was the great vase of his roses. He smiled with satisfaction.

Joy was very tired and lonely. Her elation over her job and the new friendship with Laurel had faded somewhat as she had gone into the house and discovered that Mickey was not home yet. He had been out late every night this week. She simply must have a talk with him tomorrow, or at the latest, Sunday. Surely he would not have to work Sunday. She had been too hurried that morning to do more than waken him and remind him that breakfast was on the table for him.

The worry was haunting her eyes as she came to the door when Harvey rang. She looked tired and pale and Harvey did not miss the weary droop of her shoulders. His own exuberance flooded the lonely little living room, overwhelming it. He seemed to bring into its cramped confines a breeze of the great successful world outside, a whiff of glamor, exciting, intriguing.

To Joy's tired vision the little room seemed suddenly narrower, hotter, more unbearable than ever. All at once she found herself wondering what some of her old friends were doing tonight, although she had not thought of them for days.

But Pembroke Harvey was holding out to her an enormous box of chocolates and talking briskly.

"Well, well, my dear!" he approved. "What a change you have wrought! Clever clever gal! All you need is a sow's ear and you could make a silk purse out of it!" He laughed at his own witticism.

"But now," he went on pompously, "how about a little holiday from the horrors of your lot? It might feel good to escape for a time the unsightliness here and step back into your own world again, wouldn't it?" His teeth gleamed beneath his red lips under the little dark mustache.

"Come, Cinderella, let's have lights, flowers, music, gaiety. How about Saturday night, yes?"

Joy started to shake her head, but Harvey came over close to her and laughingly took her face between his hands and held it so that she could not turn it.

"No, no, naughty!" he said. "Don't say no to me! Let's play, just for one night. You have worked so hard!" He released her almost immediately and she could not resent the little familiarity, it had all been done so laughingly.

She smiled, falling in politely with his gay bantering mood.

He took her moment of relaxation for consent and made sure of his advantage.

"Saturday night at seven I will arrive with the pumpkin coach, my dear. And lest there be a single inharmonious note, tell me now what color you will be wearing. Blue? Sky blue? Or pink—you would be luscious in pink. No, yellow, is your color, made to order for you. I have never seen you in yellow, do you know that?"

Joy had to giggle a little as he rattled on, taking her swiftly with him back into her old world of lightness and trivialities. Of a sudden it seemed the most natural thing in the world that she should be asked for a date, and flattered in this way. Then it came to her to realize how swiftly and unnoticeably clothes had receded from her recent vision. From the midst of her turmoil of thoughts about washing machines, and roaches, and gloves, she would probably just snatch a dress, any dress, out of her closet and put it on if she went with this man, which she had not by any means decided to do.

But Pembroke Harvey had decided, if she had not. And it was hard to change that gentleman's mind if he wanted something very much. Without her knowledge she found herself saying good night to him, having committed herself, or rather having heard him commit her to going out Saturday evening.

Well, no doubt it would be good for her to have a change. And now that she had a real job she had a right to celebrate.

But as she went upstairs she was thinking about Laurel and planning for Friday evening rather than for Saturday.

And the next morning on the way to work, Laurel asked her if she would come and have supper with them before they had their music.

Laurel had gone home the night before full of eagerness over her new friend. She was pleasanter even to Steve than she had been since he came home.

She greeted him when he came in with something of her old teasing tone. "Well, you sure did pick a winner after all! How come she ever looked twice at you is what I want to know?"

Steve was so glad to have his sister like herself again that he welcomed the chaffing. "So do I!" he agreed laughing.

"Humph!" sneered his sister, though good-naturedly. "Don't get your little heart set on her, mister. That gal has gone places and done things."

Laurel was setting the table for dinner, going in and out of the dining room where Steve sat straddled backwards on a dining room chair watching her, his chin on its back. She did not see the gleam of triumph in his eyes as she praised the girl he had found.

"I asked her over tomorrow night," continued Laurel, appropriating Joy as her own friend rather than Steve's find. "We'll have ourselves a spot of music. Liven up this dead old dump a bit."

Mrs. Donovan came downstairs just then. She had been asleep most of the day. Her eyes were red and dull. She started to complain of a headache until she heard Laurel say something about music. She looked from one to the other of her children and slowly realized that the hostility which had disturbed the atmosphere for some time was lacking.

"Did you say music, Laurrie?" she asked in a weary voice. "That would be nice. Yes, do have some music."

Steve cast a keen glance of wonder at his mother. She had not been willing to play or sing ever since his father died, much as she had loved it before. Could it be that his mother was rousing to take an interest in the household pleasures too? It seemed unbelievable. He put his head down on his hands for an instant to hide his relief. Joy had wrought this wonder! Or had she? Was it perhaps the God to whom he had appealed who had performed this thing which he had sought to do and could not?

Laurel came back into the dining room with a hot baking dish full of macaroni and cheese and set it on the table and then she too glanced at Mrs. Donovan in surprise.

"Yes," she said, "I've asked Joy Applegate to come over for music tomorrow night, Mother. And if I thought the family would be *decent* to her," Laurel looked straight at her mother and paused, "I would ask her to come to dinner!" The last words came with a defiant rush. That was as near as the Donovans had ever come to accusing their mother of the habit she had fallen into. They were a reserved family, respecting each other's rights, perhaps overmuch, and sealing up hurts within their hearts to burst out in bitter explosions at odd times. True to form, Mrs. Donovan acted as if it were the most natural thing in the world that her daughter should invite someone to dinner, although the girl had not done so for nearly two years.

"That would be nice," was all Mrs. Donovan said, but Laurel felt that her mother had accepted the challenge and perhaps she would rise to the occasion.

Still it was with a good deal of apprehension that Laurel went into the house the next night when she and Joy drove home from work. Joy drove on home to get freshened up, promising to be over soon.

Fearing the worst, Laurel had arranged to have a simple supper that she could fix herself if she had to, when she got home at night. She could excuse her mother, of course, by saying she had a headache, unless this would be one of those rare occasions when her mother would insist on appearing whether she was fit to or not.

But the lights were on in the kitchen and dining room, the table was set and she found that her mother had made hot rolls and an apple pie.

With vast relief Laurel ran upstairs to slip into a cooler dress and wash her hands. She heard Steve come in whistling. It almost seemed as if the Donovans were going to start living again.

Joy went wearily into her house, wondering if Mickey might possibly be home yet. She saw no sign of him, but just in case he should come she fixed a tempting plate of thin cold ham slices which she knew he liked, a big plate of fresh red tomatoes with a little fancy jar of mayonnaise, some crisp potato chips and hot rolls which she had just got at the baker's on the way home.

There was a dish of applesauce dark with brown sugar and cinnamon for dessert. Joy had fixed it up a little after taking it out of a can. She set the table daintily just as they always used to have it, and then she wrote a loving little note telling him where she was, and that their new neighbors wanted them to come over. She knew Steve would be glad to bear her out in the invitation to Mickey too. Now if only he would come home early enough to find the invitation and come.

She slid into the tub finishing with a cold dash and a quick rub and felt almost rested after her second hard day at the unaccustomed work. She put on the little dainty yellow frock that she had worn the day she first met Steve. Somehow it always seemed to belong to the times when they were together.

Then she gave a brush to her curls, ran downstairs, and started eagerly up the street.

How little she had thought those few weeks ago when she stood on the pavement outside this row of houses, that she would soon be having a neighborly dinner inside one of them and liking it!

Mrs. Donovan had been a strikingly handsome woman, Joy could see that. Her deepset dark eyes under dark brows were set off by cream colored skin. The other time Joy had seen her she had been so stunned by the woman's condition that she had not noted her looks particularly. Tonight Mrs. Donovan had taken pains to comb her wealth of dark hair low in her neck and she had fastened it with a sparkling comb as she used to wear it. Her children noticed her with pleasure.

She welcomed Joy with a nervous cordiality, sinking spasmodically from vivacity into dull silence. Joy took pains to ask her questions to try to draw her out and when she touched on the subject of music she saw the fire of interest begin to glow in those dark eyes.

Then Laurel came in to the living room with a tray of glasses.

That tray had almost been the cause of another rift in the Donovan family. Steve had sauntered out to the kitchen before the guest came to see if he could be of any service. He found his sister preparing cocktails. Without thinking he exclaimed,

"Oh, no, Laurel! Not that!"

Laurel looked up at him defiantly.

"And why 'not that'?" she asked imperiously. "Is your girl too goody good to have a drink? If you ask me, I think you'll find she is used to doing things the right way. *Everybody* serves cocktails before dinner. You know we always did when we had company."

"But Laurel—" Their mother was right in the dining room and Steve could not bear to say aloud "That was before mother got to drinking." Laurel knew what he meant but she chose to pretend that she didn't.

" 'But Laurel'!" she mimicked. "Go 'butt' somebody else if you like. I'm running this dinner."

Steve shut his lips tightly. He must not have a quarrel now. No telling what his temperamental family might do. It would be like Laurel to get angry and refuse to come down at all for the dinner even though she herself had invited the guest. What could he do? Oh God! Here is a time when I need You again, he cried out silently.

In an even tone of voice he said, "I sort of think Joy won't take it. But if you must have them, why not serve some ginger ale too and let her take her choice? Then perhaps you can say 'I told you so' to me." He managed a friendly little chuckle. Steve dreaded lest his mother should take too much and disgrace them before their guest but it seemed the best compromise he could make.

Laurel looked at him an instant, thinking it over.

"Okay, smarty, I will," she said. "You'll see."

But when she came in with the tray, politely murmuring the names of the drinks to Joy as she passed them, Joy happened to be looking at the stern face of Steve who stood opposite. He moved not a muscle of his face, but she quickly grasped the tensity of the moment. It was true that she had been more or less accustomed to the serving of cocktails all her life. She had never liked them, but had been used to taking a sip with everyone else.

Now she realized that this custom was pain amounting to torture for Steve. What must it mean to him, with the background of shame and suffering that had come into his life? Suddenly she knew that she would never again take a drink. If it could bring sorrow like Steve's, she wanted nothing to do with it. All in an instant she made her quick decision, graciously answering:

"Ginger ale, if you please!" She smiled but left no doubt as to her determination.

Without a shade of change in her expression, Laurel gave her the glass, and only Steve knew how crestfallen she felt. He carefully refrained from any triumphant look toward Laurel, then or later, for he had learned that it did not pay to try to humble his sister's fierce pride. Perhaps God could do that, but not her brother. Yet a gladness stole into his face and voice which Joy noted. She wondered if it could have anything to do with her choice.

Mrs. Donovan was sitting on the couch next to Joy and, wonder of wonders, she followed suit with a smile. Steve found himself breathing easier. Great little mother! When she did anything she did it wholeheartedly and she was evidently determined to do the right thing by her family tonight.

They had a pleasant meal, Laurel and Joy doing most of the chatting. Steve was content to let the two of them grow in their friendship without his interference.

After dinner he waited happily on the little family, quietly anticipating any need of a chair, or a better light for the piano. He was content to let Laurel monopolize the girl he adored, if it would help Laurel back to her old wholesomeness again.

Joy sat down at the piano and lightly idled through a few rippling chords and runs, playing a snatch of Chopin, Mozart, anything to break the ice.

Steve slipped out to the kitchen to help his mother with the dishes, and to let Joy start Laurel off all by herself. Soon they heard Laurel's glorious voice, softly at first, then with more confidence. Mrs. Donovan took her hands from the dishpan and drying them, went to the door to watch. The old fervor began to creep back into her face, and Steve could have cried for joy when he saw it. If he could get his mother interested in her music again that might help a great deal.

Song after song they tried, Joy exclaiming with delight over Laurel's lovely voice. Once they came on a duet. Joy turned impulsively to Mrs. Donovan who was sitting in the corner listening raptly.

"You come and sing with Laurel, won't you, Mrs. Donovan?" Joy coaxed.

The woman came to with a start. "Oh my, no, child! I haven't sung for years. Oh, no!" She shook her head. But a wistfulness came into her tone, and Joy meant to try again some time.

Joy found her house dark when she reached home and still no sign of Mickey. The nice supper had not been touched and the little note was just as she had left it.

The worry crept into her heart again. Surely he didn't work late every night. He must be spending these evenings with the gang. The boys probably fooled away a lot of time uselessly. Surely there was nothing really wrong going on. Her father had once asked Mickey the names of some of the boys, and had seemed satisfied that they were of good families. Oh, Mickey was basically a good boy. It was his recent sullenness that troubled Joy more than anything. She was certain that he would defend himself when he did come home by saying sulkily that nobody cared anything about him anyway and why should he stay at home? It seemed as if there were no way to penetrate the stubborn front he had chosen to wear lately. If she made an attempt to check on him or tried to get in touch with his friends to find out what he was doing he would resent it terribly and perhaps leave home altogether. At all costs she must not antagonize him, she thought. But she did decide that she would rise early enough tomorrow morning to reason with him gently before she went to work. She was too tired tonight to wait up for him.

But she slept so soundly that she was almost late for work and had to rush off without seeing him.

## ∾ *Chapter* 19 ∾

JOY HAD HOPED to be able to get a job that would give her Saturdays off, so that she could catch up with her work at home, but she had to be all day at the store and she was dead tired when Saturday night came.

Mickey was gone as usual and she confided her worry to Steve when he came to fix the laundry fire. Steve agreed to try to look him up.

After Steve had left Joy suddenly remembered her date with Pembroke Harvey. Oh, she *could not* go out and be festive tonight, she thought. She was too worn out and worried.

But there was less than an hour before Harvey would come for her. She could not in decency call him up and call off the date now. There was nothing to do but go through with it.

She glanced at her watch and saw that there was precious little time to primp. She grabbed a blue and white chiffon from her closet and after a sketchy shower she slid into it. But she gave a squeal and a shudder as a big brown roach fell out of it. Would she *ever* get rid of those loathsome creatures!

She did not know how like a little blue and white angel she seemed as she hurriedly descended the stairs to greet her escort.

He pompously presented her with a box. Joy thanked him automatically and took out a corsage of exquisite white orchids.

"You wouldn't tell me what color so I made it white!" He seemed to take a childish pride in his gift.

He took Joy to an exclusive restaurant for dinner. But all the time she had the feeling that he was taking more pleasure in letting her see that he knew how to entertain her, than he was in her company. It did not occur to her to wonder how Harvey could afford such lavish entertaining if the company he worked for had failed.

A man and a girl whom Joy had known passed their table once. The girl, Enid, stopped and gushingly greeted her. "Where have you been keeping yourself?" she said to Joy. "We all decided you must be away. Do you know, darling, I saw a girl at the glove counter in Wolfe Brothers yesterday that I could have sworn was your twin sister!" she laughed at the absurdity. Her trilling voice carried across two or three other tables and people turned to look. Joy felt her cheeks burn. But she held her head high and looked Enid steadily in the eye with a smile.

"It was not my twin sister," she said. "I was there in person. I am a 'woiking goil' now," she laughed. "If you want any gloves, come to me!"

Enid's face fell, and she swept Joy with a haughty look.

"Oh!" she said. "I didn't know. Do excuse me!" And she started to turn away with her companion.

Joy felt the scorn of the girl scorch over her in waves.

But Pembroke quickly broke into the embarrassed silence. "Yes, our little Joy is trying new experiences. Maybe she will write about them some day." He gave an empty laugh. "But this won't last long. I can promise you that. She will soon be back among you ladies of leisure."

Enid raised her eyebrows at Joy and gave a little polite laugh and went on.

But Joy looked at Harvey. "What was your idea in giving that impression?" she asked him. "I'm not ashamed of working. It's probably being very good for me."

Harvey smiled indulgently.

"Oh, no need to let the world think you are poverty-stricken," he said. "Besides, it may not last long. That was one thing I wanted to have you all to myself for tonight, so that I could tell you something."

"I know how hard all this change has been for you, little girl," he said, looking down into her eyes. Joy turned hers away. She had a feeling she wanted to close the door to her heart lest he should look in.

"I have been spending all my time and strength since this thing happened, in trying to find a way to build up the business again so that you and I will come out on top. I think I am going to be able to do it. It will take some reorganization, perhaps. I may have to ask you to sign some papers—but I won't bother you now with all that." His voice held a trace of nervousness and he hurried his remarks. "I just want you to know that it will all come out right. I have spared no effort to make it do so, for *your* sake, my dear girl."

Joy gazed blankly back at him with hope timidly striving to win the upper hand in her thoughts.

"You must know that I admire you," he said, looking deeply again into her eyes.

All Joy noticed was the wet redness of his lips smiling below his mustache, and the way his eyebrows slanted up at the corners, for all the world like a picture she had seen of Mephistopheles.

She shook her thoughts trying to get them back into normal position. What a ridiculous thing to think while the young man was actually making love to her!

She answered him in a light vein. "That is very nice of you," she said smiling, "and I must thank you again for the gorgeous roses. They fairly fill my little hut to overflowing and help to hide many of its discrepancies."

He gave a gratified smile.

"Roses are gorgeous, aren't they?" he agreed. "I like to

think of them around you. They are your proper setting, but not half so lovely as you, my dear!"

"Oh, thank you!" she returned with mock formality.

"I mean it!" he said lowering his voice and filling it with deep emotion.

"I mean it with all my heart," he repeated solemnly. "I have always admired you, but tonight you look especially lovely."

She smiled graciously.

"And I have something else to tell you, too, Joy." He pronounced her name as if she were a valuable possession. "I think that the business matter will soon be straightened out and I want you to get ready to marry me."

He spoke with assurance as if he were conferring a favor.

Joy had had boy friends before who had believed themselves in love with her, and had proposed marriage in various ways. She had always taken them rather lightly, considering them too young to know their own minds. This man was older, but she decided to treat him lightly, also.

So she laughed, quoting carelessly, "Oh, 'there's much to be done 'ere it comes to that!'"

But Harvey caught her glance again and held it, saying unsmilingly this time, "Yes, my girl, there *is* much to be done, and *you* can help to do it. But you will see. *I shall succeed!* And you are the one whom I want to share success with me!"

But she turned him off again and talked of other things. She began to tell him enthusiastically about the little brown church she had found, and tried to pass on to him some of the wonderful things she had heard in the Bible study there.

But he raised his well-manicured hands and the ends of his eyebrows went up contemptuously.

"My dear child!" he exclaimed. "You have got into a nest of religious fanatics, don't you know that? I thought you were above being led into such antiquated foolishness. You surely need someone to look after you! I have heard all that rot, but I wouldn't fall for it. Nobody with any intelligence could. Now don't *think* of going to that place again. You and I will find a really nice church to go to, a place of beauty where the music is true inspiration and where we will hear the best thoughts of the wisest scholars of the world."

"But you don't understand," insisted Joy. "I *have* heard a lot of the thoughts of this world's finest scholars, but none of the wise of this world seem to know God, or very few of them. Anyway, they didn't help me to find Him. These people know Him well. They are simple, humble people and they seem to radiate His love. It is a dear place. And as for learning, you should hear how well they know the Bible."

"Oh, no doubt!" sneered Harvey. "They are the kind that will quote yards of it, and don't half know what they are talking about. You may be sure they will soon break out like measles with some ridiculous theory and you will become a laughing stock if you continue with them."

Harvey made Joy feel as if he thought she did not have very good sense but she determined to have one more try.

"I think they do know what they are talking about," she maintained. "I never heard anybody before who could give a good reason for suffering, for instance. And as for knowing the Bible, you should hear this man Peter Rockland. He shows how wonderfully the Old and New Testaments fit into each other. He reads a verse from Genesis and goes to Corinthians and shows how the Old Testament pictured by physical things the spiritual things in the New."

"Poppycock!" scoffed Harvey. "I've had some pretty fine Bible courses myself and I know enough to realize that Genesis is just a mass of folklore, and as for the apostle Paul, I never did like him. He was too conceited. Come now, Joy, get the cobwebs out of your pretty head. Let's dance."

But Joy was tired and soon managed to persuade him to take her home. On the way as she paid meager attention to his punctilious conversation she tried to imagine what it would be like to be the wife of this man. He certainly was lavish in his gifts. He was good-looking in a way, and a brilliant conversationalist. But his wit was merciless at times. And then there was that little incident at the dinner table. He had been ashamed of her job at Wolfe's. It made her feel that she could not trust him wholly. It was a small thing, still she could not imagine, well, Stephen Donovan, for instance, doing what Pembroke Harvey had done, nor sneering at the Bible as if he thought he could have done a better job of writing it himself. No, the taste of her evening with Harvey would not be pleasant to remember.

But Stephen! The thought of him brought a glow of pleasure. She did not know that Steve was still out, far out of town, perched at that moment on the rail fence on which he had taken refuge once before.

Steve had been on the point of going out after supper to look for Mickey. He had just started out his front door when he saw the gray coupe draw up in front of Applegate's. Then he saw the immaculate gentleman in evening clothes go in. Stephen stood stock still and stared at the Applegate porch. Almost immediately the gentleman reappeared with Joy, escorting her down the steps. And Joy was gowned in an evening dress of cloudy blue. She looked so lovely that Steve's heart twisted in a wrench of jealousy. He could not take his eyes from her as they got into the car and drove away.

The world seemed suddenly black. All the troubles Steve had had in his young life seemed as nothing compared to this. He had never felt such pain before.

He tried to reason with himself, in vain. Why should not a girl like Joy have men friends? Why should she not go out for an evening's enjoyment? He should have asked her himself. Yet he had tried to be so careful not to force his attentions upon her. He had felt that she was so far above him socially that it would have been presumption for him to ask to take her out.

He walked and walked and walked, going over and over the problem, twisting and turning the hurt in his heart again and again, almost delighting in the pang it gave him.

At last he came upon the point that hurt him the most: he had been with Joy himself less than an hour before and she had said nothing about going out. She had asked *him* to help her brother but she was going gaily on her way with another man!

His first reaction was to cast to the winds any idea of hunting for Mickey. Why should he try to help a boy he had never seen, whose own sister thought so little of him that she could go out to enjoy herself, not knowing where he was? Let her get her other friend to find the brother, if she was so worried about him.

Yet in spite of the anger and grief in his heart Steve found himself going from one place to another where he thought a young boy might be found loafing. He followed all the leads that Joy had been able to give him, which were pitifully few, but there was no sign of Mickey. It was then, when he could think of no further place to search, that he found himself walking out to the hillside where he had been before.

He sat a long time on the fence. His eyes pushed through the blackness trying to make out objects whose vague shadows he saw. How like his life it seemed. All the way ahead was dark. He saw no path, no familiar landmark to guide him. No rules or standards he had ever learned would help him in his way, or ease the pain of what had happened tonight. There was not a soul to whom he could go with this trouble, not even Joy—least of all Joy! No, there was not a ray of light.

Suddenly the words Peter Rockland had read came back to him. "God who commanded the light to shine out of darkness." That was the light Steve needed, needed desperately—a light that was not of this world, a light that did not depend on this world for its brightness. He saw that he had been considering that lovely golden-haired girl as the light in his life. But there must be a light that would shine for him even when she disappointed him. Otherwise he did not see what use there would be in going on at all. He would stumble and fumble all his life.

When he started home it was long after midnight. All the houses were dark. The Applegate house too. But Steve could not remember whether there had been a light burning when Joy left or not. He did not know whether she was still out with that other man or not. He tried to refuse his mind permission to think any more about the matter that night, but in vain. At last, worn out with bewilderment, he fell asleep.

But Joy was still awake. She had determined to stay up tonight and wait for Mickey. She need not leave early tomorrow morning, so it would not hurt her to lose sleep. She sat at her open window looking out again at the stars. Every sound alerted her nerves. She heard Steve come down the street and then heard his front door close. Surely if he had any news about Mickey he would call her. But no call came.

She heard the clock strike two, and then three. She curled up in her big chair for comfort. Before she knew it she was fast asleep. And she was not disturbed, for that night Mickey did not come at all.

## ↜ *Chapter 20* ↝

SUNDAY MORNING STEPHEN awoke to the stabbing pain of his thoughts of the night before. He began all over again the bitter round of reasonings. The eagerness which he had felt for the Bible class at the little brown church had left him. No doubt Joy would be going there this morning, but he could not bring himself to go with her. The sweet fellowship they had had sharing the same book last week was over forever, he thought.

When it came time to go to the Bible class, Steve did not go. He paced up and down or stood at the window gloomily staring out and gritting his teeth. He called himself a fool all the time he did it, yet he kept right on. He longed to tear out of the door and rush to the church, but he would not give his feet permission. He had not seen Joy go by, but he supposed he had missed her in his pacings back and forth.

He was truly disappointed not to go to that class and hear Peter Rockland again. But he knew that if he went all he would be able to think about was Joy. He would keep seeing that other dapper young man in his immaculate get-up handing Joy into his natty coupe.

It was after nearly an hour of such brooding that Stephen finally became ashamed of himself. He looked at his watch. He had missed the class, the thing he had looked forward to ever since last week. But there was no reason why he should miss the church service. He would be late for even that now, but no matter. He would slip into the back seat and that would keep him out of Joy's sight.

As soon as he had made up his mind to go, he found himself eager to set off. In spite of the pain it gave him he was longing to have a glimpse of Joy again.

But Joy had not gone to the Bible class either. She had been awakened from her brief sleep in the big chair by the hot sun shining full in her face. She sprang up and ran to Mickey's room. It had not been occupied!

Frantic, she rushed downstairs but there was no sign of him there. A righteous indignation seized her. This was going too far! She was more angry than alarmed, for she had little doubt that he had spent the night with one of the boys. He had likely tried to call her last night and she had not been there. That was it, of course. She was quite a little relieved at so plausible an explanation and her ire was somewhat calmed. Still she would like very much to see Steve and find out if he had discovered anything about her brother last night. She looked at the clock. It was late, too late for the Bible class. But she would be in plenty of time for church. She made a hasty toilet and started out.

She took a seat in the center where Steve would be sure to see her when he came in. The room filled and the service began but Steve did not come. She twisted around as much as she dared but she could not see him. She was disappointed and a little anxious. It must be that something at home had kept him. Perhaps his mother was in a bad state and he had to stay with her. Had he, too, missed the Bible class? Perhaps he had been there and, missing her, had gone back. Then she fell to wondering if his absence had anything to do with Mickey. What if Mickey had run away and Steve had gone after him?

And all through the service Steve sat far behind her, his heart aching.

Neither of them heard a great deal of the sermon that morning. Only once did Steve forget his troubled heart and lose himself in what the minister was saying. The man had a quiet gentle way of speaking, pausing sometimes to let his hearers think.

Once he looked straight at Steve, or so it seemed to the young man, and said,

"You who are here with a troubled heart this morning, listen to the One who says, 'Peace I leave with you, *My* peace.'"

The speaker smiled and his smile seemed to Steve like a blessing.

"Now don't think for a minute that that peace is a vague sort of feeling that you are floating on beds of roses, and that you get it by going to meetings and looking holy!" The minister made a long face in imitation of a self-righteous prig. A low laugh went around the congregation in which even Steve joined. The minister laughed a little, too. Then he resumed:

"There are two kinds of peace described in the Bible; first, peace *with* God, second, the peace *of* God. You can't have the second unless you first have the first!" He gave another twinkle of a smile.

"You can have peace *with* God only because Jesus Christ died on the cross. God took your sin, the cause of dispeace between you and Him, and piled it *all* on His Son and put Him to death for it. Now God has nothing against you, and you are eligible for the second kind of peace, the peace *of* God.

"But if a man prefers," he went on, "to be punished for his own sin, rejecting the great sacrifice that God's Son made in love, then God has *that* against that man, that he has spurned His Son! There can be *no* peace for that man."

There was a hush over the people.

"Do any of you want to be *that* man?" asked the minister solemnly. "A man who will *never* know peace?" His eyes roved lovingly over his people. Steve felt as if God Himself were wooing him in that look of love. He saw clearly for the first time in his life why Jesus Christ died, and his heart bowed in thanksgiving.

"Have you been neglecting the love that bought peace for you?" asked the speaker gently. "Don't do it any longer!" Perhaps you would like to tell Him now in your heart that you accept that great offering for your sin? Let's all bow our heads."

There was a moment's silence. Steve did not know that the burning intensity of his gaze had already told the speaker that there was a young man who had been thirsting for his message of peace. He was not aware that he had nodded his head ever so slightly when the man asked that last question. And he did not know that Joy's blue eyes were brimming with tears and that she had forgotten for the time being to look and listen for Steve to come and sit with her. But he did become aware that the awful struggle in his soul had ceased. A quietness had taken possession of his heart. It was as if God had entered in. He wanted now to get away and be alone with this God who had so unostentatiously come in answer to his cry.

While the last hymn was being sung he slipped out the door and started to walk. He did not notice which way he walked. He was thinking over what he had heard and beginning to understand a little of the things of the Spirit of God.

As he came to a busy corner a newsboy thrust a paper across his way. Steve pushed past the newspaper and crossed the street. Then suddenly the words the boy had shouted made sense to him. He wheeled and recrossed, reaching frantically for a coin.

"Paper! Boy! Here!" he called and almost snatched the paper from the astonished urchin's hand. He stepped to a convenient low stone wall around a yard and opened the newspaper.

He searched the big headlines. Nothing there. No doubt the boy had hunted through the columns until he had found an item that he thought would attract the curiosity loving crowd. Clever newsboy.

Then all at once a two-inch story caught his eye. He read it breathlessly, then jammed the paper under his arm and rushed to the corner to hail a taxi.

Inside the taxi he put his head down in his hands.

"Oh God!" he cried in his soul, "Help now!" and for the first time as he prayed he was aware that the God to whom he cried was there, right with him in the taxi. There was no hopeless wondering. He knew that help would come and there was a great peace in his heart in spite of the sorrow that this news item might bring to Joy. He kept calling upon God for deliverance for his beloved. And as he did so, he found himself saying, "You know I love her, Lord!"

But the girl for whom he prayed was walking homeward in a kind of joyous perplexity.

The minister's words had gone deep into her heart and she, too, knew for certain that nothing would be just the same again for her. She would never be alone. Even though Stephen Donovan had not met her this morning and she was disappointed, God had met her! And that was everything. She had humbled herself before Him and had accepted His great sacrifice for her sin. Now there was peace.

She had a feeling she wanted to find Steve right away and tell him, let him know that it was all true, what they had wondered about. But although the front door was open when she went past Donovan's house, there was nobody about, and Joy went slowly down to her own house.

Inside she called, hoping against hope that Mickey might be there. She had bought some frozen chicken to fry. They had nearly always had it on Sundays at home, ever since Joy could remember. Surely, she had thought, he would be home for Sunday dinner. He would know that she would be there expecting him.

The fear clutched her heart again that maybe he really had

run away. Oh, what would happen to her father if he ever found out? And she would never forgive herself either, for she saw as she never had seen before that her own sharp words must have cut him often and her own interests had absorbed her so that he must have felt left out at times.

She glanced at the clock. She simply must take time to run down to the hospital and spend a little while with her father before dinner. The Applegates had always had Sunday dinner in the afternoon, about four o'clock. She dreaded to leave lest Mickey should come, but she would leave him a note. She had continued to hold to the hope that he had spent the night with one of his gang. When he came she would make him understand that he would have to let her know where he was after this.

She racked her brain again and again trying to recall the last names of some of Mickey's friends but the only ones that came to her were a Smith which was useless to hunt for in the telephone book, and a McKeown whose phone did not answer.

She sighed as she set the table and put out the chicken to defrost. She got ready the materials to mix up some muffins from a prepared package she had bought. She had some frozen peas that she could do in the pressure cooker at the last minute. Emmy had showed her how to use that. There were big red beefsteak tomatoes to slice and some fresh shoe-string potato chips. She would slip those in the oven as she took out the muffins. For dessert she had discovered a luscious looking box of fresh fruit, also frozen. It would be melted to about the consistency of sherbet if she took it out when she came back from the hospital. Mickey would love it.

She stood and surveyed her preparations well satisfied. She had spent quite a bit on this meal, yet even so it did not compare with the lavish table her father had always provided. Still, it seemed attractive, and it was worth everything to have things nice for Mickey to come home to.

As she worked she found herself praying, "O God, bring

Mickey home! Bring Mickey home! Please give me another chance with him. Take care of him and bring him home."

At the hospital she found her father doing well, and Dr. MacKenzie had left word that before another Sunday he should be able to go home, but "No discussion of business yet!" he had warned.

She rejoiced gently with the dear patient, delighting in the glad loving light in his eyes. It was still very difficult for him to talk plainly. But the doctor gave some hope that that might improve in time. It would be wonderful to have him home. But the worry was always there about how she was to explain where they were living. Perhaps her new Saviour would work that out for her.

She told her father a little about the church where she had been the last two weeks and she thought he seemed pleased. She did not stay long for she had a constant urge driving her to get back and see if Mickey would come home to Sunday dinner.

When she got home she skipped up the steps and into the house, calling again, "Hi, Mickey!" but her voice rang back emptily at her ears, and she could tell by the silence that no other person was in the house.

With a heavy heart she started out to the kitchen. She would keep on pretending he was coming, anyway. And maybe Steve would turn up soon and have some news for her. Where could he be? She wondered whether to cook the dinner or to wait. She got all the things out of the refrigerator and then went to the front window again. It was only a quarter to four. Everything would cook quickly. Why not wait?

So she went back and set them all inside in the cold again, then sat down by the front window with the little red book that Peter Rockland had given out. But she could not keep her mind on it. After a while she looked at the clock again. A quarter after four now! Surely if Mickey had been going

to come back he would be here by now. At last Joy began to
be really frightened. She had been counting a great deal on his
coming home to Sunday dinner. That had always been the
one time when the family had tried to be together. She felt
she could not stand this anxiety much longer. If Mickey did
not turn up soon, she would call the police to find him no
matter how furious that would make him.

Nervously she looked out the window again, then she went
out onto the porch and looked up and down. There was no
sign of Mickey or of Steve either. She had to force back the
tears. The world was such a lonely place.

Finally she went up to her room and got down on her knees.
She was not aware of how long she had been there when she
heard footsteps coming down the street. Two pairs of footsteps. But they were slow, not eager steps. Hastily brushing
the tears from her eyes she ran to the front window.

## ⌁ *Chapter* 21 ⌁

IN THE TAXI Stephen read over again the news item that had galvanized him into action. As he studied it the second time he realized that it might mean nothing at all, and yet he dared not pass it up as a clue that might lead to finding Mickey.

The story was told dispassionately, with few details: "Three boys, all under fifteen, were apprehended on Friday evening when they were caught breaking into a house in the northeast residential section. They admitted to having taken small amounts of money from several places within the past week."

Two of the boys had given their names and addresses and had been bailed out by their parents who had asked that their identity be undisclosed. The third boy gave a fictitious name and address. He was being held in the hope that his disappearance would soon be reported. He had given his age as fourteen; he was of sturdy build, with reddish-brown hair, the story said. The address of the police station was given and a few more items about the burglaries. Steve's face contracted with pain as he thought of what this might mean to Joy if the boy turned out to be Mickey.

He paid the driver and hastened into the building. After a talk with the officer in charge he was led to a small cell at the rear.

He had never seen Mickey, although Joy had showed him a picture taken some time ago, and had described him. He felt confident that he would recognize him.

There were three or four people in the cell. A couple of drunks, probably picked up in the park the night before, an impudent looking youth, and a boy with copper curls.

The boy was seated with his back to the cell door, his head in his hands, the picture of despair.

The officer called him and he looked up for an instant. Steve's heart turned over. There was Joy all over again, only etched in copper. And the beautiful dark eyes were sullen instead of glad like hers.

The boy glanced at the visitor for a moment, then put his head down again. He had never seen the man.

But Steve went over to him and touched his shoulder gently. "Mickey!" he said softly.

The boy looked up with a startled, angry glare. Even as he did so he suddenly realized that he had given himself away in responding to his name and he shrank away from Steve's touch.

Steve gave a nod to the officer and he led him out of the cell, where Steve spoke to him again.

"Your sister's waiting for you, kid," he said in a low tone. "I've come to take you home."

The boy glanced up at the tall stranger, despair in his eyes. "Does she—*know?*" he demanded fiercely under his breath.

Steve shook his head and Mickey went quickly on the defensive again.

"Who are you?" he blazed. "I don't know you. Let me alone and get out. I can take my medicine."

"I know you don't know me, but I know you," smiled Steve. "That is, I know your sister and I've seen your picture. Come on, we're going home."

"I haven't any home! Get out!" repeated the boy, a sob bulging up beneath his gruff words.

"I know about that, too, kid. But that will work out all right sometime. And right now home is where your sister is. She needs you. She has been worried about you." As he said that

Steve had a passing recollection of the bitterness he had felt last night about Joy. But strangely enough the bitterness had disappeared. He knew how he would feel if he were in this poor boy's position and his heart went out to him.

Steve had not planned yet how he was to deal with Mickey when he got him out of there. He had thought yesterday that he would give the boy a good thrashing when he found him, but now all he could feel was pity.

But what would he say to Joy to break the awful news to her that her brother had been in jail last night, instead of working at an honest job as she had hoped?

Steve had paved the way for taking him out. He had arranged identification and bail with the officers there, and promised to take custody of the boy at least until his father should recover sufficiently to look after him. The police were evidently glad to get the matter temporarily settled and have him off their hands. They assured him he could arrange for a private hearing with the judge later.

But in spite of Steve's friendliness and what must have been relief to the boy to be out of that cell, free, he was sullen and hostile as they walked out of the building.

Steve laid his big hand in a friendly way on the boy's shoulder as they went. He not only wanted the boy to know that he was back of him, but having been a boy himself he guessed that one impulse of the youngster would be to run as soon as he was free; so he put a warning pressure into his grip.

He felt the sturdy shoulder start to wrench itself away as soon as they were at the outside steps and he tightened his grip till the boy winced.

"None of that, kid," he said, quietly, a stern look on his face. "I've taken you on, and you're not going to skip. I could easily catch you, you know that. Besides," he broke into a smile, "I like you, and we're going to find the way out of this mess together."

The copper-colored eyes glared up into the brown ones in

an instant's measuring glance. Steve's steady look held them, and when Mickey dropped his eyes at last Steve knew that his first battle had been won. Mickey respected him and would obey.

They walked rapidly away from there, through the city traffic. Steve had had some thought of calling a taxi to take the boy home as quickly as possible. But he suddenly realized that he was not in any state of mind yet to go home. He must not be allowed to meet his sister in this mood. A long walk would be good, after the inactivity of the two days in the cell. Then perhaps he could have a talk with him.

They spoke very little as they walked. Steve took his hand off the boy's shoulder to let him understand that he was going to trust him. But there was an invisible compelling on Steve's part as they turned corners or crossed highways.

They had walked nearly two miles, and had passed the place where they would have turned to go to Emerson Street when Steve saw the boy glancing up at him uneasily. But Mickey was too proud to speak first or ask any questions.

Steve said, "We'll take a bit more walk first before we go home, and get the air of that place out of your lungs. Let's get out where we can be quiet and hash this thing over."

So, rather grumpily, Mickey trudged on beside him.

Steve headed for the old fence on the hilltop where he had been before to get his vision cleared. As he walked he tried to think how he would have felt if he were in Mickey's place, and what would be the angle of approach to this bitter disillusioned young soul.

As they climbed the hill he noticed how the lad's feet dragged with weariness. No doubt he was tired. He had probably slept very little since he had been arrested. Good. It would be much easier to deal with him tired and discouraged than fresh and ready to fight him. It occurred to Steve to wonder whether that was what God had had to do with his own soul—get him completely down before He could speak to him. He remembered what had taken place in his own heart scarcely more than an hour ago. He was conscious still of the presence of God.

When they reached the top of the hill he turned toward the fence saying, "Let's take a blow here."

He swung his leg over the top rail and Mickey followed. Even then Steve did not start talking immediately. Mickey was evidently bracing himself for a sound scolding, but Steve had no such plan. He felt infinitely sorry for the boy, and realized that he had had punishment enough for the time being.

At last he said, "It's tough, being a boy, isn't it, kid?"

Mickey looked surprised at this method of attack. But he merely gave a grunt of assent.

"I mean people expect a lot of you and you don't always know how to go about doing what you're supposed to."

Mickey continued to look his amazement. This did not sound like any lecture he had ever had, at home or in school.

"I know *I* didn't," Steve went on confidentially. "My dad died a couple of years ago and there were things he asked me to do and be that I couldn't seem to get the hang of at all. Not for a long time. It wasn't till everything got about as black as it could for me that I began to see the light. You've had a pretty tough time, haven't you, Mike?"

Mickey gave one quick look up at this stranger who so amazingly had turned out to be a friend, and nodded, struggling with an awful lump that would clutter up his voice. Then all of a sudden he turned his face aside, sprang from the fence, ran pell mell over to the far side of a big tree near by, flung himself down on the grass and burst into great shaking hoarse sobs.

Steve let him alone a few minutes. He knew how the boy would hate to have someone watch his tears. It would probably be good for Mickey to let out in this way all the grief and shock that had been pressing against his heart in the last weeks since his father had been taken sick. Very likely these were the first tears he had allowed himself.

At last when he was quieter Steve climbed down from the fence and came over and sat down on the grass beside him.

After a silence he said, "It wasn't worth it, was it, kid?"

Without raising his head from his arms on the ground Mickey's copper curls moved slowly, despairingly from side to side.

"What'd you do it for?" Steve probed gently.

Another silence, then Mickey mumbled from between the grass blades, "I wanted to help Joy. She thought I didn't know or care that she was havin' a tough time, but I did. I couldn't do anything else that would bring in any amount that would do any good."

"Did that do any good?" Steve's tone was not condemnatory, only searching.

The copper curls shook again, and the boy's shoulders started to heave once more.

"You know, your family care a lot for you," reminded Steve, "and this is going to hurt your sister."

"Oh yeah?" snorted Mickey disparagingly, turning his head and looking up sullenly. "That's where you're wrong. *Nobody* cares much about me! Only Dad and he's as good as dead, I guess. Not even the gang! One of 'em woulda snitched on me to those cops if I hadn't used our devil's threat on him in time."

Steve gazed down compassionately at the fierce young face. He did not take pains to go into the question of what the gang's dire threat might be. He had been a boy once, too. He was silent again for a while.

Mickey sat up and gazed gloomily down through the trees to the valley below. Finally he burst out, "I can't go back down there!" He pointed to the city. "There's no use. The cops have got my name now. I'd never get a square deal.

And I can't trust the gang any more. They weren't on the level with me."

Steve looked at him. "You'd like to have all this wiped off the slate and start fresh, wouldn't you?" he asked seriously.

Mickey shot a look up at him that held a sudden hope, Steve spoke so confidently. Then as suddenly he drooped again feeling that such a thing could not be.

But Steve spoke again. "Did you know that that is just what God has done for you?"

At that Mickey just stared.

"God!" he ejaculated. "Phooey!"

Steve did not register any shock at the irreverent remark. He realized only too well that he had at one time not so long ago, been almost on the point of feeling the same way himself.

He simply nodded his head with assurance and said, "I know, I felt very much like that a while ago. But I made up my mind I'd find out about God, and I did. I met Him this morning."

Mickey turned and stared at him. A leer of contempt mixed with disappointment slowly spread across his face. He had thought that he had found a friend in this man, one who spoke his own language and really understood him. Now the friend had turned to fanatical clay. His eyes plainly said, "You're cracked!"

Then Steve grinned. "You think I'm screwy," he said. "I would have thought the same a short time ago. But God got me down—never mind how—to where things looked awfully black, and there wasn't any help in anybody but Him, if there was a Him." He smiled. "I asked Him to help if He really was a God and He did. Things aren't all straightened out yet, but *I* am, inside."

The younger boy listened incredulously.

"Let me tell you something that I just lately learned myself, kid. I guess it's about the most important thing I've ever learned in my life. It's about why Jesus Christ died on the cross. You've heard the fact of it, of course?"

Mickey nodded, putting on a bored mask. In reality he knew he liked this man. He respected him. He was a right guy. And it *might* just happen that he had something.

"Well, the way I get it, it's like this," went on Steve. "Everybody has done wrong, in one way or another." He stopped and looked to Mickey for confirmation of that. The boy nodded again, dropping his eyes with sudden remembrance of his own guilt.

"Well, for some reason, God cared for people. Everybody. They had no way of getting back to Him because their sin was in the way and He just couldn't stand that. So He managed it this way. He sent His own Son down here to become man so that He could die. His Son had never sinned so God put everybody's sin to His Son's account, just like a judge *can* do; as if I would ask to take your jail sentence, for instance. Then your page in the book would be clean again. And *God* makes it as clean as if you'd never sinned! Get it?"

Mickey looked at Steve in amazement. "Of course," explained Steve, "if you paid no attention to what I had done, and insisted on serving your sentence anyway, you'd be just a fool, wouldn't you?"

"Oh, but," Mickey put in, "I wouldn't let you do that for me. It wouldn't be fair! I ought to take it myself!"

"Yes, you *ought,* but you'd have no say about it if I had *already* taken it. There would be no sense in your taking it all over again, would there?"

"No, I suppose not," said Mickey wonderingly.

"But suppose the judge were my father, for instance," went on Steve. "And after I had done that for you, you paid no attention to me, never even said thank you or asked if there was anything you could do in return, and never seemed to care?"

Mickey's face blazed up. "I *couldn't* be like that, I'd just have to—to—give my whole life to you!" he blurted out, the enormity of such a gift of grace suddenly striking home to him because of his own situation.

Steve turned a brilliant smile on the boy. "That's it, son!" he said solemnly. "That's just exactly what I intend to do for the One who did that for me."

Mickey gazed at him again, slowly comprehending. Then he looked far off again toward the distant hills beyond the city.

"You mean God really did that for us, for people?"

"He really did, kid. I just found it out, though. I don't know why I never heard it before. Maybe I was too proud to listen. It's great, isn't it?"

After a long thoughtful moment Michael said:

"It *sure* is! But do you suppose *I* could get in on it? *I've* been—a—*mess,* you know." The tears brimmed up again into the boy's sorrowful eyes.

"I haven't a doubt of it, kid," assured Steve gently. "I don't know that your penalty from this earthly judge can be remitted, but you can stand that, you know, if you have peace with God in your heart. The way I get it, He's a God who meets your need, whatever it is."

"Gee!" breathed the lad in wonder. "That would be something to live for, wouldn't it?" His eyes fairly clung to Steve's in his great wistfulness.

"It would. It is," said Steve. "I was about ready to quit, myself."

Mickey cast him a fairly worshipful glance.

"The way still looks awfully black ahead," admitted Steve, "but somehow since this morning when I sort of agreed with Him inside that I would let His death count for me, I feel as if He was just as glad as I am, and I believe things are going to work out someway, sometime. What do you say we get going?"

Steve rose and brushed off the dried bits of grass from his best suit and Mickey scrambled up and followed him. Steve looked at his watch. It was nearly four o'clock. They walked rapidly down the hill, talking a little more about what was ahead.

"I'm going to leave it to you, Mike, to tell Joy about what's happened. I have no desire to squeal on you, but I would come right out with it, if I were you. It's the best way."

Mickey's face turned white. "Oh, gee!" he gasped. "I couldn't. I just *couldn't!* Can't I just go back and say nothing about it? I promise I won't skip. You've told the cops you'll stand for me and I wouldn't let you down. Why does Joy have to know?"

"It's the only way, kid. You'd always have something to hide if you don't. And it's sure to come out through some other channel if you don't and that would be harder on her and you too."

"Oh, but, you don't know. I *can't!* She'd never forgive me."

"Listen, kid, God forgave you, didn't He?"

"Yes, but you don't know Joy."

A flash of bright pain went over Steve's face as he reflected that perhaps he didn't know Joy as well as he had thought and hoped he did.

But he said, "Never mind, you do it. There's no use going on if you don't get started right. Here's a chance for you to prove that God will meet your need, if you let Him. Why not tell Him that you are up against something too much for you and ask Him to help?"

Mickey thought over that as a new idea, and they were silent for a long time.

It was not until they were nearing home that Steve saw the boy take a long deep painful breath and straighten up, setting his chin that looked so like Joy's firm little chin. He knew then that another battle had been won.

# ⤳ *Chapter* 22 ⤳

JOY PEERED ANXIOUSLY out the front window. Sure enough there was Steve coming down the street and Mickey with him. What a relief!

She fairly flew down the stairs and out onto the little porch to greet them. Without waiting for any explanation she threw her arms around Mickey and hugged him tight, trying hard to keep back her tears of joy.

Steve stood back with serious face, watching. Mickey made no response. He stood immobile while his sister kissed him, then without making a move to go inside the house his tortured eyes looked straight at her and he spoke in a low voice as if the words were torn out of him.

"You won't want me in when you know what I've done," he said with anguish.

Joy's smiles of greeting froze and something cold gripped her heart. But she felt as if she would like to take him in her arms again and comfort him, he looked so utterly woebegone. She stood still speechless, waiting.

"I—" Mickey's voice choked, and he had to start again. "I've —been—a—*thief!*" His fists were knotted in the agony of his confession and his face was contorted with remorse. He saw the look of horror steal over Joy's countenance. Having said that much, now the words rushed out and his voice rose desperately.

"I knew you would feel that way, but this guy—" he mo-

tioned to Steve—"said I had to tell you. Say, I want you to
know he's *tops!* But let me tell you this before I leave you
forever, I know that God has forgiven me. I never heard of it
before, but I know now. And even though you can't forgive,
I'm going to live for God from now on. It's the only thing
worth while for me any more!"

The sobs were very near to bursting out as he finished but
he stood straight and brave, his chin firm although his lips
were quivering and his whole body was trembling with his
shame and the effort of his confession. Stephen, watching,
honored him.

Just an instant his sister waited, taking in the whole ghastly
truth, and then her beautiful face lit up with compassion and
joy. She drew him again into a loving embrace, the tears pouring down her cheeks now.

"Oh, my precious, precious brother!" she breathed. "Of
*course* I forgive you. It wasn't all your fault. It was mine too.
I didn't understand! I wasn't any help to you at all. I was so
upset! And, oh, kid! I'm glad you're home and safe. And—"
she stood him off and added with solemn gladness, "I'm the
*most* glad that you know Jesus Christ. I found Him this
morning, myself. And things will be different, for us all!"

She started to bring him lovingly into the house when she
suddenly realized that Steve had slipped quietly away. He was
halfway up the street to his house.

With quick understanding Joy called to him. He turned
slowly, as if questioning whether he was really wanted.

"*Please* come back, Steve," she called. Hesitatingly he started
back. The brother and sister waited on the little porch until he
reached them.

Joy turned on him a brilliant grateful smile that made his
heart wince with the pain of longing for the old basis of understanding and comradeship between them. His look was distant, grave, aloof.

But Joy was not noticing. She was trying to take in the

tremendous things she had just heard and she was so overjoyed to know that Mickey was back again and safe that she
felt only gladness.

There was a sudden moment of constraint when they were
inside the house. The news had been told, and each wondered
how to proceed from there, when all at once a clatter sounded
from the kitchen. Startled, Joy ran out to see what was going
on.

There was Emmy, just putting the chicken in to fry, and
pouring the muffin batter into the pans.

"I just got off from Mis' Landreth's Sunday dinner," announced the faithful old woman with a tinge of indignation.
"I ain't used ta not havin' my Sunday afternoons off! I figured
I'd be able to get around in time ta fix your dinner, and I see
you ain't et yet. But you're turnin' out to be a cook!" she
smiled, surveying the preparations Joy had made.

"Oh, you dear Emmy!" cried Joy. "How wonderful of you
to come and help me. Especially today. It's been a hard time.
I'll tell you about it later. Mickey has just got home, and
there is—a—guest. If you'll put on another place, I'll make
him stay too."

Joy went out to the living room and exultantly insisted on
Steve's staying to dinner.

"You are both tired out. I can see that." She lovingly swept
her hand over Mickey's tumbled copper curls. "You will want
to wash up and you'll feel fresher. Dinner will be ready in a
few minutes. I saved it for you—both!" she added with a be-
wildering smile of welcome that sent Steve's heart to racing
again. She waved them up the stairs and went out to the
kitchen to help.

They had a happy time at the table, although Steve was still
somewhat grave.

Mickey was more silent than usual. His carefree noncha-
lance was gone forever. He listened in wonder as they discussed the Bible lessons they had been hearing. It was news

to him that his sister ever went to church! He had a feeling that he had been gone from home for years and that many changes had taken place since he was last there.

It was just as they were waiting for Emmy to bring in the luscious fruit, and some little cakes that she had baked while they were eating, that the clattery doorbell sounded making them all jump and laugh. They had been talking so animatedly that they had not heard footsteps on the porch. From where Mickey sat he could see the street outside and the gray car parked there in front of the house. He gave an exclamation of disgust.

"It's that Harvey goof," he muttered under his breath. "Fer cat's sake don't bring him in here. I leave if you do!"

But Joy had already left the table and did not hear him.

"Well, well, am I just in time for chicken dinner?" sounded the suave voice of Pembroke Harvey.

He confidently opened the screen door without invitation and entered before Joy reached it. He was rubbing his immaculate hands in a gratified way, and his tongue wet his red lips as he smiled benignly.

Joy spoke rather formally. "Oh, good afternoon, Mr. Harvey. Yes, we are just finishing dinner. We were a little late today."

Steve took careful relieved note of the coolness in her voice.

"It's quite all right, my dear. Don't disturb yourselves. I can wait a few minutes. I came to take you for a ride, Joy. It is so beastly hot in this devilish little house!"

Mickey slumped in anger, and Steve's heart was tensed to await the girl's answer.

"That is nice of you, Mr. Harvey, but I couldn't possibly go this afternoon. We haven't finished dinner yet and besides I have a guest. Thank you just the same."

Mr. Harvey's eyebrows went up. He had by now arrived in the middle of the living room and was making his assured way into the dining room. Then he caught a glimpse of the handsome young giant seated at the other end of the table.

He stopped as if he had been pulled by wires.

Steve arose as Joy introduced them.

"This is Mr. Harvey, Daddy's plant superintendent, Steve," said Joy. Then turning to Harvey she said, pronouncing Stephen's name with warm interest, "Stephen Donovan is a neighbor of ours, Mr. Harvey."

Pembroke Harvey looked the young man over from head to foot, taking in his ready made suit and his dusty shoes. The slightest semblance of a sneer curled his little mustache. He made no attempt to take the hand Steve offered him at first and when he did it was as if he were handling something odd and unpleasant.

Then Harvey looked at Joy. "You don't have to wait long, I see, to get acquainted with the people in *this* section of the town!" There was that in his tone that brought the red in waves into Steve's face and his great fists suddenly showed white on the knuckles as he returned the visitor's stare. This was Joy's house. She must answer as she saw fit. This was no place to take offense or start a quarrel. But Steve had never been so humiliated in all his life. He did not even glance at Joy. He simply waited in smoldering silence.

But points of flashing blue fire had darted into Joy's eyes. She took an unconscious step or two in the little room that brought her almost to Steve's side as she faced Harvey and spoke in a steely voice.

"Steve is one of our very best friends, I'm proud to say." Then she turned on Steve her warmest smile trying to relax for him the tensity of the horrid moment.

Mickey growled fiercely, "*I'll* say he is!" His fists too were clenched in indignation and he took a threatening step toward Harvey but Steve laid a quiet warning hand on his shoulder.

Harvey smiled, a red smile, and the ends of his eyebrows slanted up. He spoke benignly as if to children.

"Oh, no offense, I'm sure. I just want you to be careful, my dear, in making acquaintances. Remember you are in the world alone as it were for the time being, and you need a little fatherly advice!" His tone remained smooth and even and his smile never left his face.

"Well, if you are content to stew in the heat, my dear," he said to Joy, "I shall be toddling along."

With icy courtesy Joy went to the door with him, too indignant to answer.

When they reached the privacy of the doorway, he said in a low tone to Joy, "I'm coming over some evening this week to bring those papers for you to sign. Just a matter of transfer of some stocks. I'll explain about them. I've managed so that you will come out very well," he told her smugly, "although it may take a little time before you actually realize any benefits."

She could not help brightening a little at that, but even her thanks were a bit cool and she said a formal good by as he took his way down the steps. Then she hurried back to her distraught dining table.

Steve was still standing, his face impassive as a statue.

Mickey burst out: "Who does that guy think he is, anyhow! What's the big idea of his barging in here as if he owned the place and us too? Whyn't you fire him, Sis? I never did like that character. I told Dad so when I first saw him. He's a lemon!" and Mickey made a disagreeable sound through his nose. Then he glanced up quickly to see if his sister was going to call him down as she usually did for his little vulgarities.

She was looking at him with sympathy.

"Mickey," she said with a twinkle, "right now I wish *I* had learned to make that noise when I was young!"

The boy looked at her in open-mouthed amazement and then suddenly the thought of his dainty sister performing in such a way sent him into peals of laughter, which served to break for him the nervous tension he had been under.

Steve's face lit up as if he had been suddenly awarded the cross of the Legion of Honor, and then he too burst out laughing.

Joy laughed with them and they all sat down again to finish their dinner.

They were still lingering over the last crumbs of Emmy's cup cakes when more footsteps sounded on the porch.

"Oh, fer cat's sake!" exclaimed Mickey inelegantly under his breath. "Who next?"

~ *Chapter 23* ~

Joy GLANCED OUT from her place at the table and then jumped
up with a quick glad cry of welcome. It was the Chatfields
and Peter Rockland.

"Come in, come in," she cried with pleasure. "How nice of
you to call." And it did not occur to her at the time to wonder
over the fact that these people did not seem like intruders,
although she had known them but a week. Yet Pembroke
Harvey had been an acquaintance of the family for over two
years, and she could not get rid of him fast enough.

With jolly cordiality the little group gathered in the tiny
living room. Mickey withheld any smiles at first when he
was introduced, recognizing quickly the names he had heard
Joy and Steve mention at the table. But it was not long before
he forgot to be prejudiced against Sunday school people and
was listening to a funny story Rockland was telling. They
were not too stuffy, he decided. At least they could laugh.

"We came to say hello, and tell you we are glad to have you
with us," smiled Jeanie Chatfield in her winning way. "And
also, we want to be sure you know about the special speaker
we are having on Wednesday evening. He is a man from
England with all sorts of medals he won in the RAF. He is
going to speak on prophecy, just what you and I were talking about after church this morning, Joy," she reminded.
"Bring your brother, too," she said. "My kid brother is coming. He has heard this man before and was thrilled to a

peanut. The man is nobody's dumb bunny, either!" she opened her big eyes wide at Mickey and gave a convincing little shake of her head. "He's as smart as they come, and always cracking jokes. He was the means of leading any number of the British soldiers to Christ. I hope you can come Wednesday."

Mickey sat in open-mouthed amazement. Never had he heard anyone talk like these people before. They dressed well, they used ordinary language, and seemed like regular human beings, yet they spoke of God continually as if He were the most important person in their lives, as if they really knew Him.

Then Steve spoke up.

"I'll make it a point to be there!" he said earnestly. "I am in the market to learn all I can. It was only this morning in church—" Joy glanced at him with a puzzled look—"that I found out that Jesus Christ is my Saviour. I intend to go on from there, but I'll have to start at the bottom!" He did not laugh, and his humility became him like a crown. An invisible thrill of wonder passed through the little group of visitors and Rockland's radiant smile beamed out as he said whole-heartedly,

"Well, praise the Lord, Steve! He's a great God, isn't He?"

"And *how!*" responded Steve with feeling. Then he turned to Mickey, laying his big hand on the boy's knee lovingly. "And here's another who has learned the same thing today, isn't that right, Mike?"

The color rushed up under Mickey's freckles but he looked up with a steady gaze at Steve and answered, "Yes *sir.*"

It almost seemed as if an unearthly brightness had flooded the little living room, such radiant sympathy and delight shone on the faces of the three callers.

Then Joy spoke up shyly. She found herself looking over at Steve as she spoke, as if she were drawing courage from him to utter what she had to say.

"Well, you two aren't the only ones," she said smiling, the pink coming into her cheeks. "I guess I'm what you people call 'born again,' too." Steve kept his big brown eyes straight on her, a light of glory coming into them that gave her courage to go on.

"And God has already done some wonderful things for me. I was worried about my brother, and asked Him to send him home safely and He did—with the help of Steve!" she smiled again, with all the gratitude of her heart in her eyes.

Then Peter Rockland burst out, his face aglow,

"Well, I guess we ought to have a praise service right here, oughtn't we?" And without any formality he simply closed his eyes and spoke to One who seemed very present there in the room with them.

"Lord, we rejoice together here in the wonders Thou hast wrought. Every one of us was a lost sheep at one time, and Thou didst seek us out in love. We thank You, Lord, for bringing these other beloved ones into Thy family. Bless them and bless their homes and loved ones in the name of our wonderful Saviour, Amen."

There was a little hush of wonder upon them all, but into the midst of it came other footsteps on the walk, and up to the front door. Joy had not lit all the lights, as dusk was only now coming on. So it was that Laurel, tapping an instant, opened the screen door to call and enter before she realized that there were strangers there.

"Oh!" she cried in embarrassment. "I'm sorry!" She started to withdraw but Joy jumped up and drew her in again.

"Come right in," she said. "I'm so glad you came just now. I want you to meet these friends of ours."

Peter Rockland instantly sprang to his feet, and Norman Chatfield also. Joy introduced them, and also her brother Michael whom Laurel had never seen.

"And this gentleman, I believe you have met before," she

laughed indicating Steve who had risen also and gave Laurel his seat.

"Well, a few times," admitted Laurel, her dark eyes sparkling with fun. "In fact, I came down here to see if you knew what had become of him. He seems to have deserted the old homestead," she laughed.

"Mike here and I had business to transact," said Steve laying his arm across Mickey's shoulder in a comradely way.

The recollection brought a spasm of suffering across Michael's face but he said nothing, only looked up at Steve as if he were a mighty hero.

Joy seated her little company again, and then said, "Sometime you must hear this girl sing," she smiled at Laurel who blushed and shook her head.

Norman Chatfield spoke up then.

"Fine!" he said. "I'm always on the ookout for more voices."

"Well, hers isn't just *a* voice," Joy assured him. "It's gorgeous."

"Wonderful!" responded Norman. "By the way, our singer for the special meeting Wednesday night is sick. How about you giving us a solo?"

"Oh, I couldn't!" cried Laurel embarrassed. "I never sang in a church in my life!"

At that Rockland, who had never taken his eyes from Laurel since she came into the room, suddenly put his head down in his hands. It was only for an instant and when he lifted it there was a look of infinite longing and earnestness as he gazed once more at the beautiful girl.

Norman Chatfield was at a loss. If this girl was not a Christian perhaps he should not ask her.

But Peter Rockland spoke up. "Perhaps Laurel will sing my favorite, Norm. I would appreciate it if you would," he said turning to Laurel as if he were asking a very special favor.

Laurel found herself compelled by his gaze and without

being aware of why, she knew that she desired greatly to please this fascinatingly earnest young man.

"I will be glad to," she said graciously.

Then he smiled, a smile like a blessing, it seemed to her, a smile that was just for her.

"I'll get it," he said, "I have the book right here in my car."

He was back in a moment, and again he bent that compelling smile upon her. "We'll be looking forward to hearing you," he said. "It has been a real pleasure to meet you, *all!*" He smiled, still looking at Laurel.

But when they were gone Laurel, feeling rather breathless and embarrassed, took it out on Steve.

"Well, what's the big idea? You stay away all day and get mother worried about you and then you wish me into some kind of a *prayer* meeting! Holy smokes! Shades of the Irish Donovans!" She threw up her hands.

But Steve only grinned. He could see that underneath her mockery she was pleased at the idea of singing, and he guessed that she liked Peter Rockland. That meant a great deal.

"Well, now that I've found momma's lost boy I'll depart," announced Laurel.

"Oh no, stay a while," urged Joy.

"Can't. I've got to go home and wash my hair and set it. I look like something the cat dragged in. I'll lose my handsome job at Wolfe's if I go looking like this." And she waved a gay farewell and went home.

"I think I'll turn in, Sis, if you don't mind," said Mickey in a small tired voice. "Gee, it looks nice here at last! I'm glad to be home, even if it is a dump."

He spoke so meekly that Joy ran to him and gave him a hug again.

"It is wonderful to have you home, Mickey. And it isn't home without you! And Mickey, if you really want to help there will surely be a job you can get till school opens."

"Wait," said Steve. "I've been thinking. There is a filling

station near the yard where I work, owned by a friend of mine. His wife is sick and I believe he'd be glad to have some help for a while. If you'd be willing to take a little less than an experienced man you could probably get the job. How about trying?"

Mickey looked up gratefully.

"Gee, that would be *swell!* Thanks awfully. I've tried most every place in the city but I didn't get to first base with anybody. Thanks heaps, Steve. And—" he hesitated, digging his toe into the deep rug at the foot of the stairs, "I don't know why you're so good to me, but—" he choked. "Oh, I don't know how to thank you!"

Steve came over to him and laid his hand again on his shoulder. "Don't try, kid," he said lovingly. "It wasn't I, anyway. I guess God had a lot to do with all that happened today!"

"I guess He must have," blurted Mickey through tears that almost brimmed over. He ducked his head and ran upstairs, calling good night.

Just then Emmy poked her head through the kitchen door.

"Oh Emmy, thank you a lot!" cried Joy. "You came at just the right time."

"Good night, honey chile. I'll be back another day." She had not failed to notice the light in Joy's face and the fine young man who stood there with her at the foot of the stairs. Also she had heard Peter Rockland's voice in prayer when she was in the dining room putting away some dishes.

"Glory be! Thank you, Lord!" she had whispered softly, standing still with her pile of plates until the prayer was over. So she left her honey child with a lighter heart at last.

Left alone together, Joy turned to Steve. "Hasn't it all been wonderful!" beamed Joy. And then she asked,

"Were you really in church this morning? I looked and looked for you to come."

Steve reddened a little.

"Yes, I was there, sitting away in the back." He grinned sheepishly.

"Oh!" said Joy lamely. Her poise suddenly left her. She could not ask *why* Steve had not come to sit with her. She blushed a little and groped for something else to say.

But Steve continued to look down at her without smiling.

"If you are wondering why I didn't go with you," he said frankly, "it's just that I got to thinking I might be a nuisance, always at your elbow."

Joy flashed him a reproachful look.

"You? A nuisance! Well, that *is* one for the book! Where would I be without you, I'd like to know? Didn't you save my life that day when the laundry stove was about to finish me?" They both laughed. "And wasn't it through you that I got a job? And wasn't it you who got me to praying? And who else but you brought my brother home, and best of all, taught him to trust the Lord? Oh, Steve!" Her blue eyes looked straight into his. "Don't you *ever* talk about being a nuisance again!" She was shaking her little gold head at him reprovingly.

It was all he could do to keep from taking her in his arms and holding her close to him. His heart pounded with the joy of what she was saying, and the sweet look in her eyes. He felt like saying, "There's one thing I haven't done for you, I didn't send those handsome roses over there on the table!" But this was a day for great rejoicing; he must not spoil it.

So they sat and talked a few minutes before he went home. They made plans for Mickey. Steve discussed the possibility of fixing up the basement for a game room. They talked of how wonderful it was that Laurel was being drawn into the company of these delightful Christian young people.

"I'd hate to have her get up there and make fun of that song," said Steve anxiously. "I wouldn't put it past her."

"Oh, I don't believe she will," consoled Joy. "Somehow I think she's more ready to listen to the truth of the Bible than she was. We'll pray for her," she promised, "and for your mother, too."

Steve cast her an adoring look.

"Well, it's been a great day!" said Steve as he rose to go a little later.

"Yes," agreed Joy. "It seems that God can work pretty fast when we let Him," she smiled in wonder.

"When we let Him, yes!" said Steve. "I guess that's the catch. And He *began* by sending *you* that day on the street."

"Oh!" cried Joy giving a little gasp, for the look in Steve's eyes as he said "you" sent the thrills through her, taking her breath. "I didn't do anything," she said, the pretty color making her cheeks flame. Then laughing impishly she added, "I was terribly bold to speak to you!" Her lashes were down, but she could not help glancing up again to see whether he thought she really had been too bold.

"You were *wonderful!*" he said with his heart in his eyes.

Just an instant he held her look, reaching for her heart, then he did not trust himself further.

"Good night!" he said in a low tone, and was gone.

But Joy stood with clasped hands, her senses whirling with the wonder of what his look had told her.

A long moment she watched him stride up the hill, listening for the last sound of his footsteps as he mounted his own porch. And still she thrilled at the memory of his voice saying "You were wonderful!"

The realization that her heart had gone with this man set her thoughts in a tumult. What had she done? Fallen in love? She must be crazy! What was this thing that had taken her so by surprise? But she hugged the precious thought of Steve close to her heart as she went upstairs and realized that the long day of anxiety and wondrous happenings was at an end at last. Or was it an end? Was it not just the beginning of more wonders to come?

# ～ *Chapter 24* ～

THE YOUNG PEOPLE finally persuaded Mrs. Donovan to go with them Wednesday evening. At first she demurred. "I never go out," she said. "And I'm not fit. I haven't the clothes. I haven't bought a new thing for a couple of years."

But Steve overruled that by sending her to buy some.

So the two families set off for the little brown church in time for Laurel to try over a verse or two of her song with the pianist.

Steve took Mickey down to show him the recreation room at the back of the church building while the others were practicing, but Peter Rockland had come early, and he stayed to listen. His eyes held that same earnest longing as before, while he watched and thrilled to the sound of the girl's marvelous voice.

"I was lost when Jesus found me," she sang.

"Oh, God," prayed Rockland in his heart, "she's lovely! But make those words real to her!"

Several older women saw the stranger there and came and spoke to Mrs. Donovan, cordially as if they really were glad to meet her. It was so long since she had mingled with the rest of the world that she was quite overcome to find people so friendly.

She listened with intensity as Laurel sang her solo and she had to wipe the tears away as she finished. Laurel had held the whole roomful breathless and there was a murmur of appreciation when she ceased.

The speaker fascinated them all. He had spent some time in the Near East, had in fact been in Palestine when the first of the Jewish refugee ships had been turned back.

"Something happened a few months ago," he began, "which was foretold twenty-five hundred years ago! God's ancient people Israel established a state of their own! After nearly two thousand years! God has never forgotten His promise to them. Many nations, including my own, have treated them miserably from time to time, but even that is according to God's Word.

"And God said that when Israel should return to their land 'the desert would blossom as the rose.' That, too, is literally coming to pass.

"Now look at the rest of the world," the speaker continued. "For the first time in history the nations are lining up *exactly in accordance with prophecy!*" He repeated various passages proving his point. "And Palestine," he said, "is the prize for which the nations are striving! Again according to God's Word.

"And now let me tell you the most thrilling fact of all! When all these things begin to happen, the Book says, then know that *He is near,* the Lord Jesus Christ. His return is the only hope for this poor earth. The United Nations will find no cure for war. Neither will any other human mind or agency. The cure for war is the return of the Prince of Peace!

"The people of two thousand years ago thought only of His coming as King, and so they did not recognize Him when He came in humility. Conversely, the people of today think of Him only as the meek and lowly One. It would seem as if they want to keep Him as He was, a humble carpenter. But He has finished the work the Father gave Him to do, the shame and the cross, and God's plan is that He shall be highly exalted, King of Kings and Lord of Lords upon this earth.

"Let us look up! This is earth's night, while He is away.

But a morning will dawn soon when sorrow and crying shall be put away. 'Weeping may endure for a night but joy cometh in the morning!' "

There was an audible sigh of anticipation as the speaker ceased. Then Norman Chatfield arose and announced a hymn and the whole company swelled into glad chorus:

"It may be at morn when the day is awaking,
  When sunlight through darkness and shadow is breaking,
      That Jesus shall come in the fulness of glory—"

Joy, surprised at the great volume of sound, glanced around. Her eyes met Steve's and there was glad understanding in them.

Laurel was in the front row, and Peter Rockland had taken the seat beside her as soon as the speaker began. She had listened in perfect amazement. All she had ever heard of the Jewish nation had been their faults.

All the way home she pelted Rockland with questions, for Laurel had a fine mind and she had been greatly moved.

But none of them knew how deeply stirred her mother had been by Laurel's singing, not only because it was her daughter but by the words of the song she sang.

When they reached home, Mrs. Donovan invited them all in to have some of the chocolate layer cake she had made that morning.

They had a merry time, interspersing their gaiety and joking with many more questions.

"Gee, I didn't know that church was ever like that, did you, Joy?" Mickey broke out once. "I never heard all those things before. The only times Dad ever made me go to Sunday school all they talked about was a club they were going to start, and the teacher hammered at us a few remarks about how we ought to keep our tempers and play fair always. Gee, most anybody knows ya *ought* to, but it's doing it that's hard.

As if his saying so would change any of us, anyway." They smiled in appreciation of Mickey's frankness.

Joy got them to singing, and then in an interval of cosy conversation Peter Rockland turned to Mrs. Donovan with his nicest smile.

"Somebody has told on you, Mrs. Donovan. I hear that you have a wonderful voice, too. I wonder if you wouldn't try over this duet with Laurel. I brought it with me hoping you would."

It was hard for anyone to resist Peter Rockland when he asked a favor. To her children's great amazement she replied, though not without some hesitation, "I haven't sung for two years, but it did me good to hear Laurel tonight, and I believe I'd like to try again. Yes, I'll be glad to."

But Laurel and Steve, true to Donovan form, acted exactly as though that was just what they had expected their mother to say.

Joy turned to the number in the book that Peter mentioned, and Laurel stood to one side to make room for her mother to look on with her. Steve merely passed his hand over his eyes to hide the flood of joy in them. This was more than he had hoped for.

Joy played a few rippling chords to give the singers their key and then the two gorgeous voices flowed out in harmony:

> "When peace, like a river attendeth my way
> When sorrows, like sea billows roll,
> Whatever my lot, Thou hast taught me to say
> It is well, it is well with my soul."

Peter Rockland closed his eyes an instant, reveling in the lovely strains, and praying in his heart for the two who sang, that the words of the song might go deep and do a wonderful work in them.

"It is well—" the voices echoed each other, and Joy's heart echoed the song with them. She was delightfully conscious of

Steve and of what this singing meant to him.

They started another verse:

> "My sin—oh the bliss of this glorious thought,
>     My sin, not in part, but the whole,
>     Is nailed to His cross and I bear it no more—"

Suddenly one voice ceased. Mrs. Donovan's hands went up to her face and they saw that she was sobbing.

Laurel's arm stole around her as, stammeringly, her mother burst out:

"I can't sing those words! They aren't true for me!" She shook her head sorrowfully. "No, they aren't true for me!" Then all at once she looked straight at Peter Rockland. "But I'd give anything in the world if they were!" she cried heart-brokenly.

A light sprang into his face, a soft light, that seemed to flood the room with love.

"Then praise the Lord!" he said, smiling quietly, "they can be true right now."

"Oh, but you don't know!" she said. "There's no hope for me. I've been an awful sinner! You don't know how I've sinned."

"I don't need to, and I don't want to," said Peter gently.

"Oh, but I've made my children miserable and it's all been my selfishness. My husband used to talk to me about God but I wouldn't listen. I was too eager then for life. I knew all the time I was wrong. And I've known it ever since but I wouldn't admit it. I've just been avoiding the issue, pretending I couldn't do any better."

Her dark eyes were flashing and Joy could see in her dramatic gestures the talent that had drawn her to the stage.

Then Peter Rockland spoke, understandingly.

"God knows all that, Mrs. Donovan. He knew it when He sent His Son to die for you. If you would like to let Him into your heart He can change everything for you."

"Yes, I would!" she cried.

"Let's just talk to Him about it," said Peter.

And then he prayed, drawing them all into the presence of the Lord, it seemed. The tears streamed down Stephen's face as Peter finished, claiming the "keeping power of that One who is able to do exceeding abundantly above all that we ask or think!"

"Now play that song over again, Joy," said Peter. "We'll have to have a praise service!" So Joy started, but Mrs. Donovan's low rich voice broke in once more.

"I want to tell you something first," she said earnestly, and there was a light of peace on her face at last. "I've found I can still sing, tonight. And since I have seen what God can do I want Him to have my voice. It is what my husband would have wanted, isn't it, Stevie?" she appealed to her son.

Steve turned a radiant look on his mother and said, "I've never told you, Mother, but I had a talk with Dad just before he died and he told me then that God was the answer in our lives. I'll tell you all about it later."

"Oh Stevie!" she cried. "It will be like a word from him! Why did you never tell me before?"

"Well, I just couldn't, Muth," he said gently.

"I know," she moaned dramatically. "I wasn't worthy. But things will be different now. You can count on that, children. And you will have to help me."

Even Laurel's eyes were misty as her mother finished, and suddenly she spoke up: "Well, I don't know what it is that has hit you all, but I know I've been miserable, and if I can get that way too, I'd like to. It must be that God is real after all, if He can mean this much to all of you."

Peter's hand reached out to Laurel's in a glad warm clasp.

"I guess we'll just *have* to have that song of praise now!" he said huskily. "I feel like shouting myself, although I never thought much of raising an uproar in meetings. Play that song again, Joy, and we'll all sing it."

They gathered about the piano, Stephen's arm around his mother and Laurel's hand held fast in Peter's. Mickey sat on the piano bench with Joy and joined in, now with a soprano squeak, and then with a bass growl.

It was late when Joy and Mickey walked home.

"Gee, didn't we have a good time!" exclaimed Mickey. "That sure was swell cake, wasn't it. And that guy Steve is tops. Those women are all right too only they weep too much for me."

"I guess they've had plenty to weep about, kid," Joy answered sympathetically.

Mickey took a few steps in silence, then he said, "Gee, that guy at church was interesting. If I had known before that God was somebody you could really go to with things, I might not have—have," he swallowed hard, "picked the way I did to try to help. Funny what a difference it makes."

"Yes, doesn't it!" agreed Joy, giving a happy squeeze to her brother's arm linked in hers. She had hard work to keep the tears of joy from welling up. And she simply must not let them overflow. Mickey hated tearful girls. She was overjoyed and astonished at the change in Mickey's whole attitude.

"I guess," she went on after a minute, "that God had to let all this dark time come so that He could wake us up, kid."

"Could be," assented Mickey seriously. "Wonder what Dad'll say, though?"

"To our living in this house, or to our liking church?" asked Joy.

"Well, both. I guess he'll be about as surprised at one as the other."

"I've told him a little about the Bible class already and I think he was pleased. But I'm terribly worried about bringing him here. I believe Dr. MacKenzie is too, although he still says Saturday, if nothing happens. I wish I dared keep Daddy there a while longer. But we really cannot afford it, I'm afraid. There isn't much left to go on. And besides, the doctor thinks his being home with us may do Dad as much good as the shock of the house would do harm. So I don't know which is best. It's another thing to ask God about, I guess."

Mickey nodded and opened the door for her. As he did so a little white card fell out. Mickey picked it up. "F. Pembroke Harvey," he read and made his own special noise through his nose. "Well, that's one time we managed to miss that stuffed shirt. It beats me why Dad ever picked him. And he thinks he's God now that Dad's not around to boss him. Here's a note on the card," he added, handing it to Joy. "Say!" he warned, "if you have any idea of taking him on steady, I'm off ya fer life. That's what he's got in his noodle, sure as my name is Mike. All these roses and the candy an' all. Say! If you can look twice at him when there's a guy like Steve Donovan in sight, you're absolutely buttons!"

Joy's face flamed scarlet in the darkness at the precious memory of Steve's look as he had said good night to her. She answered Mickey teasingly, but with a confident little lilt in her voice, "Pembroke Harvey is a very smart young man, kid. He's going places. He'll make a lot of money."

"Would you throw away your life for a little extra money?" demanded Mickey, horrified.

Joy was just on the point of saying, "That's what you almost did, isn't it?" But she caught the words in time.

Mickey was keen enough, however, to notice her abrupt stop and realized instantly what she had been about to say. His whole figure drooped at the memory of his shame.

"Okay, say it!" he burst out remorsefully. "I know what you mean. I almost did. Boy! Am I glad that God let those cops get me!" he said humbly.

"You *dear* boy!" Joy comforted, putting her arm about his shoulder and giving him a little hug. "It's tough, learning, isn't it! It has been for me too. But it's worth it!"

"Yes," agreed Mickey, "it's worth it." But his voice was sad. "If that guy Steve hadn't told me about being already straightened out with God I never woulda had the nerve to come back."

Joy had turned on the light in the living room and she looked at the card.

The writing was small and neat:

"This is the second time I have called. You do not realize how important this matter is to you. I will come tomorrow evening. Please be home."

"Well, fer the lova Pete! I like that! 'Please be home!'" mocked Mickey. "Who does he think he is? If I were you I'd be out every night from now on and let him cool his heels a little."

Joy laughed. "I guess I can't do that. He's right about it being important to me. He has a paper for me to sign that will be a big help to us, kid. He has reorganized the business, and this will safeguard our rights, he says, so that we will get something out of it."

"Oh yeah?" responded Mickey. "I'd be mighty sure before I signed anything that guy told me to."

"Oh, I guess we can trust his advice, Mickey. We have to. He is the one Dad was going to pick for a partner. And after all, he is terribly clever at business. Daddy always said so."

"It may be so," Mickey reluctantly admitted. "But I still don't like him."

"You don't have to like him, unless you get him for a brother-in-law!" chuckled Joy. "But we could do with a little more to live on, you know. It's very good of him to try to plan for us."

"Well, you mark my words, *I don't trust him.*"

Joy laughed again with sisterly condescension and they went upstairs.

But Pembroke Harvey was not laughing, over in the room on Sherbrooke Avenue that used to be Joy's.

He had been very much annoyed that Joy was not there the

second time when he had brought the papers to sign. He would feel far safer financially if he had control of those large blocks of stock which were now in Mr. Applegate's name. It was true that the Big River plant was started and the money had begun to come in. But he decided that he was carrying too great a burden of financial worry; he was bearing the load for himself and his employer too. It was only right that he should have every credit advantage possible if he was to carry on. Thus he finally settled the argument between his greed and his conscience.

He had made out stock transfers for Joy to sign. The more he thought about it the more sure he was that it was a good thing to do. He could easily make Joy see that what he had called the reorganization of the business would require all available assets. To himself he argued that he was simply serving the best interests of all concerned, especially Pembroke Harvey's, which was only natural. Every man had himself to look out for. As the transfers were to go to the business and not to himself ostensibly, he told his conscience to be quiet about it. When he was married to Joy the whole thing would be forgotten anyway for their interests would be one, that is, hers would be his. So he had decided to act and to act quickly.

Moreover, a new angle had arisen this very evening. On his second trip to Joy's house with the papers, as he was drawing up to the curb, he had seen a man at the door ringing the bell. It was dusk, but he had seen the figure plainly and there was something familiar about it, something that brought an unpleasant memory.

The man was short and slender, with the slight stoop of middle age. As he turned to come off the porch, having found nobody home, the street light caught the glass of his spectacles. Suddenly Harvey had recognized him. It was Tom Thorne!

Now what in the world had that clerk been doing around there? Harvey was not aware that Thorne was an old friend

of the family, for Tom had not often been a part of the family
life at Sherbrooke Avenue of late years since Joy had grown
up. Harvey had never happened to see him there the few
times he had come. So the only motive there could be for him
to call on Joy Applegate, Harvey thought, was that, knowing
of the Big River deal, he was on his way to tell Joy that she
had been deceived.

In a panic of fury he got out of his car, meeting Thorne
halfway up the walk.

Too desperate to control his anger at this little mousy person
who was presuming to upset the perfect plans he had laid,
Harvey blazed out at him, "What are you doing snooping
around here?" he flung at Thorne.

Poor Tom was utterly taken aback. He had been sick for
some time. He was still shaky from his illness, and he trembled with the suddenness of Harvey's attack. At first he did
not recognize the man, but when he spoke he could not mistake the voice. It brought back that dark day when he had
been dismissed. In meek terror he stammered,

"I—I—was—just stopping—to see—Joy, to make sure she—
was doing all right, sir."

"Joy! *'Joy!'*" raged Harvey in a suppressed roar. "Whoever gave *you* the right to call Miss Applegate 'Joy?' You can
get out of here and stay out. If you are caught around here
again you'll get the living daylights knocked out of you. And
you can keep the name of my future wife out of your dirty
mouth now and forever!"

"Oh! Oh! No offense meant, I'm sure, sir. I've known—"

"You've known what?" burst in Harvey. "Answer me, what
have you known? There's nothing for you to know. If you
are here trying to make trouble you can understand right now
that there is no use. You will get nowhere. Miss Applegate
understands all about what I'm doing, and is perfectly satisfied. Now get out! And don't you ever dare to go near Miss
Applegate again or I'll have you arrested."

Harvey stood over the trembling little man shaking his fist up into his face. The street lights caught the ruby eyes of the tiger in Harvey's ring and they seemed to mock Tom in devilish glee.

Tom Thorne wavered an instant in utter bewilderment and then obediently went his way, while Pembroke Harvey went up to the porch and rang the bell himself, loud enough and long enough to ease some of the fury in his soul.

Thankful at least that Joy had not been there, since Thorne would have reached her first, Harvey wrote his note. He decided that the time for swift action had come. If that mouse Thorne had tried to tell what he knew, no telling what he might try next. He must be watched, and those stock transfers must be signed immediately. So Harvey made his note as peremptory as he dared.

Then he betook himself to his gray coupe, quickly caught up with the little gray figure of Tom Thorne, lingered until he saw him catch his bus, then followed the bus until he saw Tom get off at his home and walk in.

Next Harvey drove down to a section of the city where the streets were narrow and the lights were few. He spent over two hours there, then, his business concluded, he went back to the big house on Sherbrooke Avenue, to lie awake going over and over again all his plans to make sure that no loophole was left.

All he needed now was Joy's signature. He felt sure he could get it. He had not missed the hopeful light of relief in her face Sunday night. But now that rat of a Thorne was horning into the picture! He never had liked him. Now he hated him.

Well, there was a capable man who would look after him if he went anywhere near Joy Applegate again. And by tomorrow night all of that which had been Edward Applegate's would be in the hands of Pembroke Harvey.

# ⤳ *Chapter* 25 ⤳

Tom Thorne lay awake that night also. At first he was merely stunned by Harvey's utterly unprovoked attack on him. Then as he began to get his balance again from the weakness which had seized him, he became more and more bewildered.

He had recognized long ago that Harvey was a proud and overbearing person, but he had not been aware of the hostility of the new head to him in particular. His dismissal had come as a complete surprise. He never thought ill of anyone or suspected them of unkind thoughts, because he had none himself.

But now the more he thought about Mr. Harvey's attitude tonight, the more he wondered whether there could be any crooked work going on. If Harvey had thought he was going to make trouble, there must be some trouble to be made. So he lay in the little hot room where the breath of his own treasured roses stole in at the window, and he arranged in order before him all the facts.

Joy had moved, because she had learned that the business had failed. But it was Harvey who had told her it had failed. Harvey was angry tonight for no apparent reason. There must be a reason. He had asked Tom what he knew. Then there must be something to know. And he had said, "Joy knows what I'm doing and is perfectly satisfied." Then he must be doing something about which he could expect somebody to be dissatisfied.

The worst of all was that he had said that Joy was going to marry him. That troubled Tom more than anything else. There was no accounting for the tastes of young men and maidens, of course, and he, being a confirmed bachelor, could not be supposed to be able to give advice on marriage to a young and beautiful girl. He shook his head in anxiety. At last he decided that he would spend his time tomorrow in investigations.

So bright and early the next morning Tom started out. He was not aware that anyone else started out with him. He would have been amazed to find that he was important enough to be trailed.

First he went out to Big River. It was humming with activity, and many were the casual conversations he had there. He left no stone unturned.

He returned to the city and made a few more calls, first at the bonding company where he had a friend whom he hunted up and took out to lunch. During the course of their conversation Tom confirmed the fact that the contract for work at Big River had indeed been awarded to Applegate and that the bond had been signed by Pembroke Harvey on behalf of his employer.

After lunch he visited the office of the recorder of deeds and learned that the Applegate house had not been sold. The new occupants must be paying rent, then. To whom were they paying it, he wondered.

Tom grew more and more indignant as the day wore on and proofs piled up that Pembroke Harvey had been something less than honest in his dealing with the Applegate interests.

It was while Tom was getting a cup of coffee—"half hot water, please"—at nearly five o'clock, that the man who had shadowed him throughout the day took the opportunity to call the telephone number which Harvey had given him. He made his report and got his orders.

But Tom as he cooled his coffee was turning over in his mind various methods of warning Joy about what was going on. If she was actually in love with that swindler Harvey, it might be difficult to persuade her of his dishonesty. She would not be cordial to such an idea.

Also, in the light of Harvey's threat last night Tom's timid nature inclined him to do his warning by letter or telephone. A letter might be too late to do any good, however, and a telephone was a poor excuse for a face to face talk, especially when there might be need of persuasion.

Tom Thorne's loyalty was far stronger in a case like this than was his natural timidity. So he finally decided to go to the house again. He would call her at the store to make sure she was coming home and then go straight out. That would likely be too early for Harvey to call.

So he made his phone call and boarded the bus never noticing that the same man who had grabbed the phone when he hung up was now the driver of a black sedan that was following the bus route all the way. Tom's thoughts were intent on the best way of convincing Joy that the man she was planning to marry was a scoundrel. That marriage loomed in Tom's mind as the thing most of all to be hindered. The fact that the man was apparently doing Mr. Applegate and his family out of their fortune was bad enough, but for a girl like Joy to be tied to him for life would be infinitely worse. By the time he reached the bus stop and started to walk to Joy's house he had completely forgotten Harvey's warning.

As he neared the house and started to turn in the Applegate walk a rough looking man coming on foot from the opposite direction stopped him and asked for a match. Automatically Tom started to reach into his pocket, then realizing that he had no matches he was about to offer the stranger his friendly regrets and pass on, when all of a sudden he looked down and saw the gleam of a small gun pointing straight at his stomach. It was still broad daylight, but the gun was almost hidden in the man's hand. No one would have been likely to notice it. Tom glanced around. The only person in sight was a small boy playing in a broken handcart on a vacant lot.

Tom Thorne had never had the experience of being held up. It did not seem real to him now. His soft brown eyes behind their spectacles grew wide like a child's. He started to make a feeble protest.

"Come with me!" growled the stranger flicking his coat lapel back for an instant to allow the gleam of a badge to show. The brief glimpse did not give Tom opportunity to look closely at the badge, and at first he really thought that he was being arrested. That was what Harvey had threatened. Now he *was* in trouble! And Joy would have no one to warn her. He looked up at her house frantically.

"Come on!" snarled the man under his breath. "Get in the car over here. You're *wanted!*"

Desperately Tom glanced up and down the street. But even the little boy in the handcart had disappeared.

"Get goin'!" ordered the ugly voice again. "Get in the car!" Tom obeyed and in another moment the street was empty. The black sedan had disappeared down the highway that ran at the foot of the hill at right angles to Emerson Street.

It was not many minutes before rapid footsteps sounded up at the other corner and Steve and Mickey came from the bus stop, pausing a moment to make final arrangements for going to the ball game together Saturday if all went well after Mr. Applegate was brought home.

While they stood talking little Timmy Taylor rode up on his small sidewalk bicycle and stopped before Steve.

"Hi!" he greeted him.

"Hi there," replied Steve in a friendly voice, and went on talking to Mickey.

The small boy waited in perfect composure until he had finished and then he vouchsafed in a matter-of-fact way, "There was a holdup a few minutes ago down there." He slung his thumb in the direction of Joy's house.

Steve and Mickey grinned appreciatively. They were familiar with Timmy's imagination and had often been drawn into his vivid play for a few moments, when they had been required to be pirates or cowboys.

"Who is the bandit this time?" asked Steve amusedly.

"I'm not kidding. It was real. A fella came along with a gun and made a man that was starting in to Applegate's house go off with him. I was in the handcart playing and I watched out of a hole."

Steve looked serious, but Mickey was still smiling and had already started down the street, until he heard Timmy mention Applegate.

He stopped and glanced back. Steve was giving serious attention to what the youngster was saying.

"It *might* have been an arrest," suggested the child wisely, "or it might have been a holdup. I *think* it was a holdup. Because the man with the gun didn't look like a cop. O' course he mighta been a plain cloes man."

Steve frowned. "Are you fooling, Timmy?" he asked.

"No sir, I'm not," vowed the boy. "They went off in a black Dodge sedan. The license number was L-4509. It's okay if you wanta let it go, though." He started to pedal away.

"Wait. Are you positive of this? You're not making up that number? Are you going to laugh if I call the police?" Steve urged.

"No!" replied Timmy, indignant at their lack of faith in him.

"How did you know the license number?" Mickey asked unbelievingly.

Timmy gave him a withering look of scorn.

"I always notice 'em!" he responded loftily.

"Do you have any idea who the man was that was held up?" Steve asked again.

The child described him. "He's been to Applegate's a couple o' times," he added.

"Uncle Tom!" ejaculated Mickey. "But he has no money. Nobody with any sense would try to hold him up."

Timmy shook his head wisely. "Well, they did," he insisted.

"Which way did they go?" questioned Steve.

"*That* way fast," he pointed.

"You come on in while I phone, kid," ordered Steve.

Mickey came in too, and after Steve had had a talk with the police station Mickey called up Tom Thorne's house.

"No, he's not back yet," answered his sister. "He told me not to wait dinner if he was late, but he's been sick and I'm kind of worried about him."

Mickey hung up without telling her what he wanted of Tom.

Just then Laurel walked in.

"Did Joy come home?" asked Mickey right away.

"No," she said. "I don't know where she is. Her car was gone when I came out, so I know she didn't have to stay at the store. We always agree that if she can't get away before the bus comes that I should take it, so I did. Perhaps she stopped at the hospital."

The air of mystery seemed to deepen and Steve was uneasy.

"Let's call the hospital," he suggested. But Joy had not been there.

He began to walk from the window to the front porch, then back to the telephone again lest the police should call. Timmy's eyes shone with excitement. Mickey wore a non-chalant sophisticated air, but when the minutes went by and Joy did not come he too began to fidget.

Laurel went out to the kitchen and started to help her mother with supper.

Each one offered suggestions as to why Joy was not home

yet, but none of them were convincing. They all knew that they would not have thought much of her delay if this story about a holdup had not developed.

Time went on, far past their dinner hour. Steve called the hospital again, then he called the store but only the night watchman was there. He called the Chatfields; if she had stopped in there they might have invited her to stay for supper, although surely she would not stay away without calling or making any provision for Mickey's dinner. She was not there, but they assured Steve that they would be praying for her safety. Surely she would soon be found.

Laurel and her mother put dinner on the table but no one felt like eating.

Steve had sent Timmy home to get his dinner but in a few minutes he was back again with five cookies in his hand, as eager as ever to hear news of his holdup.

At last Mickey looked at the clock for the hundredth time and said: "It's funny Joy wouldn't try to get home tonight because she was expecting that sap Pembroke Harvey. He was going to bring a paper for her to sign—something about Dad's business." Another line of worry ruffled his young brow. "I didn't want her to sign it. I don't trust that guy." Suddenly he slammed down the magazine he had been pretending to look at and straightened his leg down from its idling position across the arm of the Donovan's best overstuffed chair. A brighter look lit up his freckled face.

"Gee!" he exclaimed. "I bet that's what she's doin'. I bet she's stayin' away to avoid him. Gee! Of course! Whyn't I think o' that before?" He jumped to his feet and gave a little jig step, but it lacked confidence.

And just then the telephone rang. Its clang startled their tense nerves. Steve's hand shook as he took up the receiver.

## ∽ *Chapter 26* ∽

Tom Thorne sat trembling beside his grim-looking captor, never taking his eyes from the little point of light on the barrel of that gun.

The driver operated the car with his right hand and held the gun still pointed in his left. Tom was nervous lest in the stress of traffic driving the thing would go off unexpectedly. He edged away as far as possible.

"No funny stuff!" threatened the other man. "No use trying to jump outa the car, or anything like that. I gotcha covered. An' all I hafta do is tell people you're screwy an' I'm takin' you to a crazy house!" He gave a rickety laugh that had an ugly sinister sound to Tom.

Frightened as he was, the chief thought still in Tom's mind was Joy. Who was to warn her? Tom tried to keep his wits about him and note the turns they made. He soon saw that they were not headed for the police station. And closer inspection of his companion made him realize that he could not possibly be a legitimate detective. He was of a lower order than that.

They were speeding into the country. If they kept on they would soon cross the state line. In his fear and desperation he began to cry out in his heart silently to the only One he knew who could help him. And even more than he prayed for himself he prayed for Joy, that she might be saved from that unscrupulous man.

But even as he prayed Joy was riding along Main Street, following Pembroke Harvey.

Harvey had sprung into action when he got that second call from the man he had hired to trail Thorne. There was no time to be lost.

He went straight to Wolfe Brothers' store, and stopped at the glove counter. Joy raised her pretty brows in surprise as she saw him.

He smiled unctuously, pausing with ostentatious courtesy until she had finished waiting on a customer. The ends of his eyebrows were up and his red mouth was pursed. His little bright eyes were fixed compellingly on Joy. She felt a nervous embarrassment at his gaze. She wished he would make himself less obtrusive.

When she had finished he leaned across the counter. Joy had seen the men friends of other clerks flaunt their attentions in this way and she had despised them. She spoke coolly to Harvey.

"Good afternoon, Mr. Harvey. What brings you here?"

"You!" he said meaningfully. Then he smiled. "Seriously, I'm anxious to get that business settled for you as soon as possible, my dear," he said in a low tone. "I find there are some—" he hesitated, "enemies—of ours who are trying to make trouble. I don't want to have any hitch on your account. Couldn't we go straight over to the office now and sign the papers? Everything is there, you know." Another smile implied that he had arranged everything for her greatest convenience.

Joy hesitated, reorganizing her plans. It would be a relief not to have Harvey coming out to the house tonight. Not only because Mickey disliked him, but because she had wanted to spend the evening putting the last touches on her father's room in preparation for his homecoming Saturday. Laurel would have to go home on the bus if she went with Harvey, but

Laurel would understand. She might as well get this thing over with. So she nodded.

"I'll wait, then," said Harvey.

"Oh no, thank you," said Joy. "I will take my own car. It will save me time. I'll come right over as soon as I'm out of here." She glanced at the clock. "Only fifteen minutes now," she smiled.

But Harvey parked close to the gate lest even now she slip out of his hands. He was relieved that she showed no sign of suspicion.

He watched nervously until he saw Joy's little car fall into line behind his.

He would have preferred to have her in front of him.

But she seemed to be following meekly enough and soon they drew up at her father's office building.

He helped her out of the car, taking her arm in a close pressure that she felt was too intimate. She tried to draw away, but he held her closer. How glad she would be when this was over and she would be free of him. Or would she? He seemed to be a hard person to discourage.

As he led her back to her father's office she noted in passing little changes in furnishing and arrangement that had been made since her father's illness. It annoyed her but she shook off the trifling thought. Some day, she sighed, perhaps Daddy would be back, taking charge of things himself.

Harvey did not notice her little sigh. He was far too engrossed in his own affair.

He closed the door carefully behind them and then he elaborately drew forth his papers and pointed to the end of the page of legal terms where the dotted line ran.

"Just sign it here," he said a little breathlessly, "and then you can be done with it and get on home. I see you are in a hurry."

Joy took the pen he handed her.

"I suppose I really ought to read it first," she said in a

rather apologetic voice. It seemed now that she was here as if it was inexcusably discourteous to the man to suggest that there might be anything wrong with his arrangements.

"I've heard it is considered very bad business," she smiled, "to sign something you haven't read."

"Oh, by all means read it!" urged Harvey, proceeding to talk to Joy all the time she was reading.

He rattled on so steadily that by the time Joy came to the end of the involved phraseology she had not the slightest idea what it said. She gave a sigh and took up the pen again. She did hope she was doing right. She knew that she and Mickey simply must have more than they were making now in order to keep going at all. So with some misgivings she spread the paper out and wrote her name.

Almost too eagerly Harvey snatched it away and put another one before her, and then a third. When she had signed them all, his face was wreathed in smiles.

He came around the desk as she rose and grasped her two hands.

"Now we are all set," he said. "The next paper to be signed is our marriage certificate!"

Joy opened her mouth to discourage any thought of marriage with him when all at once he drew her close to him in a fierce embrace and planted his wet red lips on hers, drinking greedily of their sweetness. He pressed so closely to her that she was bent backward with the force of his lusting body. She struggled in pain and terror. But still his lips held hers, crushing them in the fierceness of his passion.

At last he released her and Joy sprang away with a cry. In a flash that loathsome embrace had cleared her mind. She knew that she should never have trusted this man.

She whirled and seized the three papers on the desk, tearing them across and pulling to shreds the part which bore her name. Then she made a dash for the door thinking to get out to her car before Harvey had a chance to keep her and berate her or perhaps try to kiss her again. She did not know what he might do. All she knew was that she wanted to get away and out of his unclean presence forever.

But Harvey was too quick for her. He sprang to the door and locked it, slipping the key into his inner pocket. Then he stood facing her as she stood breathing hard with horror, her eyes darting about the office to find some other way of escape.

As he watched her, knowing that she was in his power, a slow red smirk spread over his face. Joy watched in terror. He looked more like the devil than ever, she thought. The chagrin to him of what she had done in ruining his work showed in his angry eyes. But he was calm now, and intended to make her suffer for what she had done.

He stood staring her down until she was frantic with detesting him. Then he let out a slow ugly laugh.

"I see that you are not in such a great hurry after all, my dear," he said. "Perhaps you wanted to stay a little longer here with me." His purring voice had a snarl in it. "You shall wait, then, until I have copied those papers. And I am not a fast typist," he added. "Perhaps you would do better than I?" he asked archly.

But when she jerked her head away from his gaze he said, "No? Well, you may wait. Of course I wouldn't let a little childish pet, such as you were just in, interfere with your own good. I must say you don't seem very grateful to me for all the effort I have made on your behalf, but I suppose I cannot expect you to understand business affairs. The papers you tore were very valuable, my dear."

Calmly, with no sign of haste, Harvey set to work laboriously to fill in new transfer forms on the typewriter.

Joy stood where she was for some minutes. Desperately she searched the room for some means of escape. There was no door to the room besides the one he had locked, only a little door that led into a washroom. If worse came to worst she could slip in there and lock herself in. But she felt she would far rather try to get out of the building than be shut up with this man.

She studied the windows. They were too high for her to reach. To draw a chair up to them would attract Harvey's attention. The telephone was her only touch with the outside world. But the phone stood on the desk at Harvey's elbow. There was little hope of her using it.

Screaming would not do any good, for the room was air-conditioned and the windows were shut. The traffic outside was heavy and nobody would be likely to hear her. She wondered when the janitor would come by. For a while she strained her ears listening for his steps. But all she heard was the hum of wheels outside and the honking of impatient horns.

If she could only get a message to someone out there that she needed help, and ask them to call the police! But how was she to do that? She had a little pad of paper in her purse, and a pencil. She could write a note and throw it out the window. If she could only do it before Harvey noticed her!

She rummaged through her bag, her fingers feeling for the little gold mounted pencil that Mickey had given her at her last birthday, and then she drew out the pad of paper. She brought out her little mirror along with it as Harvey glanced over threateningly, and pretended to powder her nose lest he see what she was planning to do. She had decided to try breaking the window with one of the straight chairs that stood by the wall underneath. They were aluminum-framed chairs, and should not be too heavy for her to lift and wield. The crash of the breaking glass would be sure to attract someone's attention; she could throw out her note at the same instant. Surely it would be noticed. She would try anything rather than submit to that man's kisses again. Her whole body was still shaking with horror at the recollection of his hot lips on hers. She rubbed her mouth hard with her bit of a linen handkerchief to try to erase the horrid feeling. He noticed her gesture and gave another sneering laugh.

"You will learn to like a little loving before long," he said. And then he got up and came over to her, speaking in a petting tone. "You are just a little girl yet, aren't you, Joy?"

He tried to put his arms around her again and draw her up to her feet but she darted out of his grasp and stood behind her chair her eyes blazing.

"Don't you *dare* to touch me again!" she said in a tight voice. Her teeth were chattering and she was trembling all over, but she struggled to keep him from knowing it.

He gazed at her a moment smiling, and still confident. "You are very beautiful that way, my lovely little spitfire," he said pursing his lips as if he would kiss her across the space that was between them.

Joy merely stood frozen, and in a moment he went back to his work.

"I can see that you are going to take a bit of training, my pet. You seem to be something of a shrew!" He laughed. "But I have always liked a spirited girl, even if it makes a little more work! It's worth it!"

Joy bit her lip. He refused to treat her as anything more than a child. His cocksureness was maddening. It seemed to have in it a terrifying power that could compel her against her will.

He went back to his typing and with horror she saw that the page was nearly at an end. Panic-stricken, knowing that she had but little time left, she finished her note under cover of her handbag, and snapped it firmly inside the bag.

She had taken out her purse and her driver's license and put them into the pocket of her dress, but she had left everything else in it to make it heavy enough to throw easily.

She sat an instant planning her moves. They must be swift

and sure. For she would have no second chance to try, she was sure of that. She grasped her bag in one hand and then she tried holding it in the other, imagining how it should be held in order to have it handy to throw as soon as the glass was broken.

She glanced at the chairs, to see just how to hold one so that it would swing up easily above her head.

She took a deep breath. Harvey glanced up at her. She must wait until he was engrossed in his work again.

All at once he rose and went toward the light switch by the door to turn it on. Now! She rose casually to her feet and was just about to seize a chair when the telephone rang.

It was six or seven steps from Harvey's desk to the door and Joy was at the phone before he had scarcely reached the light switch.

Frantically she grabbed the receiver and without waiting to see who was calling, she cried into the instrument, "Help! Help! Quick!"

But before the first word was out of her mouth Harvey had torn the phone from her hands. In his fury, his fear lest something should still hinder the completion of his plan, he tore the wires out of the box, and the telephone lay a useless thing stripped of its power.

Joy's eyes widened in fear as she realized how desperate indeed this man must be. Wildly she ran to the other side of the room and seized the chair she had planned to use. But even as she swung it, Harvey divined her purpose and snatched her arms in a painful clutch, forcing her across the room into the little washroom where he locked her in. Yet he was smiling all the time he did it and shaking his head saying, "Naughty, naughty little shrew."

She sank shuddering against the door with a moan. Her heart was pounding with anger and fear. What *could* she do now? Then all at once it came to her that God had promised to be with her. God could not be locked in! And she began to pray, desperately, as she had never prayed before.

In a few minutes her heart grew quieter. She could still hear the tap-tap-tapping of the typewriter keys. As long as that kept up there was no immediate danger. Oh God! Send somebody to help!

# Chapter 27

THE BLACK SEDAN bearing the license L-4509 continued to speed eastward faster and faster as it neared the state line. Tom Thorne was clinging to the arm of the seat in terror. The car swayed uncertainly as they rounded a curve. The driver was still using only one hand.

Suddenly out from a side road as they flew by appeared a motorcycle. The officer on it sped ahead of them and gestured for their car to halt. He wore the dull blue uniform of the state police.

But instead of slowing down, the man beside Tom grabbed the wheel tighter, pressed the gas pedal to the floor, and tore on. There was still a chance that he could make it over the state line and elude pursuit by turning off into a side road in the woods.

Poor Tom could scarcely feel relief at the sight of the policeman, so terrified he was at the speed he was going. He had no hope of finishing this ride alive.

The roar of the oncoming motorcycles—there were two of them now—was deafening. He saw that his mad driver was keeping one eye on the mirror above the windshield.

All at once the car began to act crazily, bumping and weaving its rear about. The pursuing officers had punctured a rear tire with a bullet. But the driver merely let out an oath and tried to rush on. But in another instant a second bullet had ripped the other rear tire. Like a flash the driver jumped out and made a dash for the woods close by.

Tom grabbed the wheel of the careening car and turned off the switch. Two shots rang out and the fleeing man dropped with a bullet wound in each leg. At the same moment an officer appeared at the side of the car.

One look at Tom Thorne's terrified countenance told the police a good deal of what they wanted to know and confirmed the story that little Timmy Taylor had reported through Steve.

But it was not until after thorough questioning at the police station that they called up Stephen Donovan, who was still waiting anxiously by his telephone.

Mickey's eyes clung to Steve as he took up the receiver. Steve's face grew tense as he listened and the little group around him in the Donovan living room were breathless when at last they heard him say,

"If that's true, officer, then I'm afraid we have another chase on our hands." Then he told of Joy's disappearance. The officers evidently took a serious view of it, for Steve was asked to give all the addresses of places where she might go.

As he hung up, Steve suddenly exclaimed, "I never thought to mention your father's office. I wonder if they will think of going there." He dialed the number himself and heard a girl's voice shout: "Hel—," but the connection was suddenly broken and try as he would he could not get the number again.

As he frantically worked, he cried excitedly to Mickey, "That was Joy! I'm sure it was. She started to say 'hello,' or 'help!' I don't know which, and then we were cut off. You call the police again and send them there. I'm going down!"

He tore out the door and down to the corner where he hailed a taxi.

"Main Street and First Avenue," he commanded, "and don't wait for *any*thing."

The taxi driver welcomed the excitement and recklessly

raced downtown at a terrific pace. From time to time as neces-
sity arose he executed a perfect imitation of a police whistle.
An obstructing car would draw to one side in guilty caution.
Then the taxi driver would grin complacently and rush on.

But Steve, though grateful, was not in a mood to find it
funny. The ride seemed to him interminable. All sorts of
possibilities were racing through his mind as he sat forward on
his seat as if to push the taxi faster.

When they reached the office building Steve sprang out telling the driver to wait. He was not sure but he might have to
go farther in his search, though where to begin after this he
did not know.

He tried the front door of the building. It was locked.

Desperately he ran around the side looking for another door.
When he found it he raced to the end of a corridor calling,
"Joy! Joy! Where are you?"

Harvey, just finishing his typing, sat up startled. A cunning
look came into his eyes. He arose stealthily and went to the
door of the washroom and opened it.

In a clear loud voice he called.

"Someone wants you, Joy. You had better get over the sulks
and go and let them in."

He handed her the key to the office door as calmly as if nothing unusual had occurred, and went to his typewriter again
and sat down, pretending to be wholly engrossed in his work.

Wonderingly, with thanksgiving in her heart, Joy ran to
the door. She had not heard the voice calling down the corridor, for the two sets of walls were thick. She opened the door
and walked straight into Stephen's arms.

"Joy! Oh Joy, are you all right?" he cried, holding her close
for an instant as if he could not let her go. Then he gave a
puzzled glance into the office.

Order and quiet reigned, for Harvey had swept the torn
papers into the wastebasket and thrust the ravaged phone into
a desk drawer while Joy was unlocking the door. The peaceful

room seemed like an anticlimax. There sat Harvey at the typewriter, calmly drawing his finished sheets from the machine.

He cast a look of contempt toward Steve but he spoke in a low measured tone that was held under control by fierce effort.

"Just a minute, Joy," he said. "I have finished preparing your papers at last. I want to see you come out right in this deal even if you don't understand it." He spoke as if she were a child. "We have to have your signature, you know—"

"Signature nuthin'!" burst in a gruff voice. "Don't you sign nuthin', young lady, till *we* have a talk with this gent."

Two burly officers pushed past Steve and Joy and seemed to fill the big room with their bristling authority. The taxi driver peered in, his eyes bulging.

With impudent confidence, Harvey welcomed them all.

"To what am I indebted, may I ask, for this little gathering?"

"You'll find out in time. You're wanted for questioning."

"Very well, gentlemen, I'll be glad to go and give any information you want. Just let me gather together my things here," he said, picking up the papers on his desk.

"Ne-ver mind! We'll take care o' those!" warned the officer.

Joy stood watching in incredulity. She nestled into the comforting strength of Steve's arm about her, and he looked down and gave her a warm smile.

Just then running feet sounded in the corridor, and Mickey arrived, out of breath and white with anxiety. He looked from one to the other, taking in the whole situation.

"Fer Pete's sake!" he exclaimed, though nobody paid any attention to him. "Gee! Didn't I tell ya, Joy, not to trust that guy? Gee!"

But only Pembroke Harvey heard him as he walked past in the burly care of the law, and all he could do was to cast the boy a hot withering glance of hate.

They all had to go to the police station, except Mickey.

Steve sent him home to tell the news to his mother and Laurel
and the Chatfields that Joy was safe. Mickey would have liked
to stay to the bitter end, but Steve did not think it wise for
him to have another experience at the police station so soon.

Poor Tom Thorne was summoned and kept for a long time
giving names and addresses and facts, but he was calm and
happy behind his thick lenses as he studied the fine face of the
young man who was looking after his beloved Joy so efficiently.

Joy looked like a little wilted rose when the session was over
at last and Steve led her away. The whole experience had been
a shock to her. When they were out on the street, a little distance from the forbidding atmosphere of the police station,
Joy suddenly turned in the darkness and buried her head in
Steve's sleeve and sobbed.

Steve stopped and drew her close, stroking her little gold
head gently. He longed to take her in his arms and pour out
all the wonder of his love for her. But she was unnerved now;
he would not take advantage of her weariness.

At last she looked up with a tearful giggle, "I'm an awful
baby!" she apologized.

"You've been a soldier!" he answered gently, as he led her
to the car.

They stood there a moment out under the cool stars, glad
to be away from the stuffy atmosphere of the police station,
and a quick breathless look passed between them which each
pretended not to have seen, but a sense that something wonderful was about to happen hovered over them as Steve helped
Joy into the car and took the wheel himself. That breathless
thrilling suspense held them silent for several minutes as they
wound their way out of the city, past the turn that would take
them to Emerson Street, and up a hill road.

"Well, God sure was good to us again!" said Steve, reverently breaking their sweet intimate silence. "The best of all is
that *you* are safe!" His tone caressed her and Joy nestled closer
to him.

At the top of the hill he stopped the car and came around to her door to help her out.

"This is a place I love," he said. "I want you to see it. I'll tell you all about it sometime."

He led her over to the fence and they stood there close together gazing out over the city. Its dotting lights blinked sleepily up at the sparkling stars. The moon had just bestirred herself to rise and lay a soft coverlet of gold over the hillside. A gentle breeze, whispering as if not to waken the sleeping city, passed by and caressed the two who stood there.

Steve turned to gaze down at Joy—her head just barely reached his shoulder. Feeling his look she turned and their eyes met. Deep, deep into her heart he looked, and she flung open wide the door of her soul to welcome him. And then he smiled, a selfless smile of utter rapture. Joy smiled too, with understanding and unfathomable content. Their lips drew together in a long kiss that was a promise. The whole world seemed to stop for them; it was as if there were just the two of them together in the moonlight.

Gently Steve released her and they smiled again, the sweetness of their love drawing them close again.

"My precious, precious little joyous love!" murmured Steve. And Joy nestled closer to him burying her golden head on his breast with a happy sigh. "Oh!" he exclaimed suddenly out of the darkness. "I meant to ask you first if I might kiss you." He chuckled. "Did you—mind?"

"Mind?" echoed Joy dreamily. "Did I mind that other time you kissed me? Down in the basement on Emerson Street?"

Then they laughed together, and kissed again.

"But truly, dear, do you think you could love me enough to marry me? I don't amount to much, you know."

"Beloved," she answered, "don't you know that I have loved you ever since I first saw you that day on the street? You amount to *everything* for me! But," she looked down coyly, "you've never *said* that you loved me, you know!"

And then Steve took her in his arms and whispered close in her ear:

"It seems to me, darling, that I have loved you from all eternity! I never had known anything so precious as you that day that I first saw you. All my life will be spent in loving you, my precious Joy, the Joy of my life!"

"Steve," said Joy after he had sealed his love with another kiss, "do you suppose that God had this for us all along? That He knew about it?"

"I wouldn't be surprised," said Steve thoughtfully. "And it must be He had to wait until we were willing to seek His will for us before He could give our love to us. Ours will be one life now, won't it, darling? One life to be lived together for Him!"

"Oh Steve, I sort of think our dark time is coming to an end, don't you?"

"I believe it is, dear, at least for a while. And when dark times come again, as they are sure to, we can go through them together, knowing that the morning will soon come. Remember what Peter Rockland said that 'weeping may endure for a night, but joy cometh in the morning?' *And how* it does!" he exclaimed. "My *Joy!* My morning Joy!" He gave her another adoring look and then he suddenly realized that it was getting late.

"It will be morning in more senses than one," he laughed, "if we don't get home! And we've had no dinner, do you know that?"

"Well, now that you speak of it, I guess you are right. I had forgotten all about dinner," giggled Joy. "Do you suppose your mother saved it for us?"

"We'll get home and see what we can scare up," said Steve, handing Joy into the car as if she were a priceless china doll.

On the way home Joy exclaimed, "Why! I just realized how God has solved another problem! Mickey and I were so troubled about bringing Daddy home to Emerson Street. And now I guess we can go back to our own home, according to Uncle Tom. Hasn't God been wonderful to us!"

"Yes, He has!" said Steve, and then looked very thoughtful. "Do you know of any good man in your father's office who can take over now in this man Harvey's place?"

"No, I don't," replied Joy, suddenly feeling again as if she had greater responsibilities than she knew how to carry. "Of course Uncle Tom understands things pretty well, but he is no engineer. There were two or three assistants, and I know Daddy thought they were good but whether he would feel like trusting any one of them to carry on that big contract, I don't know. I am utterly at sea when it comes to the business end of things." Suddenly she brightened.

"Why couldn't *you* do it?" she asked with childlike faith in his superior abilities.

He laughed aloud. "I would be no more fitted to take over a job like that than—than Mickey!" Then he sobered. "I did have good engineering training in college, and I had some experience in the army, too. I had hoped to be in that work, but I had to get the first job I could find when I got home. Maybe when your father gets well I'll ask him to give me some work to do. But as for the Big River deal, that is away beyond me yet."

Joy smiled confidently in the darkness and gave his free hand a little squeeze.

"I am quite sure that Daddy will do it!" she assured him. "Oh, isn't it wonderful that he is so much better? I am so anxious for him to meet you I can hardly wait." At that Steve stopped the car with a jerk and gathered his Joy into his arms.

# Chapter 28

ALL THE NEXT day Joy went about Wolfe Brothers' Department Store as if she were at a garden party. She fitted gloves as if it were a delightful game she was playing. And more than one tired shopper left her counter feeling refreshed with just the memory of her happy smile.

And when she went for her pay that Friday evening, announcing that she would not be back, the rosy glow in her face and the shine of her eyes made the pay clerk smile and tease her: "You're quitting to get married like they all do, I can see that!"

Joy's cheeks flamed prettily as she emphatically shook her head.

"Not yet, I guess," she laughed back. "Sometime. But my father's coming home from the hospital tomorrow, and—God has done a lot of wonderful things for us!"

The tired woman gazed after the starry-eyed little glove clerk in a puzzled way and felt a faint stirring of hunger in her own heart to know, as that girl seemed to know, some of the unseen workings of the Almighty.

On Steve's advice Joy got in touch with her father's lawyer. She wondered as she called him why she had not had sense enough to go to him before. He said that as there was no lease, it would not be difficult to evict the tenants. Joy was greatly relieved also to discover that Pembroke Harvey had

never sold the furnishings after all, since the tenants had preferred to rent the house partly furnished.

By Saturday afternoon Mr. Applegate was settled again in
his own home without any suspicion of the move his children
had had to make. A peaceful look was on his face as he sank
gratefully into his own bed. Joy fussed over him lovingly
although the nurse was still on duty.

Joy called Emmy and told her the good news and she lost
no time in giving notice to her new mistress.

"I shore will be glad to be back, honey chile," she said
beaming into the telephone.

"All right, Emmy, come as soon as you can," said Joy.
"Right now, if Mrs. Landreth is willing."

"I'll do my best, honey chile," she promised.

About five o'clock Saturday afternoon there came a ring at
the front door.

There stood two tall distinguished-looking gentlemen. The
hair of one was graying, but the other man was younger and
wore a uniform.

"You won't remember me, Miss Applegate," said the older
man. "I met you with your father at the golf club a couple of
years ago."

Joy glanced at the card he offered. It bore the name of the
Atlas Corporation, and E. H. Sanderson, Vice President. Was
something wrong again? A tiny pucker came to her brow.

"We have been doing some detective work this week to try
to find you," smiled the big man. "My friend here is Colonel
John Branding. John, this is Miss Applegate. I am anxious
to have a few words with you, if I may?" he said to Joy.

"Come right in," she invited cordially, leading them into
the living room. "Things are a little disturbed here as we have
been—away. You knew my father had been ill?"

"Yes, so I understand," said Sanderson. "I called once or
twice at the office and was told merely that he was away for
a time. When I finally discovered his serious illness I won-

dered if there would not be need of some help while he is out. That is why I came today. This friend of mine—" He indicated the uniformed man, but suddenly a cheery whistle interrupted them and Steve could be heard calling softly, "Joy! Joy, darling!"

Joy's cheeks flamed pink and she had to toss the two strangers a little laugh, but her eyes were shining.

"Oh! I beg your pardon!" exclaimed Steve and then laughed with them at his own embarrassment.

Joy introduced him proudly to her guests. She was pleased to note the poise and grace with which Steve met them.

"Now," began Sanderson again as soon as they were seated once more, "perhaps you would like to tell me the whole story of what has happened. I confess I am more than a little puzzled. I brought this man over today to meet your father's assistant, thinking he might be of some use. He has just come from managing all the construction for the American army in Germany. He is at liberty now, at least for a time, and he doesn't want to be idle. I seized on him partly because he's a good friend of mine and I'd like to have him somewhere near," Mr. Sanderson gave a little apologetic smile. "But we found the assistant was not in and the office force seems to be somewhat at a loss to explain things. So begin at the beginning, please."

So Joy began. And as her story progressed the two men listened with growing admiration for the girl who had fought her way so bravely through her troubles.

When she had finished, with Steve putting in a word now and then in more accurate business terminology than Joy knew how to use, Sanderson turned to his friend.

"John," he said, "do you have any further doubt as to whether this is the place for you? You will go a long way to find a more able man, Miss Applegate, and I can promise you there will be no crooked dealings with him at the helm until your father is well."

Joy could scarcely keep from bursting into tears in her relief. She saw the shining of Steve's face and knew that he too was giving thanks for this further proof of the faithfulness of their God in answering their cries for help.

While Joy had been telling her story she had heard the heartening shuffle of Emmy's feet and once her beaming face had peered cautiously through the door of the living room to ascertain the number of guests there. Soon after they finished their discussion she called them all to dinner.

Mickey showed his delight in Emmy's cooking by taking seconds of everything and then proceeded in characteristic brotherly fashion to remark that this was the first square meal his family had had since Emmy left. Joy flushed in crestfallen embarrassment. But Steve looked up and smilingly shook his head.

"No, you missed the very first meal your sister fixed, Mike. It was the best I ever ate, even if it was served in the cellar of the Emerson Street house."

At that the stars came out and danced in Joy's eyes and she laughed in joyous recollection.

They were lingering over their coffee, when Tom Thorne arrived.

"Oh, Uncle Tom!" cried Joy rushing up to him and throwing her arms around his neck to the awful confusion of that bashful gentleman. "I haven't had a chance to really thank you for saving us. This is the man," she explained, dragging him into the dining room, "who discovered what was going on and risked his life to warn me!"

Poor Tom tried to find a convenient hole to fall through. But Mr. Sanderson and the colonel both rose to shake his hand warmly and congratulate him.

"That was fine work you did, sir," commended Sanderson. "Not only for the Applegate family but for the Atlas Company as well. No telling to what lengths that scoundrel might not have gone with his underhanded scheming."

"Yes," spoke up the colonel, "I'd like to hear all the ins and outs of it. And as it seems that I'm to take over for a while anyway, I'm hiring you back right now to take effect the day you were fired!"

When at last they were talked out and the guests were gone Steve announced, "Now let's go over to our house. Mother and Laurel are waiting to hear something we have to tell them." His eyes twinkled at Joy but Mickey looked puzzled.

"Go ahead," he said, "I'm a working man. I gotta get up early tomorra." For in spite of the change in their circumstances, Mickey had decided he liked his job and would work on until school started. Steve and Joy had appeared with him before the judge privately and after due deliberation he had been formally put into their custody for a probationary period. He was improving steadily.

Both Joy and Steve grabbed his arms.

"Oh, no," they cried, "you must come too! You may have some objections to our plans!" Then they laughed.

"Oh, all right," he grumbled in a pleased good-natured way. "Leggo of me. I'll come."

So they all sauntered over to Donovan's.

They burst in like a fresh breeze, descending on Mrs. Donovan and Laurel with joyous cries and loving hugs. Then Joy looked at Steve and Steve looked at Joy and they laughed.

Laurel pretended to pout.

"Well, you two act like a pair of fools. What is it you had to tell us? For Pete's sake get it over with and stop standing there giggling like a couple of kids!" But she had to laugh herself.

"You tell, Steve," smiled Joy, her eyes dancing.

"No, you tell, Joy. They'll take it better from you," he laughed.

"Well," said Joy her blue eyes growing serious as she gave a loving look toward Steve, "if you don't mind, Mother Donovan, we'd like to get married, if you please."

There was a whoop from Mickey who barely restrained himself from turning a handspring right in the living room, and Laurel could not keep the pleasure from showing in her face, although she said in a sophisticated way, "Oh, is that all! Anybody could have told that, this long time!"

But Mrs. Donovan rushed over to Joy, the tears streaming from her eyes, and threw her arms around her.

"You'll never know," she said through sobs of joy, "how very much you have meant to us all!"

"Oh," cried Joy, "I think it's all the other way. What would I have done without you Donovans?"

"Come on," called Laurel. "Cut out the bouquets. Time enough for those later. Bet I can call the numbers on your wedding. You'll be married in the little brown church, with a reception afterwards on Sherbrooke Avenue. Pete Rockland will be the best man, and Norm Chatfield will render a solo in his best style—"

"Yes," chimed in Joy, "and Laurel Donovan will be the maid of honor in orchid crepe, and Jeanie Chatfield will be brides-maid."

Laurel looked pleased. "And where does Mickey come in?" she teased. "Is he to be a flower boy?"

"Oh, fer cat's sake!" groaned Mickey disgustedly. "Weddings! Who wants ta get all dolled up and prance in front of people? Whyn't ya just go get married if you want to and be done with it? Although," he added with a sly mischievous glance at Laurel, "you might as well get in practice; cause anybody with half an eye can see there's gointa be another one comin' off soon and Peter Rockland will really be the 'best' man at that one. Oh, fer the *love of Pete!*"

Mickey laughed with glee at Laurel's confusion. The rich color flooded her face and she looked daggers at him, but she finally had to join in the merriment with them all.

Doctor MacKenzie made them wait a whole day more before they told even good news to his patient, although he assured them that their father seemed to be on the road to full recovery.

So it was with shining faces that Joy and Mickey came the next evening to say good night to their father.

Joy spoke in a low gentle voice.

"Daddy, there's something wonderful I want to tell you before you go to sleep. It was hard going while you were sick, and it looked pretty dark—sometime we'll tell you about it, because it has all come out right. But the best thing is that Mickey and I have come to know Jesus Christ as our Saviour. So it has all been worth it for us."

A light came into the man's pale face and his eyes filled with glad humble tears.

"My *dear* children!" he murmured brokenly. "I, too, have learned much in this time that I have been laid aside. I used to think that I was pretty good." He paused a moment to gain strength to speak. "But I have found out that there is much that I failed to teach you. And I see now that some of my own ways, in business, for instance, were not pleasing to God. Things will be different now for us all."

His eyes closed with exhaustion but there was a look of peace on his face which his children had never seen there before. They bent over and kissed him tenderly. Mickey growled a "Gee, Dad!" husky with feeling into his ear as his lips brushed his father's.

Then Joy beckoned to Steve in the doorway.

With a sweet lilt in her voice she said,

"Daddy, I want you to know the man who helped us a great deal. This is Stephen Donovan, Daddy, and you will love him —I do!"

Steve took the thin white hand in his and looked down at the fine face upon the pillow, noting the keenness of those black eyes. He stood a long moment silent and let the older man look him through and through. Then he said,

"I love your daughter better than my life, sir. May I have her?" His whole soul was shining with his love.

Then Joy's father smiled. His eyes went from Stephen to Joy and back again. Slowly, with great effort now, he said, "God bless you both! I'll wish you joy—in the morning."